ROOK

*Further Titles by Graham Masterton from
Severn House*

BLACK ANGEL
DEATH TRANCE
MANITOU
MIRROR
NIGHT PLAGUE
NIGHT WARRIORS
THE SWEETMAN CURVE

FACES OF FEAR
FLIGHTS OF FEAR
FORTNIGHT OF FEAR

Also in this series

FORTNIGHT OF FEAR

ROOK

Graham Masterton

SEVERN
SH
HOUSE

This first world edition published in Great Britain 1996 by
SEVERN HOUSE PUBLISHERS LTD of
9–15 High Street, Sutton, Surrey SM1 1DF.
First published in the USA 1996 by
SEVERN HOUSE PUBLISHERS INC. of
595 Madison Avenue, New York, NY 10022.

British Library Cataloguing in Publication Data

Masterton, Graham
  Rook
  1. English fiction – 20th century
  I. Title
  823.9'14 [F]

ISBN 0-7278-4991-3

Typeset by Palimpsest Book Production Limited,
Polmont, Stirlingshire, Scotland.
Printed and bound in Great Britain by
Hartnolls Ltd, Bodmin, Cornwall.

WEST GROVE COMMUNITY COLLEGE

SPECIAL CLASS II

Greg Lake	Amanda Zaparelli	Sue-Robin Caufield	Seymour Williams
Sherma Feldstein	empty desk	Russell Gloach	Sharon X
Beattie McCordic	Ray Vito	Elvin Clay	John Ng
Mark Foley	Ricky Herman	Muffy Brown	Tee Jay Jones
David Littwin	Rita Munoz	Titus Greenspan III	Jane Firman

Jim Rook
English
and Special Needs

Chapter One

He heard shouting and whooping in the corridor a second before Muffy came bursting into the classroom, her eyes wild, saying, "They're killing each other! Mr Rook! They're killing each other!"

Jim dropped his felt-tip pen and threw back his chair. He strode to the door and Muffy clutched hold of his sleeve. "You have to stop them, Mr Rook! They're going crazy!"

He ran down the corridor, past the lockers to the boys' washrooms. A crowd of twenty or thirty pupils had gathered outside, chanting and yelling and beating on the locker doors with their fists. "Tee *Jay*! Tee *Jay*!"

Jim yelled, "Get out of the way!" and pushed past them into the toilets.

At the far end of the washroom, two seventeen–year-old black boys were fighting. One of them – tall, and heavily built – had forced the other right back against the basins, and was knocking his head against the mirrors. Both of them had nosebleeds, and blood was spraying up the walls like graffiti.

Jim grabbed the bigger boy by the scruff of his T-shirt, and swung him around.

The boy's face was like a mask: sweaty, spattered with blood, with bulging eyes. He was so hyped up that he couldn't speak anything but gibberish. "Let go of me, man – I gotta – let *go* of me, man, I'm going to kill him – he diss me so bad – you don't even—"

"*Tee Jay!*" Jim yelled at him. Tee Jay tried to wrench himself free, but Jim twisted the neck of his T-shirt even tighter so that it was almost throttling him. Jim forced him back against the tiles and stared into his face with all the ferocity that he could muster. "Tee Jay, what in God's name has gotten into you?"

"He diss me – he *diss* me – I'm going to kill him for that – I'm going to murder that mother – don't try to stop me – 'cause you can't – you *can't*, you hear me?"

Jim kept Tee Jay pinned back against the wall. He turned to the other boy, Elvin, who was leaning over the basins with blood streaming from his mouth and nose. "Elvin, you okay? Elvin, can you hear me? You okay?"

Elvin coughed and nodded. Jim pointed to a tall fair-haired boy standing by the washroom door. "Jason! You and Philip take Elvin along to the infirmary! The rest of you, get the hell out of here! This isn't a goddamned cabaret!"

He turned back to Tee Jay. Tee Jay was still quaking with adrenaline, and he didn't take his eyes off Jim for a second, sniffing and shuffling and twitching his head. Jim could hardly recognise him. He was usually so quiet, and together, and funny, too. He was the tallest boy in the class, good-looking apart from a smattering of acne scars on his cheeks; a great basketball player. He wasn't especially bright, because none of the students in Jim Rook's class were especially bright. But he was always willing to learn – and he had never been obsessed with 'disrespect'. Not until now, anyway.

"All right," Jim demanded. "Are you going to chill out, or what?"

Tee Jay tried to pull himself away again, and the seam

of his T-shirt tore. "I'm never going to – *never!* – that mother—"

"Tee Jay, for Christ's sake! Listen to me, will you? I could have you arrested!"

Tee Jay quietened down. He attempted to jerk himself free one more time, but then he turned his face away and obstinately stared at the toilet doors.

Jim said, "Tee Jay? Come on, Tee Jay?" and when Tee Jay looked back again his eyes were crowded with tears.

"I'm sorry," he said. "It was just what Elvin said to me, man. I couldn't—"

"What *did* Elvin say?" Jim demanded. "What could anybody say to you that provokes you into attacking them like that?"

"Nothing, man. He didn't say nothing."

"So you just started beating up on him for the hell of it?"

Tee Jay wiped the blood away from his nose with the back of his hand. "Look, I've said I'm sorry, okay?"

"You think it's okay? *I* don't think it's okay. I think it stinks. I have enough of a hard job defending you guys without you behaving like mad dogs. I'm going to have to haul your ass up in front of Dr Ehrlichman when he comes back this afternoon; and Dr Ehrlichman will have to decide whether we're going to allow you to stay on here, or whether we're going to ask you to leave."

"It was a *fight*, man, that's all."

"You don't solve any problem by fighting, Tee Jay. I thought you had enough brains to know that."

"If I had any brains I wouldn't be in Special II, would I?"

Jim let go of his T-shirt and stepped away from him. "There," he said. "You're free to go. You think it's

3

demeaning to be in Special II, then clear out your locker and go home. I don't want anybody in my class who thinks that arguments are settled by hitting people. And I don't want anybody in my class who isn't proud to be in it."

He waited, and watched Tee Jay sniffing. Then he furiously banged his fist against the toilet door. "Jesus, Tee Jay! Think what you're risking! Elvin dissed you? So what? Don't tell me you're *that* goddamned sensitive. You want to sit with the girls?"

"You can't talk to me like that, man!" Tee Jay warned.

"Oh, no? So what the hell's going on? You've made more progress this semester than anybody else in the class. When you came to me, you didn't even know who Shakespeare was. You could hardly read. You couldn't add up. Christ, you thought that President Washington's first name was Denzel. Think how far you've come. But now you're ready to throw away everything you've done, *snap*, just like that, for the sake of what? Your *vanity*? And you think you deserve respect?"

Tee Jay instantly flared up again. "That's it! You *always* doing that! Bringing people down! Making them look like a fool when they ain't! You walk around your schoolroom pretending to be friends but all the time you laughing behind your hand, man. You *laughing*!"

"I'm not laughing now, Tee Jay. Get yourself cleaned up. Then report back to class."

Tee Jay shuffled over and stood over him. "I could take you, man."

"Is this the first time that's occurred to you?" Jim asked him. He held his ground. He couldn't count how many times a rebellious teenager had loomed over him and warned him that, "I could take you, man," or words to that effect. In seven years of remedial teaching he had

4

suffered one stab wound (screwdriver, upper shoulder muscle) and two missing teeth. But since he had taught over two-and-a-half thousand disturbed, disruptive and dyslexic boys and girls, he reckoned that he had probably gotten off lightly. His predecessor had been shot in the lung.

There was a moment of extreme tension – made all the tenser because Tee Jay had never challenged him like this before, and there was no predictable agenda.

But then Tee Jay said, "Ah, shit," and shook his head as if he couldn't be bothered, and slouched out of the washrooms with his hands in his pockets.

Jim watched him go, and then looked around at the blood-spattered mirrors. Behind the loops and squiggles of crimson, he could see himself, standing alone. A lean, dark-haired man of thirty-four, with eyes the colour of hazy green glass pebbles and a six-o'-clock shadow (even though it was only 9.20 in the morning.) His features were angular, slightly haunted-looking, as if he slept badly and never got quite enough to eat. He wore a short-sleeved denim shirt and a red-and-green necktie with palm trees and hula girls on it. His arms were thin and his wrist-watch looked too big for him.

Sometimes he looked at himself and wondered what the hell he was doing, trying to teach the unteachable, especially when it came to violence, like today. You could work for months on a student like Tee Jay – months of inch-by-inch progress, months of sweat and stuttering and tightly-clutched pencils – and then it could all explode, in an instant, for the stupidest of reasons, and you would be back with the swaggering, bad-mouthing streetwise numbskull that you first started out with.

Respect, he thought. *Don't make me laugh.*

Just as he was about to leave the washrooms he thought

he saw a very tall man passing the entrance. It was only a fleeting glimpse, like a shadow crossing a wall, because the man was walking along the corridor very quickly and very quietly, even though the floor was covered in polished thermoplastic tiles, which usually set up a hard rapping (stiletto heels) or a tortured squeaking (sneakers.)

Jim came out of the washrooms and looked down the corridor after him. The man was silhouetted against the sun-bright windows at the far end – even taller than he had seemed at first glance, wearing a baggy black suit with flapping trousers and a black, wide-brimmed hat, low in the crown like an old-fashioned preacher's hat, the sort that Elmer Gantry wore.

"Hey, can I help you?" he called out, but the man took no notice. "Pardon me, sir, can I help you?" he repeated. Still the man ignored him, and turned the bend at the end of the corridor and disappeared.

Jim went jogging after him. As he reached the corner, however, he almost collided with Susan Randall, the geography teacher, carrying a huge disorderly heap of books. She tipped most of them on to the floor in a flapping, slapping cascade.

"What are you doing, rushing about like a pig in a china shop?" she shrilled at him.

"Hey, Susan, I'm real sorry," he said. What made their collision all the more embarrassing was that he liked her, a lot; although she was still very suspicious of him. She had short brunette hair and pouty lips and a figure that could have won her a walk-by rôle in *Baywatch*, and today she was wearing his favourite yellow ribbed sweater. Even the boys used to whistle at her.

He knelt down and helped her to gather up the books, very conscious of the way her putty-coloured skirt had ridden up as she hunkered down next to him. He looked over her shoulder but the corridor was empty now. No sign of the man in the Elmer Gantry hat.

"Did you, uh, *see* anybody, just before we bumped into each other?" he asked.

"What do you mean *see* anybody? Who?"

God, that perfume. He had taken the trouble to find out what it was: *Je Reviens*; pretty expensive for a woman on a teacher's salary. "There was a tall guy in a black suit and a big hat. You couldn't have missed him."

"I didn't see any tall guy in a black suit and a big hat. I didn't see any guy at all."

"You must have done."

"Well, I'm sorry, Jim, but I didn't. Now do you mind if I get back to my class? I'm ten minutes late already. They'll be trashing the place."

He caught her arm, and frowned at her. "You really didn't see anybody? For real?"

"No, Jim. I really for real didn't. Now, please."

"Okay, then," he said, genuinely mystified. He stood and watched her as she tap-tapped her way toward her classroom. "By the way," he called after her. "It's bull."

She stopped in her tracks. "What do you mean? It wasn't bull at all. I really didn't see anybody. For real."

"I meant in a china shop. It isn't pig. It's bull."

She laughed; and Jim smiled, too. But when she had gone he couldn't stop himself from looking along the empty corridor, and wondering how the man in the Elmer Gantry hat had managed to disappear. It seemed *cold* in the corridor, although he couldn't think why; and there was a strange aromatic smell that wasn't *Je Reviens*. It was more like incense.

He gave an involuntary shiver, and then went to tell the janitor to clean up the blood.

*   *   *

7

By the time he returned to Special Class II, both Tee Jay and Elvin were back in their places, looking sullen and bruised. Elvin's lip was split and Tee Jay's left eye was beginning to close. The rest of the class were buzzing and twittering with curiosity and excitement, like a murmuration of starlings on a rooftop. When Jim walked in they all stood up, but the gossiping continued. Jim ignored them. Without a word, he went to the window, hoisted up a window-pole, and noisily opened it. Then he went to his desk and sat down, tilting his chair back, and clasping his hands behind his head.

He sat looking at them for a long time, and still he said nothing.

Little by little, the class began to quieten down. His silence was making them uneasy. Usually he came storming into the room and started talking right away – posturing, dramatising, gesticulating – working his class like an actor working his audience. This morning, though, he sat silent, in the same posture that *they* always adopted, chair tilted back, hands laced behind his head, eyes heavily lidded in a deliberate attempt to look disinterested and totally cool.

After two or three minutes there was complete silence. Mark Foley giggled; and his buddy Ricky Herman gave an adenoidal snort, but otherwise everybody was quiet.

Jim got up at last and walked around his desk. He looked at Tee Jay and he looked at Elvin, and then he looked at each one of his class in turn, slowly and deliberately studying their faces. There were nineteen of them in all: from Titus Greenspan III in the front, with his fishbowl glasses and his freckles, to Sue-Robin Caufield in the back with her mountains of blonde hair and her tight cerise T-shirt. There was John Ng from South Viet Nam – polite, shy and barely able to understand

8

a word that anybody said to him; Beattie McCordic with her cropped hair and her tattoo and her fierce feminist agenda, not to mention her anomia, a chronic inability to remember what things were called. She couldn't say "hammer". She couldn't remember it. She'd have to say, "that piece of metal on a stick you use for hitting nails."

There was David Littwin, who was stringy and tall and almost handsome, apart from his protruding ears, but who stuttered so badly that every sentence seemed to take forever, and the rest of the class would start making loud snoring noises and look at their watches. Rita Munoz, dark-eyed and dark-haired, with lips as scarlet as a blossoming tropical flower. Rita argued with everything her teachers said to her, simply to disguise the fact that she didn't really know what they meant.

All of the students in Jim's class were the students who couldn't fit in anywhere else. Too slow, too aggressive, too vain, too stupid, too immature; or else they had chronic learning difficulties. Some of them he knew for sure had very high IQs. But a high IQ means nothing if you can't apply it; or don't want to apply it; or if you want to apply it only to activities that are either irrelevant or anti-social.

Jim walked right up to Tee Jay's desk and laid his fingers on it. "This morning," he said, "I want to talk about respect. Do any of you have any opinions about respect?"

Beattie McCordic's arm shot up.

"All right, Beattie. Tell us about respect."

"Respect is when people give other people their own space. Like when a woman's sitting in one of those places where they serve those mixed drinks and a man comes up to her and starts hitting on her to go to bed with him, right? And she says no. So he stops hitting on her. That's respect."

"Okay, that's a reasonable definition of respect. Anybody else?"

John Ng put up his hand. "Respect is to say a prayer to ancestors."

"That's good, yes. Acknowledging the debt you owe to your fathers and grandfathers."

"And your mothers and grandmothers," Beattie interjected.

"Yes, Beattie. Can we just take it as read that every time we mention men we mean women as well, and the other way about?"

Ricky Herman called out, "Respect is when you don't eat your food off of your knife."

"Yeah and don't say 'shit' in front of your grandma," put in Mark Foley.

"And don't go around belching and scratching your ass in public," added Ricky.

"That's right. And no farting at table. That's what my dad says: 'Did you just fart?' That's what he says, and I say, 'I hope so. 'Cause if it's the dinner that smells like this, then I ain't eating it.'"

Jim looked down at Tee Jay – looked him steadily in the eye. "How about you, Tee Jay? You tell us all about respect."

Tee Jay lowered his head and shuffled his feet.

"Come on, Tee Jay. I thought you were the class expert." He waited, smiling a little, waiting for Tee Jay to say something, but when he didn't, he backed off, and returned to his desk. Beattie had been right, in her own way. Respect is when people give other people their own space, and Tee Jay needed his.

He continued on a different tack. "There was a French

writer in the 18th century called Voltaire. And he said, 'One owes respect to the living; but to the dead one owes nothing but the truth.' Well, I don't agree with that at all. Because the dead – they've done all that they're ever going to do. We can respect their achievements, but there's no point in criticising what they failed to do, because they'll never have the chance to say sorry, or to put it right.

"But the living – they have the chance to put things right, and that's why we owe them the truth, rather than respect. If one of your friends acts mean, or bad. If one of your friends starts badmouthing their parents, or beating up on younger kids and stealing their lunch money, or smoking crack, and you say to them, 'You're an idiot. You're absurd. You're wasting your life,' then that's the truth. And they don't deserve any respect until they change their ways because respect has to be earned."

Tee Jay slowly turned his head and looked across the classroom at Elvin and there was sheer malevolence in his eyes.

"Tee Jay," Jim warned him, and Tee Jay turned back. "Tee Jay, I want you to open your book at page 37 and read the second paragraph."

Tee Jay opened his English Primer and sat for a moment in silence.

"Well?" Jim asked.

"I just read it. All the way through."

"I meant *out loud*, Tee Jay. Out loud, so that we can *all* hear it."

Haltingly, Tee Jay read the paragraph, his fingertip crawling from one word to the next. His left eye was completely closed now so he had to cock his head to one side. "The season – demands – that America learn – to better duh-wuh – duh-wuh—"

11

"Dwell. To better dwell," Jim prompted him.

"To better dwell on her – choice – choicest possession—"

Jim picked up Tee Jay's book and finished it for him. "The legacy of her good and faithful men that she well preserve their fame, or, if need be, that she fail not to dissipate what clouds have intruded on that fame, and burnish it newer, truer and brighter, continually."

He put the book down. "That was Walt Whitman, talking about Thomas Paine; and if ever a man deserved respect, it was Thomas Paine. Like he *deserved* respect, because he risked his life fighting for equality and justice and what he believed to be right."

He paused, and then he added, looking straight at Tee Jay, "The day you do that, that's the day that you'll start earning *your* respect."

Jim spent the rest of the time until recess going over yesterday's homework, which had been to write a 300–word appreciation of *Rip Van Winkle*. He never set his class essays longer than 300 words; some of them had to struggle for an hour to write twenty: 'Rip van Winkles old lady was always giving him a hard time so he went to the wood and drank some stuff and woke up twenty years later and she was dead by then so that was cool.'

Others wrote 600 words of incomprehensible nonsense: 'People said that thunderstorms were thunderstorms but they werent they were all these real miserable goblin-type guys playing ninepins and Rip van Winkles knees were smoting.'

And Beattie McCordic, of course, turned Rip van Winkle's nagging wife into a feminist icon: 'He was a typical man with nothing going for him . . . who took the world easy, would eat white bread or brown, whatever was less trouble . . . would rather starve on a penny than work for a pound . . . and the whole story like blames his *wife* for nagging him to try to get his act together. Like even his dog thinks he leads a dogs life but what do dogs know and anyhow the dog was male and what do *they* know (males I mean.)'

In spite of all of his students' shortcomings, however, Jim could feel a real yearning for understanding in everything they wrote. Even in some of the most laboured essays, heavy with crossings-out and misspellings, there was a strenuous groping for knowledge, a genuine struggle to find the key to literacy. Young people in a darkened room, trying to feel their way towards the door. There were times when he could have cried over what they had written; not for himself, but for them.

'Rip van Winkle let his childrin run wile they never wore no shos and his suns pants was alus fallin down.' That was Mark Foley's essay in its entirety. But Jim could see what it was about the story that had caught Mark's attention: the careless, lazy father who never took care of his children, so that his son had to troop after his mother wearing his ragged hand-me-down galligaskins – 'which he had much ado to hold up with one hand, as a fine lady does her train in bad weather.'

In his own way, at home, Mark had suffered the same kind of experience, with a beer-gut father who owned a run-down automobile body shop in Santa Monica, so the story of Rip van Winkle was much more to Mark than just a legend. Mark had lived it; and now he had taken the first step toward expressing himself through fiction.

Who knows, thought Jim wryly, as he closed Mark's book and dropped it into his 'Out' tray. Maybe Mark was destined to be a latter-day Washington Irving.

He was turning to Rita Munoz's essay (printed in

capital letters, as usual, in multi-coloured felt-tip pens), when he happened to turn towards the window. It was dazzlingly bright outside, but he could see all the way across the schoolyard to the boiler-house. A group of boys were playing basketball right outside the boiler-house door; and Sue-Robin Caufield was leaning against a railing talking to Jeff Griglak, captain of the school athletics team and one of the brightest students at Westwood Community College for years. John Ng was sitting on the other end of the bench, eating something indescribable out a box and reading *Treasure Island*.

It was no more than a flicker; a dark shadow passing over his eye. But the door of the boiler-room suddenly opened, and the tall dark man in the Elmer Gantry hat appeared. He hesitated for a moment, looking right and left, with one hand raised to shield his eyes from the sunlight. Then he hurried diagonally across the schoolyard, and disappeared behind the science block.

He left the boiler-room door ajar. But, strangely, it seemed as if none of the students in the playground had noticed him. None of the boys playing basketball had stopped for a moment, and Sue-Robin had carried on flirting with Jeff Griglak without pausing for breath. Her hair bounced and shone in the mid-morning sunlight.

Jim frowned. He got up from his desk and walked up to the window, cupping his hands around his face to cut out any reflection. Apart from the half-open boiler-house door, everything else appeared to be normal. And yet . . .

And yet he had a gut feeling that something was badly wrong. He felt as if he had been shown a picture that had been deliberately designed to confuse him: like a painting by Rene Magritte, or one of M.C. Escher's drawings of never-ending staircases. He left the classroom and walked quickly along the corridor until he reached the swing doors that led outside.

There was laughter and chatter and shouting in the schoolyard but Jim didn't hear it. He was making his way toward the boiler-house door. He cut right through the middle of the basketball game, and smacked away the ball as it came bouncing toward him.

He reached the boiler-house and peered inside. He could see the handrail and the concrete steps that led down to the boilers themselves; but the rest was in darkness. He called out, "Hallo! Is there anybody in there?"

He listened, but there was no answer, only the deep whistling noise of the gas-fired burners. He called out again, and there was still no reply. He guessed that the man in the Elmer Gantry hat must have gone down there to steal something; or maybe to do some damage. There had been several incidents of former students coming back to take their revenge on the college which they thought had failed them. They had to blame somebody or something for their inability to make it in the world outside.

Jim switched on the overhead lights and looked down over the railings. The boiler-room smelled strongly of heat and gas, but the two large grey-painted boilers appeared to be undamaged. No broken gauges; no pipes sabotaged; nothing like that. Jim was about to switch off the light and go back outside when he glimpsed something glistening in the shadows between the boilers. A black, viscous trickle making its way across the floor. It looked like an oil leak, quite a bad one. He went down the steps, his shoes chuffing on the concrete, approached the boilers and hunkered down so that he could see between them.

The glistening fluid had crept so far across the floor that it was almost touching his toe. He dipped his finger into it and held it up; and it was then that he felt a

15

chilly, tingling feeling all the way down his back. This wasn't an oil-leak. The liquid had looked black against the concrete, but on his fingertip it was dark, congealed crimson.

Jim strained his eyes to see into the shadows. He fumbled in his pocket and found half a book of matches from the El Torito Mexican Restaurant. He struck one, and it flared up briefly, but it did little more than burn his thumb. He wished to hell he had a flashlight. There was *something* there – a dark, lumpy shape – but that was all that he could make out.

With his knees bent, he edged his way between the boilers, feeling his way with his hands. It was so hot in there that sweat was dripping from his forehead before he had even managed to shuffle six feet forward, and his shirt was clinging to his back.

He thought he heard a bubbling, groaning noise, and he stopped and listened, although the sound of the boilers was deafening.

He struck another match, and shouted, "Anybody there? This is Mr Rook! Is there anybody there?"

Again, that agonised, bubbling noise. It sounded like somebody trying to talk while they were drinking a glass of water.

Jim inched forward a little more, and suddenly he was touching something heavy and warm and wet. He shouted out, "*Ah!*" and recoiled violently.

Shaking, he struck another match; and used it to ignite the last few remaining matches in the book, to give himself a brief flare of bright light. Lying on the concrete in front of him was Elvin, recognisable only by his Dodgers T-shirt, plastered in blood. He had wounds everywhere: all over his arms, all over his face, all over his body, as if somebody had been determined to stab every inch of him. They looked like the gaping mouths of a shoal of stranded fish.

Sensing the heat from the matches, Elvin tried to lift his hand up. He let out another groaning sound; but it was the last gargling exhalation of air and blood from punctured lungs. As the matches burned down, and the light died, so Elvin died, too, and Jim was left in darkness, with the boilers roaring on either side of him.

He took hold of Elvin's sticky hand, and squeezed it, and whispered, "God be with you, Elvin. So goddamned young," and that was all he could manage to say.

Chapter Two

Lieutenant Harris knocked on the open classroom door, and stepped inside. He was short and stocky, built like a hefty little linen-chest, with a snub nose and a scrub of sandy hair and a livid red scar on his chin. He wore a sandy-coloured polyester suit with sweat marks under the armpits.

"Mr Rook?" he said. His voice was a soft, congested rasp.

Jim had been standing by the window, looking out. On his desk was the single page of Elvin's last essay, *My Best Poem*. He had taken it out of his file, with the intention of giving it to Elvin's parents. It was *Three* by Gregory Corso: three short verses, and the last verse read,

> *'Death weeps because Death is human*
> *spending all day in a movie when a child dies.'*

Jim turned around. He didn't know whether to smile or cry. The red-and-blue police lights were still flashing outside, although the ambulance and the coroner's station wagon had left about ten minutes before. Special Class II had been excused college for the rest of the day, and they didn't have to come back tomorrow if they were still too upset. Three grief counsellors had been called in, to help the students to cope with

18

what had happened. After all, Elvin had been everybody's friend. Slow, very slow; but endlessly patient; and willing to help anybody if they needed help – fixing the transmissions on their automobiles, putting up shelves, wiring plugs, running errands. Nothing had ever been too much trouble, because the best way in which Elvin had been able to communicate with people was not through words but through practical actions.

Jim had recognised that, and had let him help around the school – mending fences, draining the swimming-pool, and repairing damaged lockers. Elvin used to sing, when he was working. He loved it.

And now, at the age of seventeen years and four months, he was dead.

Lieutenant Harris prowled about the classroom. "What can you tell me about Thomas J. Jones?"

"Tee Jay? What do you want to know? That he's black? That he's not very clever? That he comes from a broken home?"

"I want to know if you think that's he capable of homicide in the first degree."

Jim turned around and looked at him. "What can I say? I guess we're all capable of homicide in the first degree, if you give us enough provocation."

"Come on, Mr Rook. You saw Elvin's body. You saw what his assailant did to him. One hundred and twelve stab wounds, that's what the medical examiner counted. Most of us would stop feeling provoked after we'd inflicted just one."

"I don't know what you're trying to say."

"I'm trying to find out from people who knew him well whether Thomas J. Jones had the motive or the psychological characteristics to murder Elvin P. Clay.

You're his teacher. You probably know him better than anybody; his mother excepted."

"I don't think he's a killer," said Jim.

"He sure isn't a babe in arms."

"Listen, he finds it difficult to read. He can't manage anything more than basic maths. His mother has three daughters and four other sons, and they all live together in a three-bedroom house in the shabbiest part of Westwood. He's intelligent and energetic, but he's also dysfunctional and deeply frustrated, like most of the kids in my class. If it hadn't have been for a garbled set of genes, he probably could have been somebody very special."

"But you caught him fighting Elvin this morning, didn't you? A pretty damned serious fight, from what I've heard about it so far. And from what I've heard about it so far, Thomas J. Jones made specific and unambiguous threats to kill Elvin, in front of several witnesses."

He took out his notebook and flipped it open. "His actual words were, 'I'm going to kill him – I'm going to kill him for that – I'm going to murder that mother.'"

Jim said, "Yes. That's exactly what he said. But he was angry. Elvin said something to upset him, I don't know what. But in my opinion Tee Jay's threats didn't really mean anything."

Lieutenant Harris gave Jim a long, pained look, as if he were feeling the first pangs of chronic indigestion. "They didn't really *mean* anything? Yet less than two hours later, you found Elvin fatally wounded in the college boiler-room, with more holes in him than a chickenwire fence."

"But Tee Jay didn't do it, did he? I talked to him already. He spent the whole of recess talking to his friends on the basketball team; and they vouched for that, too."

"Well, that's right. Except that we have a ten-minute

window. Tee Jay left his friends at approximately 11:05 and said that he needed to call his uncle. He was seen going into the main college building and he wasn't seen again until 11:15 or thereabouts."

"Did anybody see him going to the boiler-room?" asked Jim.

"No, sir. But that isn't really the point. The point is that he had just enough time to go to the boiler-room and perpetrate an act of homicide. He had the motive, and he had the opportunity. What's more, he has a considerable amount of blood on his clothing, which he freely admits is Elvin's."

"Blood from the fight in the washroom. That doesn't prove anything."

"Maybe not. But we'll be running some tests."

Jim said, "What about the man in black?"

"Excuse me?"

"The man in black. Black suit, black wide-brimmed hat. I was marking books. I looked up and saw him coming out of the boiler-room. He stopped, and took a look around, as if he didn't want anybody to see him, and then he went off."

"He was acting suspicious?"

"Well, *furtive*. That's the word. Furtive."

Lieutenant Harris tapped his pencil against his puckered lips. "He must have been. In fact he was so darn furtive that nobody else saw him. There were seventy-nine students out on that playlot this morning – *seventy-nine* – and not one of them saw anybody unfamiliar."

"You're kidding me," said Jim, in disbelief. "He walked out of the boiler-room in open view of everybody. He opened the door, looked around, and just went marching off, right through a whole crowd of kids. *One* of them must have seen him."

21

"Black suit? Black wide-brimmed hat?" Lieutenant Harris flicked all the way through his notebook and shook his head. "None of your students saw anybody like that."

"All right. Maybe not. But I sure did."

Lieutenant Harris tucked his notebook into his pocket. "So . . . do you want to give me a description?"

"You're not going to take a note?"

"It's all right, Mr Rook. I can remember it. How tall would you say he was?"

"Hard to tell, with that hat on. Six feet plus. Not heavily built. One hundred and ninety max."

"And a black suit?"

"That's right. Baggy, flappy, unconstructed."

"And what would you say was his ethnic origin?"

"Couldn't tell, exactly. The sun was against me."

"You don't even know if he was black or white?"

Jim thought for a moment, trying to remember what the man had looked like; but then he said, "No." He hadn't glimpsed anything which would have conclusively shown him whether the man in the Elmer Gantry hat was Caucasian or Afro-American or even Oriental for that matter. Both times the man's face had been turned away, or shielded by the brim of his hat, as if he hadn't wanted Jim to see what he looked like. But the mystery was, how come nobody else had seen him? Sue-Robin Caufield couldn't have been standing more than fifteen feet away from him when he came out of the boiler-room door; and Jeff Griglak had actually been facing him.

"Okay, Mr Rook." Lieutenant Harris took out his notebook again and went through a whole list of procedural questions. How old Jim was. Whether he was married or divorced. Where he lived. His telephone number and his e.mail domain name. Then he said, "Fine . . . thanks for your time."

"What happens now?" Jim asked him.

"Thomas J. Jones has been arrested on suspicion of murder in the first degree. We'll be taking him back to headquarters for questioning."

"You've arrested Tee Jay already? What about the guy in the black hat and the black suit?"

Lieutenant Harris made a complicated face, half apologetic and half dismissive. "We'll be keeping an open mind, Mr Rook."

"You mean you won't be making any effort to look for him?"

"Well . . . I have to say that your description's pretty sketchy. Quite apart from the fact that nobody else saw him, except you. I know you mean well, sir. I know that you have quite a reputation for protecting your students. That's admirable. But I have to consider the facts."

"The facts? The fact is that a guy in a black suit and a black hat came out of that boiler-room just before I went in there and found Elvin dying on the floor."

"We couldn't find any footprints, Mr Rook, except yours."

"You didn't have Tee Jay's footprints, then?"

"No. But then we didn't find Elvin's, neither. The only person who trod in Elvin's blood was you."

Jim tiredly ran his hand through his hair. "I don't know, Lieutenant. I can't believe that Tee Jay would have done anything like that. It just wasn't in his nature."

Lieutenant Harris gave a dry, thumping sniff. "In my experience, Mr Rook, it's the people we think we know the best who give us the nastiest surprises."

Jim packed up and was on his way out of the building

when he heard somebody calling his name. He turned around and saw Ellie Fox hurrying toward him. Ellie was head of the college Art Department: a petite woman with a little snubby nose and straight toffee-coloured hair held back in a band. She always wore voluminous denim smocks, jeans and sandals, and more often than not she was carrying a pencil or a paintbrush behind her ear, just in case people didn't get the message that she was an artist.

"Jim! I wanted to talk to you last week, but I was always missing you!"

"Listen, Ellie, I'm sorry – what with everything that happened today – can't we talk tomorrow?"

"But, Jim, this is important. Really."

"I'll look into the Art Department first thing tomorrow. I promise."

"It's something to do with Tee Jay. I thought you'd want to see it."

"Tee Jay? What?"

She took him by the arm, and led him back up the steps. "Come look. Tell me what you think."

He followed her along the echoing hallway until they reached the Art Department. For Special Class II, the Art Department was especially important. It was here that they could learn to express themselves in colour and light and shape. If they couldn't write, they could still tell stories – in crayons and paint. If they couldn't add or divide or multiply, they could still make necklaces of glittering beads. They could model with clay; they could paint with their fingers. Ellie Fox was an almost obsessive believer in art of all kinds. "Most of the reason people kill themselves is because they never look at pictures; or sculptures; or anything. Art brings you out. Art makes you regular, body and spirit both."

A modelling class was in progress: eight girls and three boys trying to make animals out of clay. As Jim crossed the studio, several of the students looked up from their work in curiosity, and Jim could hear a vibrant whisper travel around the room: ". . . says that Tee Jay didn't do it . . ." ". . . saw some guy all dressed in black . . ." ". . . what, The Shadow? What's he on?" ". . . well, do *you* think Tee Jay could've done it?" ". . . maybe it was a one-armed man . . ."

Ellie stopped in front of a large grey plan-chest. She opened the top drawer, and said, "I have all of their recent work in here. Anything that's creative, anything that's strong, anything that's different." Now she raised her voice so that the whole class could hear. "Provided, of course, it isn't obscene, or defamatory toward West Grove Community College or any of its faculty."

There was a burst of giggling over in one corner of the art studio, and Jim saw Jane Fidaccio quickly knock an immense clay penis off the rhinoceros that she was modelling.

Ellie drew out three large sheets of paper and spread them on top of the plan chest. They were all painted in reds and oranges and blacks. One showed a man being burned alive on top of a funeral pyre. Another showed a procession of men walking through a jungle. Jim didn't immediately find it horrifying until he realised that they were walking in line because a long stake had been driven through their stomachs and out through their backs, keeping them together like a human kebab. The third picture showed a naked woman lying on her back, eating her newborn baby even before she had passed the afterbirth.

"Tee Jay's work," she said.

"Jesus," Jim acknowledged. "These are pretty strong."

"I was going to destroy them, but I thought you'd better take a look at them first."

"Did Tee Jay ever do anything like this before?"

Ellie shook her head. "Only in the last two weeks. I asked him what they meant, and he said they were something to do with his ethnic heritage, but that was all."

"His *heritage*? He was born in Huntington Park, so far as I know. Then his father got a job as a chauffeur and the family moved to Santa Monica. What kind of ethnic heritage is that?"

"Well, I don't know," said Ellie. "But it seems to me that he's been very disturbed."

Jim picked up the painting of the men in the jungle. "You see these letters here? V – O – D – U – N. Do you have any idea what these could mean?"

"No idea at all. Tee Jay wouldn't say. He said the pictures spoke for themselves."

"Not to me they don't," said Jim. "Look . . . what's he written down the side here? S – A – M – E. Same? What does that mean? Same as what? Or maybe it's an acronym . . . Skewer All Men Equally, or something. Or an anagram. Who knows?"

"Maybe you could ask him?" Ellie suggested.

Jim nodded. She was a wise woman, Ellie; tender and wise. He said, "Can I keep these?"

She said, "For sure . . . I don't want any of my freshman students seeing them. They might get ideas."

Jim rolled up the paintings and twisted an elastic band around them. "I owe you one," he told Ellie, as she showed him to the door. "Maybe that special Rook pizza I keep on promising to make you. The one with the smoked ricotta."

"Not just yet," she said. "Let's wait till some of this dust has settled."

"Sure, Ellie. I didn't mean now."

"No," she said, as if none of the men she met ever meant now.

He went home first, to his second-storey apartment in a pink-painted concrete block just off Electric Avenue, in Venice. There was a small blue pool in the courtyard, around which the residents relaxed in the evening on rusty half-collapsed sun-loungers, drinking warm wine and reading thick blockbuster novels. This evening it was so warm that even Mrs Vaizey was outside, seventy-six years old, in a huge pair of black silk shorts and a shrivelled tube top, and one of those SpaceFace lobster visors that were thought to be such a scream about 15 years ago.

"You're looking grim, Jim," said Mrs Vaizey, shielding her eyes against the sun. "Bad day at Black Rock?"

Jim nodded. "One of our students was killed today. It's been pretty heavy all round."

"Killed? That's awful! How did that happen?"

"We're not entirely sure. But so far it seems like another student stabbed him."

"The world isn't what it was, Jim. In my day you went to school to get yourself educated, not to kill other students, or to get yourself killed."

"Well, that's right, Mrs Vaizey. But I'm not so sure that this killing is quite so simple as it looks."

The pale pink lobster on top of her head gave him a beady-eyed look and dangled its plastic claws. "You think different, do you? That's because you *are* different."

"Don't start giving me that mystical stuff, Mrs Vaizey. I respect your gifts, and I respect what you believe in, but one of my favourite students died today, and this isn't the time."

27

"Nonsense," she said. The skin on the back of her hand was like crumpled tissue-paper. "This is exactly the time. You tell me *why* you think different."

Jim glanced over at Myrlin Buffield, from Apartment no. 201, who was pretending to read *Primary Colors* but who was listening to their conversation intently. Myrlin was ninety pounds overweight, with black slashed-back hair, and bosoms, and a gold earring in the shape of a dagger; and skin as white and luminous as a freshly-caught pollock. Nobody knew what Myrlin did for a living. Nobody liked to guess.

"Why don't you come up for a drink, Mrs Vaizey?" asked Jim. "Then we can talk in private."

"Beer?" asked Mrs Vaizey, suspiciously.

"What do you think I am? Bourbon."

"In that case, Jim, I'd be happy to join you."

He picked up her newspaper and her glasses and her sewing-bag and helped her up the steps to his apartment. He didn't speak to her very often; mainly because she was always trying to persuade him to have his palms read; or his Tarot cards interpreted; or his tea-leaves scrutinised. He believed in a whole lot of odd things, but he didn't believe in fortune-telling, or Ouija boards, or ghosts. He believed that the future was unpredictable, and that when you died, you died. *Click*. The light was switched off, and that was it.

Jim unlocked the door of his apartment and ushered Mrs Vaizey inside. The calico blinds were drawn down, and it was dim and warm. It wasn't untidy, but there were several tell-tale signs that a single man lived here, and that nobody had cleaned up during the day. The cushions on the couch were still crumpled. There were dead sweet peas in the vase on the windowsill. Yesterday's paper still lay where Jim had dropped it, as well a single slipper.

Mrs Vaizey cautiously sniffed. She could smell it, too. Nothing unpleasant – just stuffy, motionless air that nobody had breathed all day.

"Where's your cat?" she wanted to know.

"The feline formerly known as Tibbles? He'll be back, once he knows that I'm here. I never let him in during the day. I'm allergic to the smell of litter-trays."

Mrs Vaizey sat down on the couch and Jim went through to the kitchen to find his bottle of Jim Beam. He sploshed out two generous glasses for both of them, and knocked his glass against hers, in salute, and to frighten away the devil. "Here's to Elvin, who died today. And here's to justice, and sense, and respect."

"I'll drink to that," said Mrs Vaizey. "Whatever the hell you're talking about."

Jim said, "I'm talking about young people who die too young, Mrs Vaizey. Elvin, you know – he didn't have much of a chance to begin with. He was so damned slow he couldn't catch a cold. His father was an invalid and his mother could never cope. But he was always so cheerful. He always made the best of what he had."

"So who killed him?"

"One of his classmates. A boy called Tee Jay. That's what the police think, anyway."

"But you think elsewise?"

"I'm not sure. Tee Jay and Elvin were having a fight, earlier on; and when the fight was over I saw a man walking down the corridor. Tall, with a black suit and a wide black hat. He disappeared before I could find out who he was. But I saw him again, coming out of the school boiler-room; and that's where Elvin was stabbed to death. I saw him, as clear as I can see you; but the trouble was that nobody else saw him. Nobody."

Mrs Vaizey knocked back her bourbon and wiped her

mouth with the back of her hand. "I think I should look at the palm of your hand, Jim."

"Mrs Vaizey, with all due respect, that's not going to answer anything."

"Jim . . . there's something different about you. I always knew there was. You got the aura."

"The aura? What's that?"

Mrs Vaizey made a circular motion with her hands. "It's a kind of a *glow* that some people have around them. Sometimes a happy person can shine like a light. But most people have more like a *mottled* effect, different colours for different parts of their psyche, if you get my meaning."

"So what colour is mine?" asked Jim. He poured her another drink.

"Yours is different. Yours scarcely glows at all. Yours is more like a shadow than a shine."

"What does that mean? That I'm depressed?"

Mrs Vaizey shook her head. "Nothing like that. It means that you're in touch with the world beyond. There's a part of you that can see *through* this everyday world right into the next, same as looking through a store window on a sunny day. You have to cup your hands around your eyes, and press your face close, but you can always see *something*."

Jim gave an amused grunt, but Mrs Vaizey took hold of his hand between her claw-like fingers with all her knobbly silver rings and clutched it tight. "What do you think you saw today, Jim? You saw a man that nobody else could see. Now, was that man alive, do you suppose, or could that man have been something else?"

"I don't know what you mean by 'something else'. What are you talking about, a ghost?"

"Maybe a ghost. Who knows? It isn't just the spirits of

30

dead people who wander through the world. Sometimes the living can do it, too."

"What, like an out-of-body experience?"

"That's one of the ways," said Mrs Vaizey, looking down at the palm of his hand. Her sharp orange-lacquered nail probed his heartline, his headline and his lifeline.

"You're very bright," she told him. "The trouble is, you're stubborn, too. You don't like taking advice from other people. You always think that you have a better way of doing things. On the other hand, you have moments of great self-doubt, when you feel that you might have taken the wrong fork in the forest. At times like these you feel that the trees are closing in on you, and that you can hear strange growlings in the undergrowth."

She looked up, and knocked back her second glass of bourbon. "Metaphor-orically speaking, of course."

Jim watched her, the way her silver hoop earrings dangled in the sunlight. He should have been sceptical but somehow he wasn't. After today's murder, he was prepared to consider almost any explanation for what had happened. If God could allow a young man like Elvin to die; then obviously they were living in a universe in which nothing was logical, and nothing was fair.

"You're very emotional, and capable of very great love," Mrs Vaizey continued. "You had a love once who let you down, and it took you a long time to get over it. But another love will appear when you're least expecting it – quite soon, by the looks of it – and this relationship will endure, on and off, for the rest of your life."

"On and off? I'm not sure I like the sound of that."

"Everybody has quarrels, Jim, especially people who really love each other."

"Well, I guess."

Mrs Vaizey probed his lifeline. He wished she wouldn't

dig her nail in quite so deeply. But then she looked up at him again and there was the most extraordinary expression on her face. She was staring at him as if she couldn't believe that he was real. She probed it some more, peering at it intently; and then she said, "I don't understand this at all."

"What's the matter?" he asked her.

"It's very strange. Normally, if somebody's lifeline is broken, you can predict when they're going to die. You know, almost to the *year*."

"And, what? Is my lifeline broken?"

Mrs Vaizey nodded. "You see here . . . way down at the bottom. It breaks up and goes every which way."

"So what does that mean? You're not telling me that I'm not going to die young, are you? My dad and my mom are both still alive."

"Jim, this break happens very, very early in your life. It means that, by rights, you should be dead already."

"What?"

"There's no mistaking it. It's very clear. It means that you died when you were eleven or twelve."

Jim laughed. "I died when I was eleven or twelve? That doesn't say much for palmistry, does it? I mean, how dead do I look?"

"There's no mistake," said Mrs Vaizey, and her voice was completely serious.

"So I'm supposed to believe that I'm dead, is that it?"

"You're not dead now; but you were once. Just for a moment, perhaps. But dead."

Jim took his hand away, and held it against his chest, as if it were injured. "Listen," he said. "This doesn't make any sense."

"I don't know, Jim," said Mrs Vaizey. "Maybe it could.

Were you ever sick, when you were a child? I mean seriously sick?"

"I went down with pneumonia once, when I was ten or eleven."

"Can you remember what happened?"

"Not very clearly . . . I was always pretty skinny and weedy when I was a kid. I went down with the grippe and the grippe turned into pneumonia. My dad and mom took me to hospital and there were all these people in white, looking after me. They were great. They took me for walks and they talked to me, and in the end they brought me back to my bed and I was cured."

"What do they look like, these people in white?"

"I don't know. I guess they were doctors and nurses. But there were dozens of them . . . all talking to me, all trying to make me feel better. And in the end, yes. I felt better."

Mrs Vaizey held out her glass and Jim filled it again. The sun had fallen, and there were wide stripes of light across the only picture which Jim had hung on the wall: a large reproduction of *The Surrender of Breda* by Veláquez, Dutch soldiers handing over the keys of the city to Spanish lancers. Jim had always taken a particular kind of strength from it, because it showed sworn enemies behaving toward each other with courtesy and understanding – two qualities which he had always tried to instil in the students of Special Class II.

Mrs Vaizey said, "Has it ever occurred to you that those people in white might *not* have been doctors and nurses?"

"I don't follow you."

"You were very young, and close to death. Clinically, perhaps, you *did* die. But, believe me, there are many kind spirits on the other side who do their best to turn back young souls before it's too late."

Jim shook his head. "I'm sorry, Mrs Vaizey. I don't believe in life after death."

"Even though you probably saw some spirits for yourself?"

"I was very young. I was probably dreaming."

Mrs Vaizey took hold of his hand again, and ran her fingernail up and down his lifeline, again and again. "The point I'm trying to make to you, Jim, is that if you've seen spirits once, you can see them again. Coming close to death, that gives you a *facility*, if you understand what I mean. An extra sense that you never lose."

Jim said nothing, but watched and winced as Mrs Vaizey pored over his palm. After a few moments, she frowned, and peered even more closely at his life-line.

"Something wrong?" he asked her.

"I don't know . . . I can't understand what this means. You have a double break and then a loop, almost, like an oxbow. You're going to have a strange meeting, unlike anything you've ever experienced before. Then something very frightening is going to happen. But that's all that I can decipher." She drew her fingernail along his lifeline yet again, and as she did so, Jim felt a searing pain. Her fingernail scratched against his skin like a safety-match, and flames sprang up behind it, right out of the palm of his hand.

"Jesus!" he shouted, and instantly clamped his hand shut. But flames burst out from between his fingers and engulfed his whole fist.

He tried to jump up, but Mrs Vaizey shouted, "No!" She snatched a cushion from the couch and pressed it over Jim's hand. She held it down for a long, long moment, and then she cautiously lifted it up again to make sure that the flames had been extinguished. Slowly, Jim opened

34

his fingers. The fire had vanished, leaving nothing but a pattern of faint red marks.

"Does it hurt?" Mrs Vaizey asked him.

Jim raised his hand and turned it this way and that. "Not really. There's a dull kind of a burning sensation . . . but I guess that's all. What the hell happened?"

"It's a warning," said Mrs Vaizey. She was so shaken that her hands were trembling. "I've heard about it but I've never seen it, not for real, not right in front of my eyes."

"A warning? A warning about what?"

"I can't tell you. There are some things that people shouldn't know."

"Come on, Mrs Vaizey. My goddamned hand just caught light. You have to tell me."

She pressed her hand over her mouth for a while, thinking. Then she said, "All right . . . I suppose you have the right. Sometimes, when the danger of death is very close, people show signs of it on their bodies. The more sensitive a person is, the clearer the signs. I knew a woman in Santa Barbara whose lips went blue; and three weeks later she was dead of cyanide poisoning. Then there was a movie producer in Westwood who kept getting these red bite marks on his arms. Before the year was out, he was attacked by two Dobermanns when he was visiting one of his friends. They practically tore off his face."

She paused for a moment, and then she said, "I've seen burns before, too, on people who have died by fire. Arm burns, facial burns. But I never saw actual *flames* before. Never. You must be even closer to the spirit world than anyone I ever met."

"But what are you saying?" Jim asked her. "You're saying that I'm going to be burned to death?"

35

Mrs Vaizey didn't answer. All she could do was to stare at him in sorrow.

"It's not inevitable, though, is it?" Jim demanded. "I mean, I can change my own destiny, can't I, now that I know?"

"I never heard of anybody managing to change their destiny before," said Mrs Vaizey, laying her hand on top of his. "Maybe *you* can. Who knows?"

Jim said shakily, "How about another drink?"

Chapter Three

Back at college the next morning the students of Special Class II were quiet and subdued, but nobody was absent, with the exception of Amanda Zaparelli who was having her braces removed. Jim wasn't surprised that they had all shown up. They badly needed to share their grief; and they needed to come to college to see for themselves that Elvin's desk was empty, and that he really had left them for ever. Jim knew that during the college semester, a class can be closer than a family, and to lose a classmate can hurt even more than losing an uncle or a cousin.

Jim came into the room tucking his blue denim shirt into his chinos. He looked and felt particularly bleary. He hadn't slept well. He had dreamed all night of shadowy figures in wide-brimmed hats, and fire; and of voices that whispered in languages he didn't understand. He had switched on the light several times to look at the marks on his hand. He had made himself a mug of hot chocolate and had stirred it and stared at it for half an hour before emptying it, undrunk, down the sink.

"I never heard of anybody managing to change their destiny before," Mrs Vaizey had told him. *"Maybe you can. Who knows?"*

"Okay," he said. "This is going to be a special day and a very difficult day. Yesterday we lost Elvin but we also lost Tee Jay, too. The police have charged him with murder in the first degree, and so far as I understand it, they're not looking for anybody else."

He walked through the lines of desks to the back of the class, so that he was standing next to Sue-Robin Caufield. Sue-Robin was wearing a very tight black V-neck T-shirt, and a thin black ribbon around her neck. Tiredly, Jim thought: trust her to make mourning look sexy. In the far corner, Greg Lake was frowning fiercely and blinking as if he were riding a motorcycle in a high wind. Greg suffered from a lack of co-ordination, and every facial expression was a deep struggle. If anybody told a joke, the rest of the class had finished laughing for at least a minute before Greg managed to arrange his face into a smile.

Jim said, "I want you all to remember one thing. As sad as we are that Elvin has gone – as *angry* as we are – and let's not make any bones about this, anger is as much an ingredient of grief as sadness – the justice system says that nobody is guilty until they are *proved* to be guilty. Tee Jay has been charged, but he hasn't been tried. So let's be mature, and wait for a jury to decide whether Tee Jay was really responsible."

"Oh, sure," said Ray Vito, turning around in his seat. Ray had a shiny black pompadour, a pasty, triangular face, and a narrow, eagle-like nose. "And I suppose OJ Simpson was innocent, too?"

"A jury found OJ Simpson innocent. Whatever I think about it, that's good enough for me."

"Oh, come on, Mr Rook. We all watched the trial. There was no way."

"You watched the trial but you weren't presented with the facts in the same way that the jury was. They listened to the facts, and they ended up with reasonable doubt. I have reasonable doubt that Tee Jay didn't kill Elvin. I saw somebody leave the boiler-room just before I found Elvin dead. I don't know who he was, or what he was doing there. I can't understand why nobody else saw him. But he must have been the last person to see Elvin alive; and he wasn't Tee Jay; so let's at least keep and open mind."

Russell Gloach put up his hand. Russell had black short-cropped hair and eyeglasses so thick they must have been bulletproof. He weighed 215 pounds and had an eating disorder which had severely disrupted his schoolwork. He couldn't sit through a forty-five minute lesson without a cake or a candy-bar or a sandwich. In spite of his size, however, his mind was quick, and he could be very irreverent. "I don't believe you saw nobody," he said. "I think you're covering for Tee Jay . . . trying to make people think that maybe he didn't do it, just maybe . . . so they'll have to let him off."

"Why would I do that?" Jim asked him.

Russell shrugged. "Tee Jay belongs to Special Class II, doesn't he? Whatever he's done. He *belongs*."

Jim looked at Russell for a long time, and then he nodded. "Sure," he said. "Tee Jay belongs."

"The point is, though, Tee Jay's been acting real weird lately," said Muffy. Muffy was small and pretty, with one of the most complicated braids that Jim had ever seen. It was looped and butterfly-bowed and decorated with ribbons and beads. She must have woken up at about five in the morning to get it right in time for college. Tee Jay and Muffy had dated for two or three weeks, but Tee Jay had been quiet and laconic while Muffy was like an explosion in a firecracker factory.

Up until yesterday, of course, when Tee Jay had exploded, too.

"What do you mean by *weird*?" Jim asked Muffy.

"Well, he was always so cool, wasn't he?" said Muffy.

"Like nothing ever fazed him, ever. But in the last two or three weeks, he went right into himself. He didn't hardly speak to nobody. You must have noticed in class."

Jim said, "I didn't notice at the time, no. But now you come to mention it." And he thought of the paintings that Ellie had shown him, the skewered men walking through the jungle, the woman devouring her new-born baby.

"I think he had some kind of trouble at home," said Muffy. "He wouldn't talk about it, but I know for a fact that he slept in his car one time; and another time he called me up at two in the morning and asked if he could crash at my place. I mean, I couldn't. My parents would've wigged."

Jim walked slowly to the front of the class. "Did anybody else notice that Tee Jay was acting strange?"

"He started bringing me down for being Jewish," said Sherma Feldstein – a dark, plump, pretty girl with a beauty spot and thick black eyebrows. "He kept saying there was only one religion and that was his. He said that all Jews were – well, he used a rude word."

"Did he tell you what his religion was?" asked Jim.

Sherma shook her head. "He tried to explain it. He kept on talking about crows and mirrors and candles; and there was something about dust, too. Breathing in dust."

"Could you make any sense of that?"

"Unh-unh," said Sherma. "And he wouldn't explain himself, either. He said if I didn't understand it now I never would."

"I noticed something else, too," put in Beattie McCordic. "He was out playing that game where you throw one of those round things over a net. It was hot and he stripped off the thing he was wearing on his top. He had all these marks on his back."

"You mean a tattoo?" Jim asked her.

"No, no. Like lumps, when you cut yourself. What do you call them?"

"You're talking about scars?"

"That's right, scars. In all these kind of like circles."

"Well, I guess if anybody wants to have circles on their back, who are we to say that they can't? He's probably had them for years."

"No, he hasn't. They're really new. Like they're still red-raw and all."

Sharon Mitchell put up her hand. Sharon was as militant about black rights as Beattie was for women's rights. She was strikingly pretty, but she was very tall, almost 6ft 1ins, and she had suffered all of her life for being gawky, and black, and a girl. She always signed her essays 'Sharon X', in honour of the Black Muslims, and Jim never called her anything else. This was a time in their lives when his students needed to be taken seriously, no matter how rebellious and irrational they seemed to be. They felt bad enough about themselves as it was. They didn't need anybody else making fun of them.

Sharon said, "Some people in Africa do that. It's a manhood thing. It's supposed to show that a boy can put up with pain; but also it shows what spirit you belong to."

"I don't follow you."

"Well, some tribes have these guardian spirits who are supposed to look after them all of their lives. The same as godparents, you know. When a boy reaches manhood, the elders choose a spirit for him, and that spirit is supposed to protect him and give him good advice and kill his enemies for him."

Kill his enemies? thought Jim, remembering the dark-suited figure coming out of the boiler-house. He said, "That's interesting, Sharon. I'd like to know some more about that."

41

"I've got plenty of books at home. I'll bring them to college and you can read them for yourself."

Jim looked around the class. "I'll be going to see Elvin's parents later today, and I'm sure that you'd all like me to take a message of condolence. Tomorrow I'd like you all to pool your efforts and make a sympathy card, so that you can all sign it.

"I've been thinking all night of what I could say to you today about Elvin. But I believe the best I can do is read you these words by Emily Dickinson."

He picked up a book and opened it. The class was so quiet that he could hear them breathing.

> "'Because I could not stop for Death,
> He kindly stopped for me;
> The carriage held but just ourselves
> And Immortality.
>
> "'We passed the school, where children strove
> At recess, in the ring;
> We passed the fields of gazing grain
> We passed the setting sun.
>
> "'Since then 'tis centuries, and yet
> Feels shorter than the day
> I first surmised the horses' heads
> Were toward eternity."

He lowered the book. Sitting right in front of him, Jane Firman had tears trickling down her cheeks. She and Elvin had both suffered from dyslexia, and they had spent hours together, struggling to make sense of their books. Elvin's sudden absence was more than she could bear.

Even Ricky Herman was wiping his eyes with his sleeve, and Sherma had her face covered by her hands.

"Okay," said Jim, gently. "Let's have a minute's silence, shall we, so that we can all say our own private prayers."

The class sat with bowed heads. For the first time ever, Mark and Ricky weren't giggling and shuffling. Russell's stomach rumbled, but nobody laughed. It just seemed to make the silence even more poignant. Life was going on as normal and Elvin wasn't here.

The minute was almost over when Jim's attention was caught by a flickering shadow on the other side of the yard. It was a bright day, and the porch that led to the main building was deep in darkness. But Jim was sure he had seen something moving. He walked slowly over to the window and peered out. At first he couldn't see what it was, but gradually he was able to make out the figure of a man, standing close to one of the supporting pillars. He was dressed in black, and against his chest he was holding a black wide-brimmed hat.

Jim beckoned to Titus Greenspan III. Titus was wearing a T-shirt with bright pink stripes across it. With his bulgy black eyes and his nervous, querulous manner, he looked like an oversized prawn. "Titus . . . come here. That's it, get out of your desk and come over here. Now I want you to look out of the window . . . over there. You see where the porch is? You see the right-hand pillar?"

"Which one is that?" asked Titus, blinking.

"It's the pillar on the same side as your right hand. No, *this* hand. Now, can you see anybody standing beside that pillar? It's pretty shadowy, but look hard. A man in a black suit holding a hat."

Titus stared and stared, but in the end he slowly shook his head.

"Is this some kind of intelligence test?" he wanted to know.

43

Jim looked back at the porch and the man was still clearly in sight. In fact he had taken a step forward so that he was easier to see.

"You can't see a man standing beside that right-hand pillar, with a hat in his hand? Come on, look again." (For a split-second, Jim was tempted to add, 'What are you, for Christ's sake, blind?' but he managed to bite his tongue.)

Titus stared across the yard for over half a minute, the tip of his tongue gripped between his teeth. At last, he said, "Nope. I'm sorry, Mr Rook. Hff. No can see."

"Ricky, come here," Jim beckoned him; and then he pointed. "Look over there. You see that man, standing in the porch? Just left of that pillar."

Ricky stared across the yard, but then he let out a whinnying noise and said, "No. Sorry, Mr Rook. I don't see nobody."

"All right," Jim told him. "Go back to your seat. Wait here everybody. Take out your poetry readers and see what you can make of page 26 . . . *Dead Boy*, by John Crowe Ransom. And don't just read it, *think* when you read it, think what it means. I'll be back in a minute."

He left the classroom and hurried along the floor-waxed corridor. He pushed open the swing door with its wire-glazed windows, into the sunshine. He ran across the tarmac yard, toward the porch. And the man was still there. The man in the black suit, holding his wide black hat over his heart. But as soon as he saw Jim running toward him, he rolled away from the pillar in a brief kerfuffle of black, and then he was gone. By the time that Jim reached the porch, panting, the door to the main building was slowly easing its way closed with a quiet pneumatic *pifff!* and the man had vanished.

Jim wrenched open the door and stepped inside. He

listened for the sound of running, but the building echoed with nothing more than the voices of teachers and the slow, plangent echoing of a piano lesson. *Für Elise* played note by hesitant note.

He walked half-way down the main corridor, looking into every classroom window. His footsteps echoed and re-echoed. This was where the most promising students were taught: the students who would graduate with honours, and find themselves a well-paying job. Very few of them would ever be really famous, or really rich. But the college had taught them to work hard, and to apply themselves; and in return most of them had realised that we can't all be Michael Jackson, or Demi Moore.

Jim's class hadn't learned that yet, and maybe they never would. But that was what made them Special Class II.

Jim stopped; and he was about to turn back; when the tall man in the black suit appeared at the very far end of the corridor, half-blurred by the sunlight, and started to tug off his gloves, finger by finger. Jim said nothing for a while, but watched him, his heart beating like an overwound wrist-watch. The man's face was so overshadowed by the brim of his hat that it was still impossible to tell if he was black or white. His head was slightly lowered and he appeared to be waiting. Jim couldn't make up his mind if he was waiting for him, or not. He certainly wasn't going to approach him until he knew for sure that he was unarmed; and even then he was going to be cautious. The man must have been at least six inches taller than Jim: square-shouldered, and brooding, and *shadowy*. Now he knew what Mrs Vaizey meant by an aura. This man carried with him a smoldering, dangerous atmosphere of his own like a thick cloud of volcanic ash. No brilliance here. No rainbow. Not even any mottled colours. He was burning up as darkly as Mount St Helen's.

It sounded as if he were *humming*, too, a strange monotonous drone interspersed with occasional growls deep down in his throat.

"I don't know who you are," Jim called out, trying to sound authoritative, "but this is college property and you're trespassing!"

There was a silence as long as the end of a tape-cassette, before it starts playing Side Two.

Then — "You can *see* me, can you?" the man replied. His voice sounded like somebody dragging a wet sack across a concrete floor.

"If I couldn't see you, I wouldn't be telling you to leave, would I?"

"Of course you wouldn't, no." The man paused again, and thought about that, and then he said, "I suspected that you could see me, the way you came rushing out of that schoolroom yesterday, before nothing had happened. There aren't too many like you, I'm happy to say. People who can *see*."

"I think you and me had better talk to the police, don't you, sir?" said Jim.

"The police? What would be the point of that? They wouldn't be able to see me."

"A boy was killed in that boiler-house, and you were the last person to leave it."

"You mean Elvin. Alas poor Elvin. I didn't know him too well."

The man was paraphrasing *Hamlet*. "Don't mock him," said Jim, although the man was probably mocking *him*, too, the English teacher.

"I don't need to mock him," the man replied. "He mocked himself. He mocked his own race."

"And that's why you murdered him?"

The man said nothing for a while. Then he held out both of his hands. "Do you know something, you and me ought to be friends. I could use a friend with the gift of sight; a friend who can actually see me. I've had friends before, for sure."

"What the hell are you talking about?" Jim demanded.

"Oh, come on, now, Jim; you know what I'm talking about. People who can *see*. Kids who were dropped on their heads. Men who were cut out of automobile wrecks. Women who tried to give birth in toilets, and almost bled to death. They could *see*, those people, but most of the time they were pretty slow on the uptake – even if they hadn't been brain-damaged. Unlike *you*, Mr Rook. You can see; but you're clever, too. I could sure use a friend like you."

"Who are you?" said Jim. He was quaking with rage, but he didn't dare to step any closer.

There was another long silence, but then the man said, "Somebody has to keep the faith, Mr Rook. Somebody has to keep the lamps lit. Some people say we should forgive and forget, but I can't do neither, and I never will."

The man's image seemed to shudder. Then, quite silently, he turned away, and opened up the door to the geography room. He disappeared inside and quickly closed the door behind him.

Jim ran to the geography room and peered in through the window. It was empty apart from the man making his way between the desks, with his back turned. Where the hell was he going? This was the only door, and for safety's sake, the windows couldn't be opened up wide enough for anybody to climb out. Jim twisted the handle, but the door wouldn't open. He rattled it, and banged on the window with his fist, but the man kept walking across the room toward the opposite corner.

But the further away he walked, the taller he seemed to be. He grew, *stretched*, as if the room's perspective had been reversed. By the time he was half-way across the room he must have been seven or eight feet tall; and when he reached the wall and turned around, he was standing higher than the picture-rail.

Jim stopped rattling the doorhandle and stared at the man in total dread. This time he could see his face, grinning at him from the top of his dark, attenuated body. It was the face of a black man, his eyes yellow, his cheeks marked with scars. The skin around his mouth was deeply lined, so that it looked as if his lips had been sewn together, like a shrunken head.

But it was his height that unnerved Jim the most. His hat almost touched the ceiling, and his arms were so long that they could reach half-way along the walls.

Für Elise continued to echo along the corridor: a plonking, mundane counterpoint to the horror inside the geography room.

Jim looked at the man for one more hair-prickling moment. Then he turned and ran to the principal's office, beside the entrance-hall. Dr Ehrlichman's secretary was arranging some flowers on the windowsill when Jim came skidding in. She had big ash-blonde hair and oversized spectacles, and she always wore fussy blouses with lacy collars and cuffs.

"Sylvia – call the cops!" Jim told her.

"Mr Rook! The police? What on earth for?"

"There's a man – it's the same guy I saw yesterday – he's locked himself in the geography room. Now, please, will you call the cops!"

Sylvia dithered, so Jim picked up the phone himself

and punched out 911. "Yes – West Grove College – will you please dispatch somebody fast before he gets away. And if you can get a message to Lieutenant Harris – that's right, he's been handling the whole investigation. Yes."

He put down the phone just as Dr Ehrlichman came out of his office. Dr Ehrlichman was small and neat, with a bald suntanned head and a voice like Micky Rooney. He always wore grey Sta-Prest slacks and a crisp short-sleeved white shirt and his favourite word was 'businesslike'. "Jim – what's going on here?"

"It's the same guy that I saw yesterday," said Jim. "The one who was coming out of the boiler-house when Elvin got stabbed. He's here. He's right here in the building."

"You've called Mr Wallechinsky?"

"I've called the police."

"Jim, listen to me. We pay good money for Mr Wallechinsky and there's a reason for that. He's an ex-cop. He knows how to deal with security problems. And you know college policy, don't you? Nobody calls the police to this college without my say-so. Can you imagine the kind of reputation we're going to get? Yesterday's incident was serious enough, without compounding it."

Jim pointed toward the geography room, his arm rigid. "Dr Ehrlichman, there's a guy in this building who stabbed one of our students so many times that even the medical examiner could hardly count how many holes he had in him. And you think Wallechinsky could deal with somebody like that?"

Dr Ehrlichman said, "Mr Wallechinsky is a good man. Sylvia – do you mind giving him a call? Let's see if we can deal with this problem in-house."

"I'm warning you," Jim told him. "This guy is not an ordinary guy. Not by any stretch of the imagination."

Dr Ehrlichman took off his spectacles and looked at Jim

bulgy-eyed. "I don't think you're the one who ought to be talking about stretches of the imagination, Jim. Nobody else saw your man in black yesterday, and so far nobody's seen him today."

"Then come look," Jim urged him.

"When Mr Wallechinsky's here – then, yes, I will."

Jim said, "I was talking to a woman last night. She's kind of an expert when it comes to things like this. She said that it's possible for some people to leave their bodies and walk around. They don't have to be dead or anything. But the whole point is, only certain people can see them. People who have come within a whisker of dying. That near-death experience gives them an ability to see things that most people can't. Dr Ehrlichman, we have invisible spirits walking among us, all the time. But the trouble is, we simply don't have the eyes to see."

Dr Ehrlichman replaced his glasses and stared at him as if he was having an afternoon off from the madhouse. "You haven't been drinking, Jim, have you?"

"Of course not. What do you want to do, smell my breath?"

"You haven't been smoking? Or snorting? Or whatever it is you people do these days?"

"I'm a teacher, Dr Ehrlichman. I don't come to college stoned or drunk or even impatient."

Dr Ehrlichman looked unconvinced, but at that moment George Wallechinsky arrived, six feet five inches of lumpy human tissue in a tight brown uniform. His face was broad, with two tiny expressionless eyes, buried in his flesh like two sultanas buried in a bread pudding.

"George," said Dr Ehrlichman, briskly, "it seems like we've got ourselves an intruder. Mr Rook says that he's locked himself into the geography room."

Wallechinsky sniffed, and cleared his throat. "How long ago was this?"

"Five minutes; not more."

"Did you ever see the individual before?"

"Sure. I saw him yesterday, coming out the boiler-house, just before Elvin was killed. In fact he was the only reason I went over there, to see what was going on."

"You sure it's the same individual?"

"Believe me, Mr Wallechinsky, there's only one guy like this."

"Okay, then. Let's go take a look. You're sure he's not a college inspector? Sometimes they send inspectors by surprise."

Wallechinsky waddled steadfastly in front of them, all the way down the corridor, his keys jingling on his belt. "This it?" He stopped outside the door of the geography room and looked inside, stooping down so that he could see the ceiling, then angling his head close to the glass so that he could see the floors and corners.

"This room is empty, so far as I can see," he reported. He tried the handle, rattling and shaking it, but it was still locked, or jammed, and he gave it up.

"Did he have any kind of weapon?" he asked Jim.

"Is he there?" Dr Ehrlichman demanded.

"Well, I can't see anything, Mr Principal, sir; but that doesn't necessarily mean that there's nothing there. He could be pressing himself flat against the wall here; or behind this here bookcase; or even under the teacher's desk."

Dr Ehrlichman pressed his nose flat against the window. "No," he said. "He's gone. That's if he ever existed at all."

Jim said, "He was there, Dr Ehrlichman. He even spoke to me."

"I'd like a talk with you later, Jim," Dr Ehrlichman told him. "Mr Wallechinsky, you'd better call the police and tell them it was a false alarm."

"I'd like to check the room first, Dr Ehrlichman," said Wallechinsky. He lifted his keyring, heavy with all kinds of keys, and picked out the one which would open the geography-room door. He inserted it, and turned.

"It's not locked," he said, in surprise.

"What do you mean it's not locked?" Dr Ehrlichman demanded. He seized the handle and shook it until he almost pulled it off.

"No disrespect, Dr Ehrlichman, sir. But I mean it's not locked."

"Then open it."

Wallechinsky reached out for the handle, but Jim lifted his hand and stopped him. "Let me," he said. He hesitated for a moment, and then he opened the door with no trouble at all. He pushed it, and it swung open, so that sunlight fell across the corridor and illuminated their shoes. Dr Ehrlichman's brown rubber-soled lace-ups; Wallechinsky's highly-polished black boots; and Jim's balding blue suede sneakers.

Wallechinsky tried to push his way his inside, but Jim held out his arm to stop him. If Mrs Vaizey was right, then Wallechinsky wouldn't be able to see the man in black anyway. Jim stepped into the classroom, looking right and left, ducking down so that he could check under the desk, then turning around to make sure that the man in black wasn't hiding behind the bookcase.

It was then that he saw him. He was no longer dressed in black, but all in white, and even his face was white, although it was still the face of an Afro-American. He looked as if he had been rolling in flour, or ashes. Even the pupils of his eyes were white, like lychees.

He was up on the ceiling, lying horizontally against the cornice, his hands crossed over his chest as if he had been laid out in a funeral parlour. He wasn't dead, though: he was staring at Jim with those milky white eyes and he was grinning in triumph.

Wallechinsky came into the classroom and circled around it with the clumsiness of a purblind bear, peering behind bookcases and wallcharts as if a man could hide in a space less than an inch wide. He turned to Jim and saw that he was staring at the ceiling, and he stared up at it, too.

"You want to tell me what you're looking at?" he asked. "You don't expect the guy to be up on the ceiling, do you?"

Jim whispered, "You can't see him, can you? You really can't see him."

"See who?"

"The intruder, that's who. He's there. Look. Use your imagination."

"You're not trying to tell me he's invisible? He's up on the ceiling and he's invisible? Come on, Mr Rook. Is this some kind of a practical joke?"

Up above them, the man grinned even more widely. Jim couldn't take his eyes away from him. He felt so terrified that he couldn't speak; but what was worse than his terror was his sense of helplessness. In all his years as a remedial teacher, he had always been able to cope. But he couldn't cope with this. Not logically, or emotionally, or any way at all. He had to stand in the middle of the geography room and admit to himself that there was nothing he could do, and that was the most horrifying feeling of all.

Testily, Dr Ehrlichman said, "Are we done now? I'm extremely busy."

"Ain't nobody here but us chickens, Mr Principal,"

53

said Wallechinsky, giving Jim an exasperated shake of his head.

"All right, then. You'd better call the police and tell them it was a false alarm."

He turned away. As he did so, the door slammed shut with such violence that the glass cracked and plaster dropped from the architrave. Dr Ehrlichman's face immediately reappeared in the window, and he was shouting something, but Jim couldn't hear what.

Wallechinsky went for the door-handle and tried to pull it open, but it was stuck just as fast as it had been before.

"Give me a hand here!" he called. But Jim could see what he couldn't see; and that was the white-faced man slowly sinking from the ceiling, slowly turning around, so that he landed feet-first on the floor only four or five feet away from them. His shoes touched the floor completely silently, and with exaggerated grace. Jim backed away, colliding with one of the desks. The white-faced man lifted his hat and dust fell off it and sifted to the floor.

"Will you please give me a hand here, *sir*?" Wallechinsky repeated. Outside the room, Dr Ehrlichman hammered on the door with his fist and shouted, "What's going on? Will somebody tell me what the *hell* is going on?"

The white-faced man was gliding toward Wallechinsky, smiling and gliding. When he was only two feet away, he stopped. He grasped his right wrist with his left hand, and twisted; and to Jim's horror, his right hand rotated, around and around, until it came off altogether. A false hand, carved out of ebony and smothered with ash. But the white-faced man was left with more than a stump. Out of his right wrist protruded a long, wide-bladed knife, which looked as if it had been grafted into his bones. It gleamed in the sunlight, wickedly sharp; and

54

the white-faced man mockingly waved it from side to side in front of Wallechinsky's face, because he knew that Wallechinsky couldn't see it.

Jim said, "George, I want you to step back from the door."

"Trying to get the damn thing open," Wallechinsky protested. "There's no reason why it shoulda jammed."

"George! Get away from the door! Now! Quick! As fast as you can!"

"Why? Do you think there's some kinda—"

Jim lunged forward and shoulder-tackled the white-faced man as hard as he could. He went right through him, as if he didn't exist, and collided with the door, splitting the wood and hurting his shoulder so badly that he spun around, saying, "Shit, shit, shit," over and over. He had felt the briefest of draughts when he passed through the white-faced man, like a fridge door opened and shut, but that was all.

The white-faced man silently laughed, and circled his arm around and around, so that his knife actually whistled.

"Don't touch him," Jim warned him. "You've done enough goddamned damage already."

"I haven't done anything," Wallechinsky complained. "Begging your pardon, sir, it's *you* that broke the goddamned door."

"Just stay back," Jim warned the white-faced man, edging away.

"I don't know what you're talking about," said Wallechinsky. "Stay back from what?"

But the white-faced man had made his way behind him, and was grinning at Jim over his shoulder, and there was something in those milk-white eyes that told Jim what he was going to do.

"Listen," he said. "You want me to be your friend? I'll be your friend. I'll do anything you want."

Wallechinsky looked deeply uneasy. "Listen, Mr Rook, I'm a married man. Three kids. A wife who's put up with me for twenty-eight years."

"I don't care what it is, I'll do it," said Jim.

"Mr Rook, sir—"

At that instant, with a sharp racketing noise, the door was kicked open from the outside, and two police officers came bursting into the geography room. Instantly, the white-faced man whipped up his knife and drew a line of blood down Wallechinsky's right cheek, a razor-thin cut that Wallechinsky could have scarcely felt, because he didn't even flinch. The white-faced man turned to Jim and said, "You've made me a promise, Mr Rook. I expect you to keep it. Otherwise, I'll be back for this fellow, and *then* you'll see what a knife can do."

He turned around and flowed out of the room as if he were no more substantial than a cloud of smoke from a summer bonfire. Jim was about to call out after him, but now he had two sceptical-looking cops in the room, as well as Wallechinsky and Dr Ehrlichman, and he decided it would be wiser for him to keep his mouth shut.

"You hurt there, buddy?" asked one of the cops, pointing to Wallechinsky's cheek. A thin scarlet stream of blood was running into his uniform collar.

"What? Hurt?" said Wallechinsky, in bewilderment; and then he dabbed at his cheek with his fingers. "Hey. What the hell happened? I'm bleeding."

Dr Ehrlichman took a clean squared handkerchief out of his breast pocket. "Here, use this. You'd better have it seen to."

"How the hell did I cut myself like that?" asked Wallechinsky. "Mr Rook, did you see what happened?"

Jim shook his head. "I don't have any idea," he lied. "It just – *happened* – just like that."

"So who are we supposed to be looking for?" asked one of the cops.

"I'm sorry," Jim told him. "I must have made a mistake. I saw somebody suspicious in the building, and I thought he came in here."

"Can you give us some idea of what he looked like?"

"Hard to say. Tall, dark, dressed all in black."

The second cop turned to Wallechinsky. "You see anybody like that?"

"I didn't see nobody. Only Mr Rook."

"Have you *any* idea how you could have gotten that cut?"

"I told you. It just happened."

"Mr Rook didn't cut you? Maybe by accident?"

"Mr Rook wasn't nowhere near me."

"Okay," said the cop. "Why don't you get your face cleaned up, and maybe we'll talk to you later."

Wallechinsky left, clutching Dr Ehrlichman's blood-sodden handkerchief against his cheek. As he did so, Lieutenant Harris arrived, wearing a lurid purple necktie and perspiring furiously.

"So what's going on here?" he wanted to know.

Jim said, "I'm sorry . . . this is all a misunderstanding. I thought I saw the same man in black that I saw yesterday outside the boiler-house."

"The same man in black that nobody else could see?"

Jim grimaced. He couldn't tell Lieutenant Harris how shocked he was; and how much the white-faced man had unnerved him. If he could hover on the ceiling and change his colour like a chameleon and cut people who couldn't even see him, God alone knew what he else he was capable of. Besides, even if Jim explained everything, there was no chance whatsoever that Lieutenant Harris would believe him.

Lieutenant Harris said, "Have you thought of talking to somebody about this guy that you've been seeing?"

"What do you mean?"

"Well—" clearing his throat, embarrassed, "—I mean like a counsellor; or maybe a psychiatrist."

"You think this is some kind of hallucination?"

"I don't know what to think, Mr Rook. You're a college teacher and from what I've gathered from most of the other members of the faculty you're a very well-respected college teacher. But you teach a difficult class, don't you? Maybe you've been suffering from stress. When people are stressed, you know, they sometimes get their heads filled up with some pretty wacky ideas."

"I'm not under stress, believe me. My class is fine. I'm fine. Everything's fine."

Lieutenant Harris shrugged. "Okay, you're fine. So you won't mind my asking you if you indulge in recreational substances of any kind."

"I smoke now and then."

"Did you smoke yesterday?"

"Unh-hunh. I never do it at school. Evenings and weekends only; and then only once or twice a month."

"So you didn't smoke today, either?"

"Absolutely not."

"You know I could easily check that out."

"Listen, Lieutenant," Jim told him, "I'm not under the influence of stress or drugs or anything else. Yesterday I saw what I told you I saw. Today . . . well, let's just say that I was a little confused."

Lieutenant Harris stared at him for a very long time without saying anything. A bead of sweat ran down his cheek and he wiped it with the back of his hand.

"Okay, then, Mr Rook. Maybe I'll talk to you later."

Jim's class reconvened after the lunch recess for a session of reading and word-recognition. Unusually for him, Jim went to the classroom early so that he was waiting for them when they arrived. No dramatic entrance this afternoon.

After they had settled down, he stood up and paced to the back of the room. "Before we start reading," he said, "I want to know if any of you believe in ghosts."

John Ng's hand shot up. "My grandfather is a ghost."

There was a loud hooting of derision from the rest of the class, mingled with spooky whistles and moans of "*wooooooooooo!*" but Jim remained serious. "You've actually seen your grandfather for yourself?"

"No, but my father said that he visited him when he was in a time of trouble, and stood at the end of the bed, and told him the proverb of the golden carp always trying to swim upstream. He was all dressed in orange and he wore an orange mask, so that only his eyes peeked out."

"I believe in ghosts," said Rita. "*And* I saw one, too."

"Go on," Jim encouraged her.

"Well, we used to use this beach-house on Santa Monica beach when we were kids and every time we went there we used to see a kid with a surfboard under his arm coming out the door. Always the same kid. Then he used to disappear in the crowd and we'd never see him again till next time. We asked the lifeguard about him and like described what he looked like and the lifeguard said it was a kid who got drowned about seven years before. He came out of the beach-house and went into the sea and like two days later they found his body under the pier."

"That's *scary*," said Sherma.

"I think that's great," said Ricky. "I mean the kid

may be dead, right, but he gets to go surfing every day."

"I d-d-don't b-b-believe in g-g-g-g—" David Littwin began. Immediately a loud chorus of snoring started up, but Jim raised his hand and the class could tell by the look in his eye that he wasn't going to tolerate any teasing, not today. "I think that when you d-die your spirit g-g-g-gets reborn in somebody else. Or s-s-something else."

"Hey, Littwin, just so long as you don't get yourself reborn as a sports commentator," Mark put in.

Jim said, "Shut up, Mark. A whole lot of people believe in reincarnation – the Buddhists in particular. Now let's take it a step further. Does anybody believe that some people can see ghosts when maybe other people can't?"

Russell said, "Are you trying to tell us the guy you saw yesterday was a *ghost*?"

"I'm not sure what he was. But I think I saw him again today, and believe me, he doesn't act like a human at all."

"Mr Rook's finally flipped," said Ricky. "Guess you've been teaching us dummies for too long, sir."

Jim smiled, but then he said, "Let me tell you what happened, and then judge for yourselves."

He walked back to the front of the class, and went up to the blackboard, with the intention of drawing a picture of the black-suited man floating on the ceiling. As he picked up the chalk, however, he saw something moving in the small window in the classroom door.

He turned and stared, and he felt that terrible cold prickling sensation up his back, like centipedes walking down his spine. In the window he saw the face of the black-suited man – black now, as he had been the first time that Jim had seen him. His fingertip was held to

60

his lips, and his yellow eyes were as threatening as a poisonous snake.

Jim hesitated, and then flipped the chalk back into the tin. "Let's forget it," he said. "It's not your problem. Let's get down to some reading, shall we? Russell, how about you? *On The Road*, from the beginning of chapter ten."

He didn't look at the window again, although he was conscious that the man was still there, watching him.

After a few minutes, however, he disappeared. Jim immediately went to the door and opened it, and looked out, but the corridor was empty in both directions, except for a lanky boy leaning over the water-fountain.

Chapter Four

He let class out an hour earlier than usual, and left the
college on his way to see Elvin's parents. He was
crossing the faculty parking-lot when Dr Ehrlichman
called out to him.

"Jim! Are you leaving already?"

"I'm going to see Elvin's parents. You know, to give
them the class's condolences."

Dr Ehrlichman laid a hand on his shoulder. "Jim . . . I
know you've been through a tragic experience, but I think
it's essential that you keep your grip on reality. It's going
to be very disturbing for your students if you don't."

Jim said, "I guess it depends on what you mean by
reality, Dr Ehrlichman. There's one reality for each of
us, and sometimes those realities don't exactly match.
Sometimes it's hard to know which one you ought to be
keeping a grip on."

"I'm sorry, Jim. I'm not here to get involved in a
philosophical discussion. I just have to tell you that if
we have any further incidents like today's, I'm going
to have to consider putting you on suspension and
requiring you to undergo – well, a psychiatric evalu-
ation."

Jim had reached his car, a '69 Rebel SST in its original
screaming orange. "I see. We can't have the staff being
as nutty as the students, can we?"

"'Nutty' is not a word we use in association with West Grove College, Jim . . . even for Special Class II. I simply want to make sure that you're mentally stable and that you're able to carry out your professional duties without you seeing phantom prowlers everywhere you look and calling the police out willy-nilly. The students come first, Jim, every single time. The students, and West Grove's good name."

Jim replied, "I'm aware of that, sir. You won't hear any more about men in black." And he meant it. His new-found friend had made it chillingly clear that he didn't want Jim talking about him to anybody.

Dr Ehrlichman seemed to be satisfied with that. He slapped Jim on the back and walked off with his bald head shining in the sunlight. Just then Susan Randall appeared, carrying an armful of books. She had her hair pinned back and she was wearing a white sleeveless blouse with pointed lapels.

"You're not headed anywhere south of Santa Monica Boulevard, are you?" she asked him.

"Sure. Do you need a ride?"

"If it's not too far out of your way. My car's in the shop and I don't relish the idea of carrying all these books on the bus."

Jim opened the door for her and she climbed in. He had never noticed before that she wore a gold ankle chain. He said, "Watch your skirt . . . I mean you don't want to get it caught in the door."

They drove out through the college gates and headed southward on Westwood Boulevard.

"Great car," said Susan. "I really love classics."

"This car's classic all right. It was crap when it was new and it's still crap."

"It's a terrific colour, though, isn't it?"

Jim shrugged. He wasn't in the mood for talking about cars. Susan watched him for a moment, and then she said, "You must be feeling pretty bad about Elvin."

"I'm feeling bad about both of them, Elvin and Tee Jay."

"You really believe that Tee Jay wasn't responsible?"

"I don't know. He *could* have done it. He had the time and he had some kind of motive. But I really don't believe that he did."

"Because of this man you saw? The man in black?"

"I'm sorry, Susan. I can't talk about it any more. I have to get a few things straight first."

"Okay, whatever. It's just that yesterday you seemed so sure."

Jim didn't answer. They had stopped at the traffic lights at Wilshire and all he could think of was the man in black glaring at him through the classroom window, his finger pressed to his lips.

As the signals turned to green, Susan said, "We've never really had the chance to get to know each other, have we?"

"I guess not. Always busy, busy, busy."

"Ron Philips said you were something of an expert on antique maps."

Jim turned and stared at her. "Ron Philips said that?"

"Sure. He said you had one of the finest collections of antique maps he'd ever seen."

Shit, thought Jim. Ron Philips, the faculty smartass. I'll garotte him next time I see him. The only antique map I'm an expert on is the well-worn Chek-Chart of Central Los Angeles in the glovebox.

"I'm totally *fascinated* by antique maps," Susan continued. "I bought a 16th-century map of the Huguenot

64

settlement in Carolina last year, but it's only a reproduction. Authentic maps are so expensive, aren't they? Ron said you have hundreds."

"Well, not quite hundreds. In fact, to tell you the truth—"

"I'd love to see them," she said, touching his arm. "Maybe I could come round sometime."

It was the touch that did it. "That would be great," he said, thinking: of all the luck in the world, the most attractive woman in the whole school has just invited herself around to my apartment, and it's all because of some stupid dumbass joke.

"Maybe Saturday?" Susan urged him. "I could bring around some Chinese food."

"Saturday? Like, this coming Saturday? The day after tomorrow? I don't know. I'll have to check my diary. And you'll have to remember that I keep all the really valuable maps in a safe-deposit box."

"Do you have anything extra-special?" she said, her eyes bright. "Go on, give me a for-instance."

"I don't know. There are just so many."

"Tell me just one."

"Well . . ." he said. "I have a chart of Martin Frobisher's voyage to Greenland in 1577, when he was trying to find a way through to China." Thinking: thank God I know some history.

"Oh, I *have* to see that," said Susan. "That must have cost you a fortune."

"Yes, well. It's pretty rare. There are only three copies in existence, and one of those is supposed to be a fake. Trouble is, nobody can decide which one." You're getting in deep here, Jim. Don't say any more.

He stopped outside Susan's neat white house on Almato Avenue and helped her to carry her books to the door. The

65

sprinklers had just finished and the concrete path was still wet. "Time for a drink?" she asked him.

"No . . . I'm sorry. I promised Mr and Mrs Clay I'd be there by four."

"All right, then," she smiled. "I'll see you tomorrow."

With that, she kissed him on the cheek. He stood staring at her as if he had forgotten his lines. This wasn't a play, and he wasn't an actor, but he simply didn't know what to say next.

"Tomorrow, then?" Susan prompted him.

"Oh, sure, tomorrow." He turned off-balance and brushed against a wet bush. "That'll save me taking a shower." Brushing the droplets off his shirt and pants, he walked back to his car. Before he climbed in, he raised his arm in a goodbye wave and Susan waved back. He felt extraordinary. It was just as if his lungs couldn't remember how to breathe. He hadn't felt this way for such a long time that he had to pull down the sun-visor and stare at himself in the vanity-mirror to make sure that it was really him.

He looked back toward Susan's house but she had gone inside now and closed the door. "Maps," he said. "Where do I get some goddamned maps?"

Inside Mr and Mrs Clay's second-storey apartment the drapes were half-drawn and Grant and Elisabeth Clay were sitting in the shadows. Jim was let in by a solemn nine-year-old girl with cornrows and white satin ribbons and a very white dress. There were other relatives in the kitchen, drinking coffee and talking in low, respectful voices. A large photograph of Elvin hung above the couch, draped in a black cloth. Beside it hung a crucifix and a 3–D picture of The Last Supper.

Jim went over and gave Mrs Clay a long, sorrowful hug.

He felt her tears through the shoulder of his shirt. Then he turned to Mr Clay and held his hand in both of his.

"We're going to miss Elvin so much," he said. "All of his classmates send you their love; and they all want you to know that they're thinking of you."

"You found him, didn't you?" said Grant. He was a short, stocky man with wire-grey hair. He was wearing a formal white shirt and a black bowtie. He spoke well, and he carried himself with supreme dignity. He could have been mistaken for a judge.

"Yes, I found him," said Jim.

"He was alive, wasn't he? That's what the police lieutenant told me."

"Only barely, Mr Clay. He died just as soon as I reached him."

"And he didn't say nothing? No last words?"

Jim shook his head. Elisabeth Clay took hold of his hand and looked up at him in tearful incomprehension. "Why did this have to happen, Mr Rook? What did Elvin do? He wasn't smart, I know that, but he always worked hard. He was always good, and kind, and Christian."

"I don't know why it happened, Mrs Clay. Every time a young man dies, I guess that every grieving mother and father ask themselves the same question. And I guess that they always come up with the same answer. Wrong place, wrong time; wrong friends, wrong situation. Sometimes I think that God turns his back, and doesn't see what's happening, not until it's too late."

Grant said, "Elvin and Tee Jay were such good friends, that's what I can't understand. And I used to like Tee Jay. He was always polite, and called us 'sir' and 'ma'am', and once he took Elvira to the beach. She's our young one. Eleven now; and all we have left. Elisabeth can't

67

have no more children. Not that any child could ever replace our Elvin."

"Do you believe that Tee Jay did it, Mr Rook?" asked Elisabeth.

Jim said, "Let's put it this way. I have my doubts. But I can't say too much about it right now – not while the police are still looking into it."

A wide, pretty woman in a black dress and a black pillbox hat came out of the kitchen and said, "Would you care for some coffee, and a piece of fruit pie?"

"Coffee would be great," said Jim.

Grant went up to Elvin's portrait and stared at it, as if he were willing it to speak. "Elvin didn't see too much of Tee Jay these past three months. Elvin didn't know too much about it, but it seemed like Tee Jay was having trouble at home. I can't tell you much more than that, because it was one of those things that you don't put a mind to, till something tragic happens, and then you look back."

"Do you have any idea what kind of trouble Tee Jay was having?" asked Jim.

"The police asked me that, but I don't have any idea at all. What kind of trouble does a seventeen-year-old boy usually have with his parents? He wants to party; he wants to stay out late; he doesn't want to do what he's told. He wants to experiment with alcohol and drugs. I don't know. All I know is that Elvin stopped hanging out with Tee Jay so much as he used to."

A young girl in a black-and-white gingham blouse was standing by the door, listening. She said, "Elvin told me that Tee Jay was getting too religious."

Elisabeth held out her hand. "Come here, honey. Mr Rook – this is Elvira, Elvin's sister. Elvira, this is Elvin's teacher, Mr Rook."

Jim said, "Good to know you, Elvira. I came here to tell your folks how sorry we are about Elvin."

"Elvin talked about you a whole lot," said Elvira. "He said you were crazy sometimes, but you always taught him more than anybody else."

"What was that you were saying about Tee Jay getting too religious?" asked Jim.

"I didn't understand that, either," put in Grant. "How anybody be *too* religious? Elvin was religious. The whole family, we go to church regular, always have. Elvin sang in the choir before."

"But it wasn't that kind of religion," said Elvira.

"What do you mean?" Jim asked her.

"I heard Elvin and Tee Jay arguing once. Tee Jay was trying to get Elvin to bite the head off a chicken. He said they should drink its blood, and say some prayers, and then they would never die."

"You didn't tell us this before," said Elisabeth.

"I couldn't. Elvin and Tee Jay caught me listening and they said I had to swear not to tell, otherwise the smoke would come and get me."

"The smoke? What smoke?"

"I don't know. But the way Tee Jay said it, I was frightened; so that's why I didn't say anything."

"Okay," said Jim. "You did good to tell us. Now why don't you cut me a piece of that pie?"

Elvira went back into the kitchen. Jim turned to Grant and said, "Does any of this mean anything to you? Killing chickens? Or smoke?" He paused, and then continued, "How about crows and mirrors and candles? Or breathing in dust?"

Grant glanced uneasily at his wife. "This isn't the time to talk about things like that. Nor the place, neither. We're devout people, Mr Rook. We don't hold with blasphemy."

"Then you know what I'm talking about?"

Elisabeth looked up at him and Jim couldn't understand the expression on her face at all. But Grant said, "Yes. I know what you're talking about. You're talking about killing chickens, to please the spirits. You're talking about crows, which are sometimes crows and sometimes men. You're talking about mirrors . . . the kind of mirrors that don't reflect your own face."

"Hush," Elisabeth interrupted him. "You shouldn't be saying such things . . . not now, not in front of Elvin's picture."

"Maybe there's somewhere else we can talk," Jim suggested. Grant hesitated, but Jim said, "I think it's important, Mr Clay. It may be too late for Elvin but it's not too late for Tee Jay."

"Come out on the balcony," Grant suggested; and so they did, and slid the doors shut behind them. Grant leaned on the railings and looked down at the small concrete yard where children were playing in a sandpit and a group of teenagers were hanging around smoking and playing techno-rock on a huge ghetto-blaster. "Kids," said Grant. There was no pity in his voice, but there was no judgement, either. "What do they have to look forward to, but this?"

"You were telling me about Tee Jay's religion," said Jim.

"I don't know too much about it, but it's like voodoo. My grandfather used to tell me stories about it to frighten me, when I was a boy. He told me all about the goofer dust which the priests blow into your face to make you seem like you're dead, although you're not. They can stick pins into you and you can feel them but you can't cry out. Then they bury you, even though you're still awake."

"Do you believe in any of that?"

70

Grant's eyes gave nothing away. "I'm just telling you what my grandfather told me."

"All right, then. What about the smoke that Elvira was talking about?"

"My grandfather used to mention the smoke, too, but I could never understand what it was. He used to say, 'The smoke can always find you; and the smoke can always do you harm; like real smoke can choke you to death. But what can you do to the smoke? You can't do nothing. It's there, but it isn't there. You can smell it,' that's what he used to say, 'but you can't touch it. You can see it, but you can't feel it. Watch out for the smoke', that's what he used to say."

"But you don't know what the smoke actually is."

"No, Mr Rook, I don't. And to tell you the God's-honest truth, I believe I'd rather not."

"Well, I appreciate your telling me," said Jim. "I was beginning to think that I was going crazy."

Grant looked at him narrowly. "You know something about Elvin's killing, don't you? Something connected with this voodoo stuff. You want to tell me what it is?"

"I'm sorry. I can't, just at the moment."

"You can't, or you won't? Which is it?"

"Mr Clay . . . I don't know very much more than you do. But I've seen some things that aren't normal at all, and I think they could be connected with Elvin's death. You've done the best thing possible: you've put me on the right track. I promise you, if I can find out who killed your Elvin, then you'll be the very first person to know."

Grant said, "Thanks," and relaxed.

The doors slid open and Elvira smiled, "Your pie's ready for you, Mr Rook."

"Thanks, Elvira," said Jim, and followed Grant inside. As he glanced over the balcony, however, he was sure that he could glimpse a shadow in the trash-crowded corner between the swings and garages. He tried to focus, but the garages were too far away. Besides, Grant was taking his arm and ushering him inside to finish his coffee.

Chapter Five

It took him over twenty minutes to find the Jones house, in a tatty triangle of scrubby hinterland right next to the freeway. It was so noisy that you had to shout at yourself to find out what you were thinking; and the air was yellow with photochemical smog.

There was a scrubby patch of grass outside the house, on which a derelict bronze Buick Riviera with no wheels was supported on cinderblocks. A small black boy with no pants on was furiously tricycling up and down the sidewalk. Glistening snot poured from each nostril and he intermittently stopped to lick it. Jim was almost tempted to give him his handkerchief, but one handkerchief wouldn't do much to solve the problem of child neglect. He had seen kids of seven and eight, openly smoking cigarettes that their parents had given them. What was a little snot?

Jim went up to the front porch and rang the doorbell, although the door was already half-open. The green paint was faded and flaking and one of the windows was cracked. From inside the house came the smell of chicken frying and the monotonous thumping of garage music.

After a while, Jim stepped inside. The house was shabby but well-kept, with lace doilies on all of the side-tables and antimacassars on the backs of the armchairs. The walls were crowded with colour photographs of aunts and uncles and cousins, as well as a garish painting of wild animals coming down to an African waterhole to drink.

He made his way along the corridor to the kitchen, where a thin bespectacled woman in a green dress was chopping peppers. He rapped lightly on the open door, and she looked up, flustered. She was obviously Tee Jay's mother: he had inherited her eyes and her nose and her firm, determined jawline.

"Mr Rook!" she said. "What brings you here?"

"How are you, Mrs Jones? I just came by to make sure that everything was okay at home."

"As good as it can be, with my son accused of killing his best friend."

"Have you seen him yet?"

"Saw him this morning, over at the police headquarters. They were fixing to find him a lawyer."

"How is he?"

"Not much different from always," said Mrs Jones, scraping the chopped-up peppers into a saucepan. "He hardly said more than two words strung together."

"Mrs Jones, I want you to know that I don't think Tee Jay did it."

"Huh!" she said, wryly. "Looks like you're the only one who does."

"I'm not so sure. Most of his classmates don't think he did it, either; although some of them said that he'd been acting kind of weird lately."

"Acting kind of weird is the understatement of the century," said Mrs Jones. "For the past three or four months, Tee Jay has been just impossible to live with. Staying out till all hours, giving me mouth. Hanging out with all kinds of low-life."

"You mean he's been behaving like any normal eighteen-year-old?"

"Maybe so. But I'm trying to keep this family together all on my own, working every hour that God sends me; and the last thing I need is rebellion and bad language and slamming of doors. I just don't need it."

She suddenly turned to Jim, and her eyes were crowded with tears. "And I don't need my son in jail, accused of first-degree murder."

"Mrs Jones—" Jim began, "if you don't want to talk right now—" But then the garage music stopped and Tee Jay's older brother Anthony appeared, wearing a Dodgers T-shirt and a baggy pair of Bermuda shorts. He was even taller and broader than Tee Jay, and he put a large, protective arm around his mother's shoulders.

"Hi, Anthony," said Jim. "I just came round to make sure that your mom was okay. You found yourself a job yet?"

"Start Monday, Mr Rook, working for Santa Monica 'Vette. The money ain't great but I'll be doing what I'm good at."

"Hope you're still reading . . . keeping your brain in shape."

"Oh, sure thing. I just finished *Native Son*."

"Have you been to see Tee Jay too?"

Anthony shook his head, and gave his mother a comforting squeeze. "Tee Jay and me haven't been getting along too good lately. Tee Jay hasn't been getting along too good with anybody, as a matter of fact. That's why he left."

Jim frowned. "You mean he doesn't live here any more?"

"Uhn-hunh. Not for three months now."

"So where *does* he live?"

"Down near Venice Boulevard. He's staying with his uncle, Dad's big brother. That was another reason we were arguing so much. His uncle's been away for years and years, right, working in Nigeria and Sierra Leone and places like that; and all of a sudden he turns up and pays us a visit. Me and mom and the rest of the family really dislike him, you know, but for some reason Tee Jay takes a shine to him. He starts visiting him two or three times a week and that was when the trouble really starts. In the end the rows get so bad that Mom tells Tee Jay to pack his bag and get the hell out. So of course, where does he go? Straight to Uncle Umber."

Jim thought for a moment, and then he said, "This Uncle Umber. Tell me about him. Why didn't you and the rest of the family like him?"

"You ought to meet the guy, then you'd know. He's, like, really heavy, if you know what I mean. He walks in through the door and he fills up the whole house. And he's full of all this stuff about racial heritage and African tradition. Real mumbo-jumbo, you know; but if you try to disagree with him he gets totally aggressive, and treats you like you're some kind of traitor to your race."

Jim said, "I think I'd like to meet this Uncle Umber of yours."

"Believe me, Mr Rook," said Mrs Jones, "you wouldn't. If I were you, I'd leave well enough alone."

"All the same, do you have his address?"

Anthony tore the corner off a piece of kitchen-towel and wrote it down. "He's a blowhard, okay? So don't take him too serious."

"*Ly*," Jim corrected him. "It's 'serious*ly*'."

"Right, well, that too," said Anthony.

Uncle Umber's address near Venice Boulevard turned

out to be one of four apartments over Dollars&Sense, a small cut-price supermarket in a scabby street lined with ten-year-old automobiles and overflowing trash cans. The upper part of the building was painted white, but at one time it must have been light green, because the paint was scaling off like skin-disease.

There was an intercom speaker and three doorbells, one without any identifying card, one saying Puchowski, and the other 'U.M. Jones'. Jim pressed it and waited.

Nobody answered, so he pressed it again, and then again. At last a deep, crackly voice said, *"Who is it?"*

"Mr Jones? My name's Rook, Jim Rook. I'm Tee Jay's teacher. I wonder if I could have a word with you."

"You'd better come on up, Mr Rook. I've been expecting you. It's Apartment 1."

The buzzer sounded and the door unlocked, but Jim hesitated. *I've been expecting you?* He didn't like the sound of that. Maybe he should back off, and leave Mr U.M. Jones for Lieutenant Harris to interview.

The buzzer sounded again. *"Are you coming on up, Mr Rook, or is there something that's bothering you?"*

"I'm coming."

He pushed open the door and found himself in a gloomy, airless hallway with a single fluorescent tube dangling from the ceiling by its wires. He climbed the concrete steps until he reached the first landing. Then he went up to the black-painted door marked '1' and knocked.

The door was opened almost instantly – and there, to Jim's horror, stood the tall dark man from college, hatless now and dressed in a long black kaftan. He was grinning at Jim with a gleeful ferocity, baring his teeth.

"It's *you*," Jim whispered. He wished to God he had

77

a crucifix or a vial of holy water or whatever it was that kept supernatural creatures at bay.

"Yes, Mr Rook, it's me. But don't look so shaken. I'm only Tee Jay's uncle, after all."

"Oh, no. You're a hell of a lot more than that. I don't know what you are or who you are, but don't try to tell me that you're 'only Tee Jay's uncle'. You murdered Elvin Clay."

Uncle Umber gave a light, dismissive shrug. "So what do you propose to do about it? Call the police? Make a citizen's arrest?"

"There's no point in that if nobody else can see you. You said so yourself."

Uncle Umber's brow furrowed. For the first time, Jim noticed that he had a pattern of cicatrices on his forehead, tiny self-inflicted scars in an arrow-pattern that met between his eyes. "Nobody else can see me? What are you talking about?"

"Don't play games," Jim told him. "Nobody can see you but me, and even I can't feel you. But you murdered Elvin Clay and by God I'm going to find some way to make you pay for it."

Without a word, Uncle Umber stepped out of his apartment and swept past Jim to the opposite door, Apartment 2. Jim felt his silky kaftan sliding against him, and he could *smell* him, too: that distinctive incense aroma that had been left in the college corridor the first time that Jim had encountered him. He stood back while Uncle Umber knocked at the apartment door; and then knocked again.

The door opened and an elderly man in a grey short-sleeved shirt appeared, with a checkered napkin tucked into the collar. His face was grey and his hair was grey and even though it was thinning it stuck up at the back like a cockatoo's crest.

"What is it?" he demanded, querulously. "I'm trying to eat my supper here."

"Zygmunt," said Uncle Umber, with all the showy patience of a stage magician, "can you see me?"

The elderly man stared at him as if he were mad. "What the hell do you mean, Umber? Of course I can see you. I just don't happen to *want* to see you, that's all. I'm trying to eat my supper."

"Zygmunt," said Uncle Umber, "before you go . . . can you tell this gentleman where I was yesterday morning round about eleven o'clock a.m.?"

"You was in your apartment, wasn't you?" said the elderly man. "I saw you going in round about quarter after ten and I saw you coming out again just before two."

"You're sure of that?" asked Uncle Umber.

"Of course I'm sure. You couldn't have left without closing the street door, and when I hear that street door shut, I always look out to see what's what."

"There," said Uncle Umber, in triumph. "I don't appear to be the man that you say I am, do I? Other people can see me; and I couldn't have possibly killed Elvin, because I was here; and I have a witness to prove it. Even if I *had* managed to leave without Zygmunt hearing me go, I could never have reached West Grove College in time to do the dirty deed – now, could I?"

He came up to Jim and stood right over him; and this time Jim could actually *feel* his aura, vibrant and dark. His eyes were yellowish, with bloodshot rims, like the yolks of fertilised eggs. He laid his hands on Jim's shoulders and gripped him hard. It hurt, but Jim did his best not to wince.

"You said you could see me but you couldn't feel me?" Uncle Umber growled. "How does this feel?"

Jim said, "You don't frighten me, Mr Jones. I know what I saw and I know what I felt. Or rather, what I *didn't* feel."

"So call the police," Uncle Umber suggested, lifting his hands away from Jim's shoulders and holding them up wrist-to-wrist as if he were waiting for handcuffs.

"I came here because of Tee Jay," said Jim. "Not because of you. All right, you can prove to the police that you didn't do it. But what about Tee Jay? No matter what else you are – if you're his uncle, how can you let him take the rap for a crime that *you* committed?"

"He won't," said Uncle Umber. "The police don't have any witnesses. They don't have any forensic evidence. They don't have anything but circumstantial evidence – except, of course, *your* story that you saw me leaving the boiler-house, and they won't believe that for a moment. Plus, one more thing."

"What's that?" asked Jim.

"One of your class will suddenly remember that he saw Tee Jay at the very time that he was supposed to be stabbing Elvin Clay."

"What the hell do you mean?"

"He saw him smoking behind the science block, that's what I mean."

"But the cops have talked to every student in the school. Nobody saw him doing that."

Uncle Umber tapped his forehead with a long, dry finger. "They will, Mr Rook. They will." He held out his hand in front of his face, palm uppermost, and gently blew. "All you have to is to puff a little dust their way, Mr Rook, and they will remember anything you want them to remember, forever. Polygraph proof."

He beckoned Jim toward his apartment. Inside, it smelled even more strongly of incense, and Jim sneezed three times before he could go any further. There was a dark hallway, its window shuttered, its walls painted oxblood red. Three skulls were hung in a triangle. They had twisted horns and pointed noses, and they were probably nothing more bizarre than oryx, but Jim was beginning to think that anything was possible. Standing in one corner, half-hidden by the thick black velvet drapes, was an ebony statue of a beautiful naked woman with the head of a snarling dog.

Uncle Umber led Jim into a large living-room, whose walls were entirely lined with black-and-red fabric. It was furnished with two leather sofas the colour of clotted blood, a black carpet, and a huge coffee-table strewn with books and magazines and strings of beads and all kinds of other bizarre detritus, such as bones and feathers and wedding-veils. One side of the room was taken up with charts and diagrams and something that looked like an astrological map, although it was covered with drawings of scorpions and beetles and oddly-deformed children.

In the opposite corner stood a wooden carving of seven naked men, all joined together with the same long spear.

Jim said, "I've seen that before."

Uncle Umber looked at him in surprise. "You've seen the piercing ceremony? Where?"

"I mean I've seen the same image. Tee Jay drew it in his art lesson."

"Tee Jay is very expressive, Mr Rook. Very creative. He is also very proud. He finds it difficult to do what he's told."

"There are times, Mr Jones, when, for the common good, everybody has to do what they're told."

Uncle Umber went across to a small antique desk, pulled open the drawer, and rummaged around inside.

81

A few moments later, he reappeared, carrying a small linen bag tied with thin black string and sealed with black sealing-wax. He grinned, and held up the bag between finger and thumb, and shook it. "Do you know what this is? This is memory powder, the people in Dahomey used to call it *loa* powder, because they thought it was made by the lesser spirits, so that they could see Vodun."

"Vodun?"

"That's right, Mr Rook. Vodun, the greatest god in Dahomey Fon folk belief. It was after Vodun that voodoo was named."

He held it out and Jim took it. He sniffed it, and it had the strangest smell, a smell that reminded him of dreams and drying grass and some long-lost flickering picture of his mother, turning around in front of a sunlit window to say—

He looked up, and Uncle Umber was smiling at him. "Memory powder," said Uncle Umber. "But you never know if the memories are true; or if they're false. I could give you a memory with memory powder, and even a lie-detector wouldn't be able to show if you were telling the truth."

"So what am I supposed to do with this?"

"It's very easy, Mr Rook. All you have to do is to blow the powder over one of your students, and then tell him or her that – why, didn't they see Tee Jay smoking behind the science block at the time when he was supposed to be stabbing his friend?"

"That's it?"

"That's it, Mr Rook. The memory powder will do the rest."

Jim offered him the bag back. "I can't do anything like that, Mr Jones. All of my students are my own personal responsibility. If any one of them should come to any harm—"

Uncle Umber flared his nostrils. "Don't try to be pious with me, Mr Rook. You promised that you were going to be my friend. Unless you do this thing, your class will suffer a tragedy like nothing they have ever experienced before."

"Listen, Mr Jones, if you touch any one of them—"

"You'll do *what*, Mr Rook? You'll kill me, and spend the rest of your life in jail? You said you came here for Tee Jay's sake, didn't you? *This* is for Tee Jay's sake."

Jim said, "If Tee Jay *wasn't* smoking behind the science block, then where was he? If he didn't have anything to do with Elvin's death, then why do you have to cook up this cockamamie alibi?"

"You don't understand. Tee Jay had to be there when Elvin died, to see."

"You mean he *was* in the boiler-house, after all? He stood there and watched you cut Elvin to pieces? You're sick, Mr Jones. You're very, very sick."

"I'm just keeping the lamps lit, Mr Rook. Far more terrible things have been done in the name of Christianity."

Jim said, "Forget it. I'm not going to poison any of my students. No way."

Uncle Umber gave him another grin. "Then try it on yourself first. Go home, and tell yourself one thing that never happened to you, and then sniff a pinch of the powder, and see what happens. It won't kill you, I promise. It's only made of roots and hair and ground-up bones. I wouldn't hurt you, Mr Rook. Like I said to you before, I need a friend."

Jim looked Uncle Umber in the eyes, trying to challenge him, trying to show him that he couldn't

83

play with children's lives. But there was no feeling at all in Uncle Umber's eyes, nothing but cold-blooded indifference, that in the end he had to turn away.

"All right," he said. "I'll do it. But only for Tee Jay's sake. And when Tee Jay's free, I want you to send him home to his family, where he belongs."

"Tee Jay will only go where he wants to go, Mr Rook. He's an independent spirit."

Jim had hardly been home five minutes when there was a knock on the door and Mrs Vaizey came in, wearing a wide floppy straw hat, a pink bikini with a lobster motif on it, and a white nylon cardigan. "Jim! I was hoping to catch you!"

He quickly opened one of the kitchen cupboards, took down the china jar in which he usually kept his snipped-out shopping premiums, and dropped the bag of memory powder into it. He didn't want Mrs Vaizey to get wind of what he was doing. "How're you doing, Mrs Vaizey? Haven't run out of bourbon, have you?"

"No – no – nothing like that, sugar. I've been doing a little research today, on your behalf, and I've found out some *very* interesting things."

"Oh, yes?" said Jim. He went to the fridge, took out a can of Coors and popped the top, noisily sucking up the froth.

"How long have you had that cheese?" asked Mrs Vaizey, peering into the dairy shelf. "It looks like it's ready to run the 200 metres."

"It's gorgonzola, Mrs Vaizey. It's supposed to look like that. Now what are these very interesting things you found out? I'm kind of bushed."

"Oh, yes . . . well, I looked it up in *The Occult Review*. In the past ten years, there have been fifteen recorded cases of people who claim that they have seen other people when nobody else can – just like you and your man in black."

"Are these ghosts we're talking about here?"

"Ohhh, no. Not ghosts. Not ghosts at all. Every one of those manifestations was the image of somebody who was actually living at the time. But here's the interesting bit: they *all* emphatically denied being at the locations at the time they were seen."

Jim thought of Uncle Umber, with his eye-witness evidence that he had been back at home when Elvin was killed. Jim had seen him at the college, and yet all the time he had been back at his apartment near Venice Boulevard. "So what's your conclusion?" he asked Mrs Vaizey.

"I think my first hunch was absolutely right. The man you saw was having an out-of-body experience. His physical body was lying somewhere else, in a state of trance, while his spirit went out walking."

"I saw him again this morning," said Jim. "He came to the college and confronted me. He said he wanted me to be his friend."

"Well, he would. Spirits have only limited powers, outside of the body; and out-of-body experiences are very taxing. If he were to stay out too long, his physical body would be at risk of a stroke or a heart-attack."

"What I don't understand is how he can be nothing but a spirit and at the same time be able to hurt people. He was floating on the goddamned ceiling, for God's sake, and when I tried to push him he just wasn't there. Yet he cut our security guard's face, right in front of me; and of course he stabbed Elvin, too."

85

Mrs Vaizey said, "Spirits have been known to bruise people. You can wake up in the morning and find purple fingermarks all over your body. They've strangled people, too. A force doesn't have to be visible or touchable to do you harm. You can't see the wind but it can blow you over. You can't touch smoke but it can make your eyes water."

"Smoke . . . that's it," said Jim. "That's just what Elvin's sister was talking about. She overheard Elvin and Tee Jay talking about sacrificing a chicken, biting its head off, and they told her to keep quiet about it or else the smoke would get her. Elvin's father said his grandfather used to give him the same warning, when he was a little boy. If he didn't behave himself, the smoke would come to get him."

"It's not just 'smoke'," said Mrs Vaizey. "It's '*The* Smoke'. It's what they call out-of-body experiences in Haiti. A man can rise from his body in the night to steal things that he wouldn't be able to take in his physical form; or to make love to a woman who would never normally let him touch her; or to take revenge on his enemies."

"Voodoo," said Jim. "He said so himself."

"You mean you *talked* to him?"

Jim nodded. "I talked to him in his spirit form, at the college, and I talked to him in the flesh. He wasn't difficult to find. He's Tee Jay's uncle, his father's brother, a guy called Umber Jones. He virtually admitted what he's done; but then there's absolutely no way of proving it, is there? The guy was at home, and he's got himself a witness who's prepared to back him up."

"And he wants you to be his friend?" asked Mrs Vaizey.

"He's threatened to hurt some of my students if I don't."

"Oh, yes; and he would, too. What does he want you to do?"

"I don't think I ought to tell you. I don't want any one of my students put at risk."

"I can't help you if you don't confide in me, Jim."

Jim shook his head. "I can't. I'd never forgive myself if anything happened to any of those kids."

Mrs Vaizey pressed her hand over her mouth and stood thinking for well over a minute. Jim stood watching her, feeling as if he had been riding on a rollercoaster all afternoon, shaken and tired and slightly sick.

At last Mrs Vaizey lifted one finger. "There's only one thing we can do," she said. "It won't be easy, but I don't see any alternative."

"Any alternative to what?" asked Jim.

"Give me a drink," said Mrs Vaizey, and she waited while Jim poured her the last of the bourbon. She swallowed a large mouthful, and then she ran her tongue around her teeth. "If you want to use The Smoke, you have to have a *loa* stick, a spirit stick. Every *houngan* has one, so that he can draw symbols in ashes to summon the spirits. I guess you could say that it's the voodoo equivalent to a magician's wand. It has to be carved from a ghost oak, from Western Africa, and it has to be carved from a ghost oak which grows in a cemetery . . . a tree that's been nourished on human flesh.

"Without his *loa* stick, your new friend will still be able to leave his body, as we *all* can, but he won't be able to call on the spirits to help him, which means that he won't have the power to hurt anybody in the physical world."

"So what do you suggest we do?"

"As I say, there's no alternative. We have to take it away from him."

"But how the hell do we do that? We can't exactly break into his apartment and go rummaging through his closets, can we?"

Mrs Vaizey looked up at him and her expression was deadly serious. "Not in the flesh," she said. "But we can do as he does, and leave our bodies, and visit him as ghosts."

Jim said, "Come on, Mrs Vaizey. This is beginning to leave the ground."

"But it's true. Everybody can leave their body, if they wish. You did, when you nearly died, and you almost didn't come back."

"All right, let's say for the sake of argument that it's possible. But even if it's possible, how do you do it?"

"I'll teach you, if you like. But you won't have to, not this time. If you tell me exactly where this Umber Jones man lives, *I'll* do it."

"Is it dangerous? I can't let you do it if it's dangerous."

Mrs Vaizey gave him the briefest flicker of a smile. "Yes, Jim, it's dangerous. But life is dangerous, and we don't stay in bed all day, frightened to go out, just in case an airplane falls on our head, or the ground opens up underneath our feet."

"Look, if there's any risk at all, I'd rather do it myself."

"*No,*" she said, with surprising firmness. "If your friend were to find you when you were out of your body, you wouldn't stand a chance. You don't try to do your own wiring, do you? You call an electrician. This is one job that you ought to leave to a professional."

"Well . . . if you say so," said Jim. "But I can't say that I'm too happy about it. When do you want to do it? Tomorrow maybe?"

"Tonight. *Now*. The sooner the better."

Chapter Six

Mrs Vaizey prowled around Jim's apartment, sniffing the air and rearranging books and ornaments.

"Which way's east?" she asked.

"Er . . . that way."

"East is very important. All evil spirits come from the east. You don't mind if I use your couch, do you?"

"Of course not."

"Then go down to my apartment, go into the kitchen, and open up the left-hand cupboard. You'll find two brass incense-burners inside, and a pack of incense. Bring them up here, and we'll see what we can do for you."

Jim said, "How do you know all of this voodoo stuff? I knew you read horoscopes, but I never realised that you were into black magic, too."

Mrs Vaizey went over to the couch, picked up a newspaper that was sprawled across it, and rearranged the cushions. "I wasn't always an old lady living in a low-rent apartment block in Venice, you know. My father used to work for the State Department. I spent most of my girlhood in France and Morocco, and a year-and-a-half in Haiti. We had a Haitian housemaid who taught me all about the *loa*. There is Legba, who seduces women; and Ogoun Ferraille, who looks after men when they are fighting; and Erzulie, the spirit of purity and love. Then of course there is Baron Samedi, who devours the dead.

"By the way," Mrs Vaizey admonished him, "you mustn't call it 'black magic'. It has some of the same rituals as black magic, like sacrificing chickens. But it's a mixture of Fon culture and Roman Catholicism, and it has the power of both."

Jim said, "I'll go find your incense, okay?"

In less than twenty minutes, his apartment was thick with incense smoke. The only light came from a single table-lamp with a nut-brown shade. Mrs Vaizey was lying full-length on the couch with her eyes closed, her cardigan drawn around her wrinkled brown stomach. She had spread a sheet of newspaper on the rug and drawn a complicated design with white ash that Jim had brought her from the barbecue. "Any ash that has been used to burn flesh will do," she had told him, and he just hoped that Oscar Mayer wieners counted as flesh.

Now she was muttering a long, droning incantation which seemed to Jim to be a mixture of Latin, French and some other language which he couldn't understand. He recognised fragments of it, bits and pieces of the Catholic mass, and something to do with *'sang impur'*, or bad blood, and and *'la mort et la folie'* – death and madness.

She had allowed Jim to sit and watch her, but she had made him promise not to move and not to say a word. He stayed in his armchair in the darkest corner of the room, while the incense-smoke eddied all around him. He coughed twice, and she opened her eyes and gave him a disapproving look, but it was obvious that she was entering into some kind of a trance, because her pupils were unfocused and her eyelids were trembling. He had opened another can of beer but so far he had left it untouched. Mrs Vaizey's droning was so hypnotic that he was practically falling into a trancelike state himself.

"*Libera nos a malo*," she mumbled. "*Panem nostrum quotidianum da nobis hodie.*"

Without warning, it suddenly felt as if the air in Jim's apartment were under intense pressure. He went momentarily deaf, as if he had closed a car window at high speed. Mrs Vaizey shuddered, and her left hand fell sideways across the couch. Her mouth was open but she had stopped chanting, and her face was the colour of cheap newsprint. She let out a reedy little gasp, and then another one, and then her head dropped back and she looked as if she were dead.

She had warned him about this; but he was anxious, all the same. He got out of his chair and walked across the room and crouched down next to her, taking her hand. Her fingers were very dry and very cold, like a lizard with silver rings around its legs. He felt her pulse and it was so weak that it was barely detectable, but this was another aspect of out-of-body adventures that she had warned him about. "The body can't live for very long without a soul. That's what makes humans what they are."

He hesitated for a second or two, but then he reached his hand over her face and lifted her eyelid. Her pupils were totally white, as if she had suffered a heavy concussion. "Mrs Vaizey?" he said, quietly. Then, louder, "Mrs Vaizey! This is Jim Rook! Can you hear me, Mrs Vaizey?"

He shook her shoulders, but all that happened was that her head lolled from side to side. She felt as if she were dead – and not only that, she felt as if she had been dead for two or three days. "Mrs Vaizey? Mrs Vaizey? Can you hear me, Mrs Vaizey?"

The pressure in the room gradually eased. Jim continued to hold Mrs Vaizey's hand, but he sat back, more relaxed. Her pulse may have been faint but it was regular, and showed no signs of faltering; and she was breathing distinctly, with her mouth open, like someone involved in a very deep dream.

He looked up, and it was then that he felt the ice-bath sensation of total shock. Here he was, holding Mrs Vaizey's hand while she lay on the couch. But Mrs Vaizey was also standing by the front door, staring at him.

At first he couldn't speak. His throat was completely constricted with fear. But then he managed to say, "You've done it. My God, you've done it."

She made a complicated sign in the air with her hand; like a benediction. Then she spoke, and her voice sounded reedy and distant, as if she were speaking on an answerphone in an empty office, with nobody to hear her. *"I'm going now, Jim . . . I'll bring back the loa stick . . . and then you can . . . mmmmmlllooowwaaaaahhh . . ."* Her words trailed away into a long, echoing distortion.

She waited for a long, long moment, still staring at him. Then, abruptly, she turned, and walked through the door. It was open only a half-inch, but she seemed to flow through it in the same way that Uncle Umber had flowed through the door of the geography room, like a shadow, like smoke.

After she had gone, Jim looked down and realised that he was still holding Mrs Vaizey's hand. That is, he was still holding the hand of Mrs Vaizey's *body*, but this was a body without a soul, not dead, but not capable of life. He let go, and folded her arm over her cardigan. Then he sat back and watched her in the way that people at airports watch the arrival gates, waiting for their friends and their loved ones to reappear.

He checked his watch. He still hadn't touched his beer. It was 7:06 precisely.

At seven forty-five he got up and went to the window. Over Venice, the sky was the colour of a bruised cheek. He hadn't smoked in years but he felt like smoking now. He glanced back at the couch. Mrs Vaizey hadn't moved, although she had whispered once or twice, nothing that Jim had been able to follow. It was strange, standing over another human being who was so utterly helpless. He couldn't tell where she was or what she was doing. He began to wish that he had prevented her from going. The incense was all burned out now, but his apartment still smelled like a church.

All of a sudden, Mrs Vaizey's right arm flapped up. She twitched on the couch as if she were falling asleep, and her reflexes had tried to jerk her awake. She said something like, *"Agnus—"* but then she fell back into her coma.

Jim knelt down beside her and felt her forehead. She was cold, desperately cold, and her pulse-rate seemed fainter than ever. *Oh Christ*, he thought, what's going to happen if she dies? How am I going to explain the presence of a dead seventy-five-year-old woman on my couch, wearing nothing but a bikini and a cardigan?

He thought of dialing 911. After all, Mrs Vaizey's life was worth more than his reputation. But then Mrs Vaizey appeared to settle again, and breathe more evenly, although her fingers kept on trembling, and her head flopped from side to side, as if she were searching for something.

Maybe she was. Maybe she was searching for the loa stick.

It was almost eight o'clock. Jim sat on the end of the couch, worriedly drumming his fingers against his half-empty beer can. Mrs Vaizey's condition hadn't changed, but now and again she had whispered a few words, and once she had almost sat up. He wished to God that he had a way of knowing where her soul was, and what she was doing. She had said that Umber Jones would probably keep his *loa* stick well-hidden. What if she couldn't find it? What if Umber Jones found her first?

Eight-fifteen came and went. Mrs Vaizey was still breathing and her heart was still beating, but she felt as cold as if she were dead. Every now and then her fingers jumped or her feet shifted, but it seemed to Jim as if she were further and further away. This was a body that had no soul, and somewhere near Venice Boulevard there was a soul that had no body – a whole personality, disassembled.

Jim took hold of her left hand and chafed it between his, in an effort to warm it up. "Mrs Vaizey, come on. It's time you came back. Forget the spirit stick. It isn't worth it. We'll find some other way of dealing with Uncle Umber."

Mrs Vaizey murmured, *"Monstre . . ."*

"Come on, Mrs Vaizey," Jim urged her. "Just come back. You said it yourself: your soul can't stay outside of your body for too long."

"Monstre . . ." Mrs Vaizey repeated. *"Monstre . . ."*

"Please, Mrs Vaizey, you don't have to do this. You'd be better off coming back and then we can work out some different way of doing it. Come on, you know all about voodoo. There must be *some* way of getting rid of Uncle Umber without risking your life to do it."

At that instant, Mrs Vaizey's eyes opened. She stared up at Jim, and her expression was one of total desperation. Not fear. It was that stage beyond fear, when people have given up hope that they're going to survive, and simply want to die with the least pain possible.

"Mrs Vaizey!" said Jim, and clutched both of her hands, tight. "For God's sake, Mrs Vaizey, hang on in there!"

"*Monstre!*" she screamed, her mouth opening so wide that she almost dislocated her jaw. "*Monstre!*"

Jim slapped her. He didn't really know why. Maybe it would shock her into waking up. Maybe it would bring her soul back.

She started to shudder, gently at first, but then faster and harder, until the whole couch was jostling and the cushions dropped onto the floor. She flung her head from side to side, and thick white foam began to boil out of her mouth. Jim gripped her wrists and tried to keep her still, hoping that she was going to tire, but she kept on thrashing and shuddering so violently that he could scarcely hold her.

Suddenly she stopped, and glared into his face. He had never seen so much concentrated fury and contempt, and he was so alarmed that he almost let go of her. "You bastard!" she spat at him. "You liar! You told him you were going to be honourable! You told him you were going to be his friend! A fine friend you turned out to be!"

Then, right in front of his eyes, something terrible began to happen. Mrs Vaizey's mouth puckered inward, as if her face were nothing more than an empty rubber mask. Her nose collapsed into her mouth, and then her cheeks were drawn in, too. Her eyes stared at him mutely, as glutinous as oysters, before they, too, were sucked down into the crumpled hole where her mouth had once been. She was literally consuming herself – disappearing down her own throat.

Her head unrolled into her neck with a sticky, slithery sound unlike anything that Jim had ever heard before. It was Mrs Vaizey's brain-tissue, sliding down inside her.

She was still tense, still quivering, even though she had no head. Jim let go of her wrists, and stood up. Her shoulders were beginning to be dragged into her neck now, as well as her cardigan. Her arms were pulled in, right up to the elbows, and for a moment the two of them protruded from her neck, jostling together as if they were waving. Her hands were pressed together in a momentary mockery of prayer, and then they disappeared, too.

Jim backed further and further away, but he couldn't keep his eyes away from her. Her collarbone stuck up beneath her skin in a V-shape before it was dragged inward. Her ribcage dropped inward, rib by rib, and Jim heard her lungs collapse with a punctured sigh. She was only two-thirds of a woman – headless and armless, yet her stomach continued to swell, and swell, and her flesh and bones and gristle and fat continued to pour into it.

Her legs doubled back under her, and her feet were drawn into her stomach first, before her shins and her knees. For a moment there was nothing on the couch but a grossly-distended stomach with two suntanned thighs on either side of it, and Jim was horribly reminded of a giant Thanksgiving turkey. Then there was a last crackling noise, as her thighbones were drawn in, and all that remained was a lumpy, bloody stomach-lining, as big as a garbage sack filled to bursting with offal and bones and connective tissue. It was stretched so thin that

Jim could see Mrs Vaizey's right hand pressing against it, with all her silver rings.

Shaking uncontrollably, he managed to walk stiff-legged to the kitchen, where he vomited warm beer into the sink. He was cold and sweating and he couldn't even begin to think straight. He couldn't understand what he had seen, or how it had happened. However, he was sure that Umber Jones had done it. What had Mrs Vaizey said? *It's a mixture of Fon culture and Catholicism, and it has the power of both.*

After a long while he rinsed out the sink with a sharp blast of cold water, and then splashed water in his face. It was no good him falling to pieces. Mrs Vaizey must have been aware of the danger of what she was doing, and yet she had volunteered to do it, anyway. Maybe she had wanted to end her life doing something strange and spectacular, instead of slowly ebbing away in a sunset home.

Now he knew why Mrs Vaizey hadn't allowed him to come along with her. Sending your soul out to burgle a man like Uncle Umber wasn't a game for novices. God alone knew what kind of spell he had worked on her, to force her to devour herself.

He went back to the living-room and confronted the terrible thing on the couch. Somehow he was going to have to dispose of it, without anybody finding out. Fortunately, nobody had seen Mrs Vaizey come up to his apartment, as far as he knew. But it would be madness to call the police. What would he say to them? "She just sort of imploded"? "She ate herself"? "Her soul was out burgling this voodoo *houngan* and he got real angry and turned her inside out"?

He went to the bedroom and dragged the quilted

cotton cover off the bed. It was bright red, which would help, in case Mrs Vaizey's stomach-lining burst. There were maroon pools of blood inside it, as well as viscous yellowish fluids and a half-digested spaghetti bolognaise.

He spread the bedcover on the floor next to the couch. Then he laid his hands on Mrs Vaizey's remains, and gently rolled them toward the edge. They were so disgusting to touch that he had to stop for a moment, and close his eyes, and take five or six really deep breaths. He hadn't realised that they would still be warm, and how much all of her limbs and organs would roll and slither together when he started to move her.

But, mercifully, the stomach remained intact, even when it dropped on to the floor with a dull, soggy thump.

He rolled the bedcover around it, and tied each end with cord. Then he went back to the kitchen and scrubbed his hands until they were sore. He could see himself in the mirror next to the telephone, but he thought he looked like a stranger. *He* didn't dispose of dead bodies, not Jim Rook, the teacher. He spent his evenings marking papers or going to concerts or meeting his friends – not trussing up the mutilated remains of old ladies.

He called his father in Santa Barbara. "Dad? It's Jim. Yes, I know, I meant to call you back but everything's been so hectic since yesterday. No – well, the police have one boy in custody, but I'm not at all sure he's the one who did it. No."

He paused, and then he said, "Listen, Dad, is it okay if I borrow the boat tomorrow evening? Well, just for three or four hours. Well, I've met this girl and I thought it might be romantic to take her out for a picnic on the ocean. I think I need to take my mind off things. Okay. Fine. No, that'll be fine."

He hung up. He hated involving his father in getting rid of Mrs Vaizey's body, but he couldn't see any other way out. If he tried to bury her, there was always a chance that somebody would dig her up, and he wouldn't be able to feel safe for the rest of his life. But scattered in the ocean, her remains would be lost forever; and he thought that somehow it would give her back the dignity and peace that Umber Jones had so savagely stripped away from her.

For now, he dragged Mrs Vaizey's remains into his small spare bedroom and pushed them under the bed. In the small hours of the morning, he would carry them down to his car and lock them in his trunk.

He took the cushion covers off the couch and took them down to the laundry in the basement. They weren't badly stained, but even the smallest trace of Mrs Vaizey's DNA could prove fatal. As he switched on the machine, Myrlin Buffield came in, from Apartment 201, carrying under his arm a purple plastic basket crammed with withered shorts and misshapen T-shirts.

"Hi Myrlin," said Jim, attempting a grin.

"Hi yourself," he replied. He began to stuff his clothes into the next machine, but every now and then he gave Jim a sneaky little sideways glance.

"What?" asked Jim, after a while.

Myrlin shut the washing-machine door. "Was your apartment on fire before?"

"On fire? Of course not. What do you mean?"

"I happened to be passing and I smelled this strange like *burning* smell."

"Oh, that! *That* burning smell! I was burning some incense, that's all."

100

"Incense?" said Myrlin, darkly, as if to say, "Everybody knows why people burn incense."

"I'm into this meditation thing," Jim told him. "Tibetan transcendental yogarology. You have to burn incense to get into the mood."

Myrlin slowly scratched his behind and continued to stare at Jim like a baleful child. "You know that there are *rules* in this apartment block?"

"Against Tibetan transcendental yogarology?"

Myrlin lifted an imaginary roach to his lips and deeply inhaled.

"Against drawing in your breath?"

"You know what I'm talking about," said Myrlin.

"I wish I did, Myrlin. I really wish I did."

He went back to his apartment with his damp cushion-covers. He locked and chained the door behind him and stood for a moment with his back against it. The shock of what had happened to Mrs Vaizey had left him feeling exhausted, and his hands were still trembling. He went into the kitchen and poured himself a large whiskey, which he drank without taking a breath.

He poured himself another one, but he didn't drink it immediately. Instead, he opened up the kitchen cabinet and took down the bag of memory powder that Uncle Umber had given him. He found a small knife and cut the hairy, waxy cord that fastened it. Inside, when he unfolded it, there about a tablespoonful of fine brownish dust, as soft as ground cinnamon, with a pungent aroma that reminded Jim fleetingly of something from his childhood. He tried to focus on it, but it was gone, and he was left with an unexpected sense of loss.

He pinched a little of the powder between his finger

and thumb. So this was the drug that could enable you to remember people and events and places that you had never known. He wondered what it would be like if he could remember being wealthy, with a twenty-bedroom house in Bel Air and a pair of matching Maseratis; or his affair with a ravishing French movie actress in Provence, days of sun and kisses and chilled rosé wine. Or if he could remember seeing his dead brother Paul only last weekend, for a game of tennis and a long walk along the shoreline.

If you could remember it, did it matter that it hadn't happened?

He drew out a chair and sat down. He decided to remember something comparatively modest – something which could be easily tested. He decided to remember that Susan Randall had kissed him and told him that she had fallen in love with him the moment she first saw him. I mean, that would be harmless, right, because she obviously quite liked him anyway.

He held the dust up under his nostrils and cautiously sniffed. Then he sniffed again, more sharply this time. He sneezed, and sneezed again, and then he clamped his hands over his face. He felt as if he had breathed in spice-flavoured fire. It burned his sinuses and made his eyes feel as if they had swollen up to three times their normal size. He sneezed yet again, and stood up to get himself a glass of water from the sink.

He saw the sink. He reached out for the tap. But then suddenly the world was at a different angle, and the floor was tilting. He tumbled over sideways, hitting his shoulder against the table, and lay on his back sweating and trembling. He thought he could hear voices. He thought that there were other people in the room, people with dark faces and dark suits and sunglasses. He thought that he could hear drums; or maybe he could only *feel* them, throbbing through the floor.

He was aware of a sudden wind, blowing through the room, and a whispering voice that said, *"Ah, oui . . . il est triste . . . il est solitaire . . . ha-ha-ha . . . un spectre qui se glisse le long des allées ses pas l'ont conduit . . . de son vivant, ha-ha-ha . . ."*

He thought that there was somebody crouched down next to him, staring him right in the face. A black man, with pitted cheeks and a high sheen on his forehead. A black man with eyes that were filled with blood.

He heard a bell ringing, shrill and urgent. He sat up, shocked. At first he didn't know where he was. He felt as if he had been away for years. But then he managed to grab hold of his chair, and ease himself up. The bell was still ringing and it was his doorbell.

For a moment the bell stopped, and somebody started knocking. Then the knocking stopped and the bell started again. Then there was ringing and knocking together.

With his arms held out on either side to balance himself, he made his way to the front door and opened it.

It was Mrs Vaizey's son Geraint, a short bullet-shaped man with greasy black curls and a bright red face. He was wearing a jungle-patterned shirt and huge Bermuda shorts. "Hey, I've been ringing for five minutes," he protested.

"How did you know I was in?"

"That Myrlin geezer told me. He said to keep on trying on account of you might be taking some kind of trip or something."

"That Myrlin geezer should keep his nose out of other people's business."

"I'm looking for my old lady," said Geraint, trying to

peer past Jim's shoulder into his apartment. "You seen her, or what?"

Jim could never understand how a civilised, well-educated woman like Mrs Vaizey could possibly have given birth to a coarse, overweight loudmouth like Geraint. Geraint ran a video rental store, with a big line in horror and violence.

Jim shook his head. "I haven't seen her since yesterday – sorry."

"Myrlin said she might of come up here."

"Well, Myrlin's wrong, I'm afraid."

"I don't know . . . she's not in her apartment and look at the time. Add to that her door wasn't locked. She never goes out late."

"Maybe she went to the 7–11."

"Yeah, right, and maybe she went on a six-week hiking tour to Guatemala. She left her door unlocked, for Christ's sake, and a salad on the table."

"If you're worried, why don't you call the police? She could have had a memory lapse or something . . . she could be wandering around anywhere."

There were beads of clear perspiration on Geraint's upper lip. "I don't know . . . maybe I should just go look for her. What can the cops do that I can't?"

"Well . . . I hope you find her. She's probably okay."

"What are you, Mr Blue Sky or something? She's probably lying battered to death in a stormdrain."

Jim closed the door, and made sure that he put on the security-chain. He gingerly touched the tip of his nose and it was still a little tender, but his eyes weren't so swollen and he was able to walk back across the living-room without overbalancing. He went into the spare bedroom, and stood for a long time without switching on the light, because he didn't want to see what was lying under the bed. But then he had the idea that Mrs Vaizey's remains might start shuffling out from under the bed on their own, waggling from side to side in his blood-red bedcover like a giant maggot, and he switched on the light instantly.

The bedcover was still there, motionless. He hunkered down next to the bed and prodded it, just make sure, and all he could feel was softness and heaviness.

He left the room and switched off the light. He crossed the corridor to his own bedroom, but then he stopped. He hesitated for a few seconds. Then he went back and turned the key in the spare bedroom door. He didn't believe in life after death, especially a death as grisly and complete as Mrs Vaizey's, but then what was the point in taking chances?

He hadn't meant to sleep. He had meant to wait until there was nobody around, and then take Mrs Vaizey's remains down to the parking lot. But Geraint was coming and going for hour after hour, and Tina Henstell had some noisy friends in for drinks, and Myrlin didn't switch off his bedroom light until well past one o'clock, and even then he was probably watching his neighbours from his darkened window.

Jim slept badly and went through hours of frightening dreams. He kept hearing those muffled drums, beating through the house in a rhythm that became increasingly reckless. He felt that he was in the grip of a power that was beyond understanding: a huge malevolence. He saw fretwork balconies and thunderous skies. He heard feet flying through the rainswept grass.

He heard somebody running and jumping close behind him. *"Ha-ha-ha! Ha-ha-ha!"*

He woke up just after seven. A big grey quail was

sitting on the rail outside his window, tapping with its beak on the glass. His sheet was all sweaty and wrinkled, and he had been sleeping at the wrong end of the bed.

"Go on, scram," he said to the quail, and knocked on the window with his knuckle. But the quail stayed where it was, cocking its head to one side.

He climbed out of bed and shuffled out of the room, stretching and yawning. His nostrils still felt a little sore and his mouth was as dry as a sheet of Grade 2 glasspaper. He went through to the kitchen and opened the fridge, taking out a quart of orange juice and drinking it straight from the bottle until it ran down his chin and soaked the neck of his T-shirt.

Wiping his mouth, he saw the little bag of memory powder on the table. He knew that he had tried it last night, but he couldn't think what false memory he had tried to lodge in his brain. Maybe it didn't work. If he couldn't even remember what memory he had wanted to remember, what kind of memory powder was that?

All the same, he tied up the bag and put it on the kitchen counter next to his wallet and his keys and his mobile phone. He had seen what Umber Jones could do when he tried to double-cross him. He didn't want anybody else to end up devouring themselves; not for his sake, anyway.

Besides, he knew for sure now that Tee Jay was innocent, and if it took one of Uncle Umber's spells to get him free, then so be it.

He showered and dressed and made himself a cup of what railroad workers used to call 'horseshoe' coffee — coffee so strong that a horseshoe would float in it. He wondered if he ought to check on Mrs Vaizey's remains, but what was the point? She wouldn't have *moved*, would she? All the same, he thought he ought to drape the spare

106

bed with a double bedcover, so that nobody could see that there was anything underneath it. Juanita wouldn't be back to clean up until Monday, but you never knew. The building super might come in for some reason or another. Jim was quite sure that he wouldn't, but he *might*; and Jim didn't want to be sitting in college all day fretting about that million-to-one chance of discovery.

He unlocked the bedroom door and cautiously opened it. The red bedcover was hunched under the bed, just where he had left it. He approached it as if he expected it suddenly to move, even though he knew what was in it, and that it would never move again. He sniffed the air two or three times to make sure that it wasn't smelling. He had smelled a dead body only once before – when an elderly man had died all alone in the next apartment, but he had never forgotten it. It had been a stomach-churning reminder of what he, too, would one day become.

He went to the closet on the far side of the room and took down a large white woollen bedcover that he occasionally used in the winter. He unfolded it, and he was about to spread it right over the spare bed when he noticed something.

A greyish dust had leaked out of the side of the bedcover in which Mrs Vaizey's remains were wrapped.

Hesitantly, Jim prodded the bedcover with his foot. More dust trickled out, almost as fine as talcum powder. He knelt down and laid his hand flat on top of the bedcover, trying to feel what was inside it. Immediately, it collapsed, and he jumped back in fright, ricking his ankle.

He waited for a moment, panting, wondering what to do. He didn't want to open up the bedcover to see what had happened to Mrs Vaizey's remains, but he knew that he would have to. He approached it again, and very carefully took hold of one corner between finger and thumb, and drew it back. A small landslide of dust fell out on to the floor.

Bolder now, he dragged the whole bedcover out from under the bed, untied the string that held it together, and opened it out. Inside there was nothing but a heap of thick dust, with one or two small bones in it, fingers and toes and the curve of a rib.

He tried to pick up the rib but that, too, fell into dust. Mrs Vaizey's remains had been reduced to ashes just as effectively as if she had been cremated. Jim could see now that he was facing a man of extraordinary supernatural powers, and the problem was that they were like nothing he had ever heard or read about before. The way in which Mrs Vaizey had consumed herself had no parallel in American or European culture – none that Jim had ever heard of, anyhow – and the way that she had crumbled into dust bore no resemblance to any Western phenomenon, such as instant mummification or spontaneous combustion. This was African magic – strange and strong.

He went to the kitchen and came back with a black plastic bag. He lifted up the bedcover and sifted all the dust into the bag, and then knotted it. Mrs Vaizey's remains weighed no more than a heavy cat. Any dust that he had spilled he sucked up with his vacuum-cleaner. At least the poor woman's body was going to be easier to dispose of.

Half-way down the steps he met Myrlin again, who was wearing an olive-green nylon shirt and a nasty look. "There's still no sign of Mrs Vaizey, you know," he said, accusingly.

Jim said, "Maybe she just got tired of living here, that's all."

"What you got in there?" Myrlin asked him, nodding toward the bag.

"Just memories," said Jim. He went to the parking-lot, opened his car, and put the bag into the trunk. "Just memories," he repeated to himself, so quietly that Myrlin couldn't hear him.

Chapter Seven

This morning, in English, they discussed *Dead Boy* by John Crowe Ransom.

" 'A boy not beautiful, nor good, nor clever,
black cloud full of storms too hot for keeping,
A sword beneath his mother's heart – yet never
Woman bewept her babe as this is weeping.

" 'He was pale and little, the foolish neighbors say
The first-fruits, saith the Preacher, the Lord hath taken
But this was the old tree's late branch wrenched
away.
Grieving the sapless limbs, the shorn and shaken.' "

Jim sat on the edge of his desk swinging his leg as he listened to the class stumble out the poem line by line. He wore his reading glasses perched on the end of his nose. When they had finished, he said, "He didn't sound like much, this kid, did he? So why were his mother and the elder men so hurt that he was dead?"

Titus Greenspan III put up his hand and said, "I don't get this stuff about the tree."

"Ah, yes, but the tree is the whole point. Greg – why do you think the tree is the whole point?"

Greg Lake's face went through a slow series of incredible distortions as he tried to think. He took so long that it gave David Littwin the opportunity to put up his hand and say, "It w-w-w—"

"Okay, David, take it easy," Jim encouraged him.

"It w-wasn't a real t-t-tree he was t-talking about, it w-was a fuh. A fuh. A family tree."

"That's exactly right. The mother and the elder men were grieving because their old Virginia heritage had been put at risk by this one boy's death. No matter how stupid he was, no matter how badly-behaved, he was one of them, one of their line."

He walked up and down between the desks. "Your heritage is something more than you are . . . something to cherish and be proud of. John here honours his ancestors . . . Rita here celebrates the Day of the Dead . . . Sharon has traced her ancestry right back to Sierra Leone."

He reached the end of the room, and turned around, and as he did so he froze. Umber Jones was standing in the corner, next to the flag, his eyes concealed behind tiny black-lensed spectacles. He was watching Jim and his teeth were exposed in a lipless smile.

Jim had a good idea why he had come. He wanted to make sure that Jim made use of the memory powder, so that Tee Jay could be released. Jim stayed where he was, right at the back of the class, while Umber Jones continued to stare at him, and grin.

Russell Gloach said, "What if you don't have no ancestry? Like, I was adopted. What are you supposed to celebrate then?"

Jim didn't take his eyes off Uncle Umber. "You can celebrate the fact that your mom and your dad both wanted you enough to call you their own. It's just like a new branch being grafted on to a tree. It came from another tree, sure; but now it's an integral part of the tree that accepted it. You're part of the Gloach heritage

111

now, no matter where you came from; and I happen to know that your mom and dad are very proud of you."

As he was speaking, Umber Jones began to glide toward him, without even moving his feet. He came right up close, so that Jim could see every pockmark in his face, and every white whisker that protruded from his night-black skin.

"You're not going to let me down, are you, Jim?" he asked, in his harsh, heavy whisper.

"Seems to me like the elder men were more worried about their heritage than they were about the dead boy," put in Amanda Zaparelli. She spoke with hugely-renewed confidence now that her braces had been taken out.

"No," said Jim.

Amanda frowned. "I just thought – you see here where it says about the elder men looking at the casket—"

"You saw what happened to your friend, didn't you?" breathed Umber Jones. "You sent her looking where she wasn't welcome. The same thing could happen to you."

"What the hell are you harassing me for?" Jim demanded.

Amanda turned around at looked at Sue-Robin Caulfield in astonishment. The rest of the class twisted in their seats and stared at Jim with expressions that showed they were deeply impressed. Jim had always been outspoken, but never *this* outspoken.

Jim jabbed his finger at Umber Jones and said, "I don't know what you're trying to do, but by God I'm going to find a way to stop you."

"Way to go, Mr Rook!" called out Ricky Herman. "Let's shut Amanda up for good and all!"

"I hope you're not going to be rash, Mr Rook," said Umber Jones. "Before you could say the Lord's Prayer,

I could leave this whole class dead and dying." He looked around at the walls. "This room could use some redecoration, don't you think? How about a nice shiny red?"

"I'll do it," Jim promised him. "Just wait until recess, and I'll do it."

"Hear that, Amanda?" laughed Mark. "If I was you, the minute I heard that recess bell, I'd run like fun."

Uncle Umber laid his hand on Jim's shoulder. "I'm pleased to hear it. Believe me, Mr Rook, you're going to be the best friend I ever had. You and me, we're going to go far together."

Jim was aware that the class were all staring at him. He lowered his arms and stood with them rigidly by his side. "Get the hell out of my class," he told Umber Jones, between tightly-clenched teeth.

"What's that, now?" asked Umber Jones. "Wasn't sure that I heard you too good."

"Get the hell out of my class," said Jim, much louder. His students started swivelling around and staring at each other and saying, "Me? What, me? He wants *me* to get the hell out? Hey, Mr Rook, is it *me* you want to get the hell out?"

"Couldn't hear you," Umber Jones taunted him.

Jim lost his temper. "This is my class and these are my students and I'm responsible for every one of them. You've already caused enough grief, so help me. I'll do what you want me to do. But get out of my class before I do something that both of us are going to regret."

"Oh, no," grinned Umber Jones. "Only *you* are going to regret it."

With that, he folded his arms and glided backward across the classroom, until he reached the chalkboard.

"I'm keeping my eye on you, Mr Rook," he said. "And

don't you forget it." With that, his outline appeared to waver, as he were no more substantial than smoke, and of course he wasn't. His darkness blew sideways, and curled around, and funnelled itself into the surface of the chalkboard. Jim heard a deep, soft rumbling sound, and then he was gone.

Jim walked stiffly toward the chalkboard and touched it with his fingertips. Its surface was hard and cool and perfectly normal. But as he stood there, a curved white line appeared on the board, drawn in chalk; and then another. With a drawn-out squeaking noise that set his teeth on edge, a picture of an eye appeared, almost three feet across; and underneath it, the words VODUN VIVE.

The class was totally silent. Jim turned around and looked at them and didn't know what to say. It was only when Mark said, "Sheesh, that was so *cool!*" that they suddenly started talking and bantering again.

"How did you do that, Mr Rook?" asked Ricky. "Like, you didn't even use your hands."

"Not like you, Ricky," said Jane Firman. "You're *all* hands, you are."

Jim lifted his hand for silence, and then he said, "It was a trick, okay? Nothing but a trick. At the end of the semester, if you all pass with better-than-average grades, I'll show you how it's done."

He couldn't tell them about Umber Jones. If he did, there was no knowing what Umber Jones would do. But it was becoming increasingly difficult for Jim to keep his presence a secret, and Jim was beginning to feel that he was doing it on purpose: taunting him, provoking him, so that Jim would really snap and Umber Jones would have an excuse to slaughter the whole class.

It was interesting, though: Umber Jones could have

114

slaughtered them anyway, without an excuse. He was invisible, to everybody except Jim. Nobody believed in his existence, which made him uncatchable. Jim wondered if there were some restraints on his behaviour – if, like vampires, he needed to sleep in a coffin filled with his native soil, or if he couldn't endure crucifixes, or garlic-flowers, or if he had to stay out of the sunlight.

The recess bell rang. The class gathered up their books, laughing and chattering. Jim stood by the window with his back to them, just to make sure that Uncle Umber wasn't out there somewhere, just waiting to do them harm.

Six years ago, Jim had married quickly and misguidedly, and he had never had children. But then he didn't need children of his own; he had them already. Beattie and Muffy and Titus and Ray. During college hours, they were his family. Out of hours, as he sat marking their essays, they were still with him, because each essay was like a letter, trying to explain what they thought he had taught them . . .

'Mark Twain says about Huck Finn that "there were things he stretched but mainly he told the truth" but when you think about it whole of *Huckleberry Finn* is "stretched" because it's a story. Stretching is a way of saying something in a way which people are going to remember.'

He was still standing by the window when Sharon X came up to him, carrying three books. Today she had decorated her hair with dozens of tiny beads and she looked especially pretty. "I brought you those books I was talking about," she told him. "This is the best one. *Voodoo Ritual*. It tells you just about everything you need to know about voodoo."

"Thanks," he said. "That's kind of you."

He thought she would go then, but she didn't. She stood beside him as if she wanted to say something more.

"I'll take care of them, I promise," he said.

"You saw him just now, didn't you?" Sharon asked him.

He put the books down on his desk and didn't answer.

"He was here, wasn't he? *That* was who you were talking to, not Amanda at all. I watched you, and you weren't even looking at Amanda, you were looking right in front of you, like there was somebody standing there. And there *was*, wasn't there?"

Jim looked at her seriously. "Let me just put it this way, Sharon. You're in danger, all of you, if I say one single word."

"But he drew that eye on the chalkboard, didn't he? You weren't standing anywhere near it."

"Sharon, let's forget about it, okay? You know what they mean when they say that even walls have ears."

"That's an evil eye," said Sharon. "And Vodun, he's the head spirit of voodoo. That means 'Vodun Lives'. You only see that eye when Vodun's watching you, to make sure you don't take his name in vain, or do nothing to displease him."

"Sharon, thanks for the books . . . but I'm not going to say any more."

But Sharon was persistent. She picked up *Voodoo Ritual*, licked her finger, and quickly leafed through it. "You're talking about seeing a person when nobody else can, aren't you? Like you can really *see* this dude, can't you, when the rest of us can't? But there's a way that you can show him up, so that everybody else can see him, too."

"Oh, yes?" Jim was growing impatient. He would

116

rather have studied Sharon's books at leisure; and besides, he needed to get out into the yard and see if he could persuade Ricky Herman to breathe in some of the memory powder. It wouldn't work, he was sure of it. *He* wasn't aware of remembering anything that had never actually happened to him. But it was what Umber Jones wanted him to do, and he would do it.

"Here, look," said Sharon. "Death dust."

"Death dust?" asked Jim, abstractedly. He was still looking out of the window, spooked by every shadow. Was that the oak trees dipping in the breeze, or was it a man in an Elmer Gantry hat, walking across the grass?

"Sure, look. 'Spirits can only be seen by *houngans* and people with special gifts. Otherwise they are invisible. But spirit-hunters used to take bags of death dust with them when they went to exorcise huts and houses. They would toss the dust around the room, and if there was a spirit present, the dust would cling to them, making them momentarily visible.'"

Jim said, "Let me take a look at that." He flicked back and read the two preceding pages while Sharon watched him, fiddling with her beads.

"'A *houngan* has many ways of disabling or killing his opponents. If they use The Smoke to leave their physical bodies and to visit his dwelling-house, he can cast a spell on their body while they are away, when the body will be unconscious and defenceless. There are many spells he can cast. He can put the body into a deep sleep which may last for days or even years. He may cause it to choke; or to suffer a stroke. He may paralyse it, or set fire to it. One of the most gruesome spells is *Se Manger*, when the victim literally devours himself.

"'If the physical body is killed, the spirit will be forced to wander for ever in the Half-World. The physical body

117

itself will decompose very quickly into death dust. Death dust is still remembered in the Christian funeral ritual 'ashes to ashes, dust to dust.'"

"Does that help?" asked Sharon.

Jim closed the book and nodded. "It makes sense out of something that didn't make sense. I'm very glad you brought it in."

"It's my ancestry," said Sharon, with pride.

Jim went out into the yard and wandered around, talking to some of the students. He was conscious that – whatever they were talking about – they always changed the subject as soon as he approached, but then he always used to do the same thing when *he* was a student. The age gap between seventeen-year-olds and thirty-four-year-olds is about 4 million light-years. Jim was patient with them, though. He knew a secret which they didn't know: in another seventeen years, *they* would be thirty-four, too.

He was just about to stroll across to the bench where Ricky was telling a group of girls about the night he had raced his Camaro at 95 mph along Mulholland Drive when John Ng approached him.

"Mr Rook . . . something weird happened in class this morning."

He was obviously embarrassed, but Jim shrugged and said, "Sure. What was it?"

"That time you were talking strangely."

"Yes, what about it?"

John took a silver neck-chain out of his T-shirt. On the end of it dangled a dull black stone. "Look," he said.

Jim held it in the palm of his hand. "Great. Nice-looking stone. Now, John, if you'll excuse me—"

But John clutched his sleeve to stop him. "This is not a stone, Mr Rook. This is a crystal. It comes from a *dzong*, a sacred Buddhist temple. It is supposed to protect me from evil."

"And?"

"It's supposed to be clear, and sparkling. It only turns dark when something is troubling me. It has never turned as dark as this before."

"So what does it mean, when it goes as dark as this?"

"It means that a very great evil has come close to me. It happened at the same time that you were talking strangely."

Jim hesitated, but he knew that he couldn't lie. John was clinging on to his sleeve so tightly and there was such a worried look on his face that he would have to tell him the truth – or part of the truth, at least.

"Somebody was there, in the classroom," John insisted.

"Well . . ."

"Mr Rook, we have spirit-walkers in my religion, too. Monks who can leave their bodies and visit the sick and the dying."

Jim glanced around to make sure that the man in black was nowhere in sight. "Yes," he said, "I did see somebody. The same man I saw when Elvin was murdered. I could see him, but none of the rest of you could. I could hear him, too, and talk to him."

"He is very evil," said John, emphatically.

"Well, that's why I don't want to tell you too much about him. The less you know, the safer you'll be."

"Who is he?" John asked him.

"I think it's better if I don't tell you. Not just yet."

"But what does he want? Why has he come here to West Grove College?"

"I'm sorry, I can't tell you that, either. But I'm doing everything I can to get rid of him."

119

John took his hand away, and then said, with great simplicity, "You're frightened, aren't you?"

Jim nodded. "Yes, I'm frightened. Not for myself. But I don't want this character hurting my class."

John said, "With respect, Mr Rook, if we are in any kind of danger, wouldn't it be better if we knew about it, all of us? On your own, you may find it a hard fight to get rid of this spirit. Together, we would be strong. My father says that evil loves the darkness; but shrivels up when you shine a light on it."

"Your father's a thoughtful man."

John went off to join his friends, leaving Jim standing alone, thinking. Maybe he was right, and the Smoke spirit of Umber Jones *should* be dragged out into the open. But then he thought of Elvin, bleeding from scores of stab-wounds; and Mrs Vaizey, disappearing into her own mouth; and he knew that if any one of his students was killed or injured, he would never able to forgive himself.

Half-way across the wide, parched lawn that ran all along the east side of the college buildings, he saw Ricky sitting crosslegged, talking and laughing with Muffy and Rita and Seymour Williams, a spotty, friendly boy with heavy-rimmed Clark Kent glasses. Jim felt in his pocket for the bag of memory powder and loosened the ties around it. Then he approached the group at what he hoped was a casual stroll, even though he was so tense that his teeth were clenched.

Ricky looked up and shielded his eyes against the sun. "Hi, Mr Rook. What's happening?"

"I, er, found something in the boys' locker-room."

Ricky immediately blushed scarlet with guilt.

"No, no," said Jim. "It isn't anything that belongs to you." He took the bag of memory powder out of

120

his pocket and held it up. "It's some kind of powder. I didn't want to turn it in to Mr Wallechinsky, though, until I knew what it was. No point in making a fuss if it's harmless."

Ricky said, "Let's take a look at that, Mr Rook. I'm the class expert on suspicious substances." He winked at Seymour and Seymour gave a goofy laugh. Jim had a strong suspicion that Ricky and Seymour and some of the other boys had occasionally smoked grass in the boys' washrooms, but he had never been able to catch them at it. He handed him the bag and watched as Ricky opened it and peered inside.

"Doesn't look like nothing that *I* ever saw before," he remarked.

"Anything," Jim corrected him.

Ricky wet the tip of his little finger and dipped it into the powder and tasted it. He wrinkled his nose up and said, "Urgh. Doesn't *taste* like nothing I ever saw before, neither. Tastes like – herbs, and leaves, and kind of . . ." He paused, his eyes suddenly unfocused. "Kind of – *yesterday*."

"It tastes like *yesterday*?" scoffed Seymour. "What does yesterday taste like? Your old gym socks?"

"Sniff it," Jim coaxed him. He had never felt so guilty and irresponsible in the whole of his teaching career, but he didn't dare to think of the alternative.

Ricky took a pinch of the powder and snorted it up his nose, in the same way that Jim had. Immediately he let out an explosive sneeze and then another. "Jesus Christ!" he swore. "What the hell *is* this stuff?"

"Maybe it's the same stuff that Tee Jay was smoking," said Jim, hunkering down close beside him. Ricky stared at him with watering eyes. "You know . . . when you saw him behind the science block, the time that Elvin was killed. That's where he went, didn't he, at five after eleven? So he couldn't have gone to the boiler-house."

"Unh?" said Ricky and then promptly fell backward on to the grass, knocking his head.

"Hey, is he all *right*?" said Jane, leaning over him.

"Ricky?" said Seymour, crawling over toward him on all fours and staring into his face. "Ricky, can you hear me, man?"

Jim picked up the memory powder and pocketed it. "It's all right . . . he's hyperventilated, that's all." He knelt next to him and gently patted his cheek. "Ricky . . . come on, Ricky, you're fine. Come on, Ricky, wake up now." Thinking: my God, I hope I haven't done him any harm . . .

Ricky said something blurry and then he opened his eyes. He looked at the four faces peering down at him and said, "What?"

"You fainted," said Jim. "You must have breathed in too deeply."

Ricky sat up, smearing his nose with the back of his hand. "Jesus, that stuff *smarts*, Mr Rook. I don't know what it is but it sure ain't coke."

"I'm sorry," said Jim. "I didn't mean for you to get hurt."

Ricky sneezed again. "Doesn't matter," he said. "My sinus hasn't been this clear all summer."

"I think I'll just drop the bag in the trash and forget all about it," Jim told him. "Whatever it is, I don't think it's the kind of stuff that anybody would voluntarily put up their nose."

He was about to leave when Seymour said, "Hey, Mr Rook . . . what was that about Tee Jay? You know, smoking behind the science block."

"What about it?"

Seymour blinked. Jim could almost hear the cogs whirring inside his brain. "Well . . . if he was smoking behind the science block, then he couldn't have killed Elvin, could he? He couldn't have been in two places at the same time."

"The trouble was, nobody actually saw him," said Jim. "He *said* that he was smoking behind the science block but the police couldn't find any witnesses."

Ricky said, "Wait a minute. *I* saw him."

"You're putting me on," said Jim. "Why didn't you tell Lieutenant Harris?"

"I don't know. I just – I don't know. I just didn't."

"You definitely saw Tee Jay smoking behind the science block between five after and a quarter after?"

"Sure. I'd swear to it. He left the other guys, then he went behind the science block and lit up. I could see him all the time. I guess I didn't say anything because I thought he was going to get into trouble for smoking."

"Ricky," said Jim, taking hold of his shoulders. "Tee Jay is facing a charge of murder one. That's a whole lot more serious than smoking."

Ricky pressed the heel of his hand against his forehead. "I don't know why I didn't say anything before. It's like it must have slipped my mind or something."

"Well, now that it's *unslipped* your mind, maybe we'd better talk to Lieutenant Harris and see what we can do to get Tee Jay free."

"Sure. Sure thing." Ricky kept shaking his head, like a confused dog. Seymour and Muffy and Jane looked at each other in bewilderment. It seemed so unlikely that Ricky had taken two days to remember that he had seen Tee Jay smoking at the time of the murder. On the other hand, if he could get Tee Jay released, what did it matter?

123

Jim said, "Come with me. Let's go tell Dr Ehrlichman. Then we can call the police."

They walked across the grass together. Ricky said, "This is incredible, isn't it? I mean, because of me, Tee Jay's going to go free."

"Lieutenant Harris will give you a pretty thorough grilling. Be prepared for that."

"I'll tell you something, Mr Rook. He can grill me till I'm well done. I saw Tee Jay smoking. I swear it. I saw him with my own eyes."

They had almost reached the main administration block when Susan Randall came out of the main entrance, talking to George Babouris, the physics teacher. She was wearing a blue checkered blouse with the collar turned up, like Doris Day, and a short navy-blue skirt. Jim slowed down as he approached her and a wide smile came across his face. He was beginning to think that she must have been avoiding him this morning, for some reason. Maybe she was teasing him. After all, hadn't she kissed him and told him how attractive she had always found him – how masterful?

He walked straight up the steps, put his arm around her waist, and kissed her on the lips. "Hi, sweetheart. I've got some good news."

Susan smacked at his arm and took two steps back. "Jim!" she protested. George Babouris, big-bellied and black-bearded, stared at both of them in total astonishment.

Jim raised both of his hands in mock-surrender. "What's wrong?" he asked her. "I just came to tell you that—"

"You *kissed* me, that's what's wrong. You kissed me right on the mouth."

Jim was bewildered. Yesterday she had been so

passionate, and now she was treating him as if he were some kind of sex molester. "Listen," he said, "you don't have to blow so goddamned hot and cold."

"What are you talking about? When have I ever been hot?"

"You didn't exactly behave like the Snow Queen yesterday afternoon."

"I said I was interested in seeing your maps, that's all. That's hardly a proposition."

Jim turned to George and gave him one of those oh-ho-ho man-to-man looks. "She's only interested in seeing my maps!" he grinned.

This time, Susan slapped his face, so hard that it stung.

"What the hell was that for?" he protested.

"What the hell do you think it was for? Do you want me to report you to Dr Ehrlichman for sexual harassment?"

"Now, wait a minute," said Jim. "Yesterday afternoon it was 'Jim, I fell in love with you the second I saw you.' Now it's assault and battery. What's going on?"

Susan stared at him in disbelief. "Are you some kind of psychopath, or what?"

Jim looked around. George Babouris was giving him a very odd, old-fashioned kind of look; and even Ricky was keeping his distance. He began to get the feeling that something was very badly wrong and that he was seriously out of kilter with everybody else. He said, "Okay . . . maybe there's been a misunderstanding," and he backed away. "Come on, Ricky, we've got something more important to worry about."

Chapter Eight

Tee Jay was released at ten o'clock that evening, after Lieutenant Harris had interviewed Ricky for over four hours. Ricky offered to take a polygraph test but Lieutenant Harris knew that he couldn't take Tee Jay in front of a jury with no murder weapon, no fingerprints or footprints, and an independent witness whose testimony seemed to be so sincere.

Jim waited at police headquarters all that time, sustained by three cups of wishy-washy coffee and three sugared doughnuts. Tee Jay's mother hadn't been able to come, although Jim had phoned her and told her to expect some good news. Tee Jay's brother hadn't wanted to come and so far there was no sign of Uncle Umber.

Lieutenant Harris came out into the reception area in his shirtsleeves, dabbing at his forehead with a balled-up handkerchief. Tee Jay came up close behind, accompanied by his attorney and two uniformed officers. He stared at Jim as if he didn't recognise him.

"Okay," said Lieutenant Harris. "He's free to go. I just wish his friend had come up with this information the first time I asked him. The first twenty-four hours of any investigation are always the most important. Now he's put us back forty-eight."

"Come on, Lieutenant. At least you haven't charged an innocent man."

Lieutenant Harris pressed his handkerchief against the back of his neck and looked at Jim as if innocence had about as much to do with criminal justice as the price of fish.

Tee Jay's attorney came up to Jim and shook his hand. He was a barrel-chested Afro-American with immaculately-topiarised hair and a silk necktie with hot-air balloons on it. "Assume you're Tee Jay's teacher?" he asked. "You did a great job, bringing Ricky in. Tee Jay would've been real hard to defend, otherwise." He paused, and then he put his arm around Jim's shoulders and said confidentially, "Be a good idea to keep an eye on Tee Jay, though. That boy has some attitude problem. Keeps banging on about African culture and the power of the spirits and all kinds of stuff like that. Told me I was selling out, working for white men. And this is not your average Black Power thing, either. He was chanting and singing. Practically drove everybody nuts."

"Thanks," said Jim. "I think I have a handle on this thing."

"Oh, yes?" The attorney waited expectantly, and then he said, "You're not going to tell me what it is?"

"Sorry, no. I've been told to keep my mouth shut."

"You can't even give me a clue? I mean, I like to keep abreast of what the kids on the streets are into. Helps me with my job."

At that moment, the swing doors opened and Umber Jones walked in, still wearing his Elmer Gantry hat. The reception area immediately seemed to shrink, and even the tallest cops looked as if they were undersized.

"Here's your clue," said Jim, stepping away. The attorney gave him a baffled frown, but then he stepped back, too. Uncle Umber's sheer size and presence were overwhelming. His skin gleamed uner the fluorescent lights like polished black wood. He went up to Lieutenant Harris and said, "My nephew free to leave, officer?"

"For now, yes," said Lieutenant Harris. "We may want to talk to him again. Meantime, I'd appreciate it if he stays in the Greater Los Angeles area and stays out of trouble. I trust you may have some influence in that direction."

"Oh, I've got influence," grinned Umber Jones. He cracked all of his knuckles, one by one, waiting for Tee Jay to sign his release papers and collect his watch and his money and his leather belt. As soon as Tee Jay was finished, he took hold of his arm and guided him toward the door. On the way, he stopped beside Jim and said, "You did what you were told, Mr Rook, and I'm pleased about that. Now there's something else I want you to do for me."

Jim shook his head. "No way, Mr Jones. This is where you and I stop being friends. There's nothing I can do to prove that you stabbed Elvin and that you killed Mrs Vaizey, but I don't want to see you or hear from you ever again."

"I'm sorry you feel that way," said Umber Jones. "I really thought that you and me were going to be bosom friends for the rest of our lives. Still – even if you don't want to be my friend, you can still run a couple of errands for me, now can't you?"

"Forget it. I'm doing nothing for you, ever again."

"You sure are eager to see your children suffer, aren't you?"

"I warned you before. You leave my students alone."

"You *warned* me? Ha-ha-ha-ha-ha. And what are you going to do if I maybe just cut them a little? Give them some nasty scars? Or what if I burst their eardrums and turn them all stone-deaf? Or poke out their eyes? Or give them the fire sickness so that they feel like they've been doused in blazing gasoline?"

"I told you to leave them alone. If you hurt them, by God I'll find a way to bring you down."

"No you won't, Mr Rook, because there is no way. Now . . . stop your blustering, it doesn't suit a man in your profession. All you have to do is wait and I'll send you a messenger, telling you what to do."

"Go eat yourself," Jim suggested, bitterly. "Go turn yourself to dust."

Uncle Umber ushered Tee Jay to the doors. In all the time that they had been talking, Tee Jay had glanced at Jim only once, and his expression had been very difficult to read. All the same, Jim was sure that he had seen a glimmer of the old Tee Jay, somewhere behind those indifferent eyes – a flicker of his eyelids to show that he wasn't totally under Uncle Umber's influence.

Then they were gone, and the swing door briefly showed Jim a reflection of himself, standing with his hands in his pockets, looking tired.

Lieutenant Harris came up to him and sniffed. "What was all that about?"

"Just a word of thanks from a grateful uncle."

"You can't kid me, Mr Rook. I know my body language. That looked more like a toe-to-toe confrontation to me."

"Mr Jones has a forceful way of demonstrating his indebtedness, that's all."

"You intellectuals," said Lieutenant Harris. "What would you call it if the guy hit you in the beezer? A palpable expression of discontent?"

Driving west on Santa Monica Boulevard, Jim couldn't help smiling at Lieutenant Harris's remark. He had never thought of himself as an intellectual. He certainly hadn't come from an intellectual family. His father had sold earthquake insurance, and when Jim was born he had just lost his job. Jim had been brought up in a house where T-shirts were worn until they had holes in them and it was always meatloaf on Sundays and water to drink instead of Coke. He had never had many friends because none of his classmates wanted to come back to his place and eat plain bread-and-butter and watch television in black-and-white.

Jim's first ambition had been to make a name for himself as a Western movie star, like Clint Eastwood. Then he wanted to be a secret agent, like Napoleon Solo. Later, he changed his mind and decided to be an architect. But more than anything else he wanted to be wealthy. He wanted to give *his* children peanut butter on their bread, and Dr Pepper to drink on Sundays.

While he was still at high school, however, his father started his own marine insurance business, and it instantly flourished. By the time he graduated, his parents had moved to a large, comfortable house in Santa Barbara, and Jim was able to take English at UCLA, with the half-formed ambition of being a famous writer. He had a car. He had a generous allowance. He thought he was happy at last.

But while he was still in his freshman year, his cousin Laura came to stay and his cousin Laura changed his life overnight. Jim had last seen her when she was only six years old. Now she was eighteen – a startlingly pretty blonde with long shiny hair that she could sit on and blue eyes that absolutely mesmerised him. What he couldn't understand, however, was why she acted so shy. She seemed to have no confidence in herself whatsoever, and she always seemed to prefer to stay inside and watch television rather than go out and have fun.

Jim appointed himself her unofficial cheerer-upper. He took her swimming, he took her dancing, he took her to parties. He was so breathlessly infatuated with her that he felt as if he were drowning; and it was plain that she liked him too.

He wrote her a love poem, embarrassingly titled *My Golden Girl*. He gave it to her while they were sitting on the beach. She studied it for a moment and then handed it back to him and smiled and said nothing at all.

"You don't like it?" he asked her.

"I don't know," she admitted. "I can't really read it."

That was the first time Jim encountered dyslexia. Laura had no verbal thoughts at all. Everything went through her head like a movie without a soundtrack, and she simply couldn't connect printed words to objects or actions or ideas. At school, both her teachers and her classmates had treated her as if she were ignorant or stupid, and once a teacher had ripped up her work in front of the whole class.

She had often been punished for being late, too, because dyslexics have no sense of time.

The next day Jim went to the university's psychology department and took out nine books on dyslexia and reading dysfunction. He studied them all and then he contacted one of the authors, Professor Myron Davies at Boston University. With Professor Davies' help, he devised a way of teaching Laura to recognise words, using charts and diagrams and pictures.

He taught her the sentence, 'I can jump' by holding a can of baked beans and jumping off a kitchen chair.

Laura stayed with the Rook family all the way through

131

the summer vacation and slowly Jim taught her to read stories and poems and magazine articles. She became bolder, and more confident, and by the time she was ready to go home, she was able to read whole pages of text, even if it did take her more than a quarter of an hour.

But he never made love to her; not once. And in December she wrote him a Christmas letter saying that she had found a new boyfriend and that she was 'crazy in love'. But she also said that Jim had given her, 'a miracel, a whol new life.'

It had taken Jim almost six months to get over her, and he had never really gotten over her, not really. He would die remembering what she looked like, on the beach, those fine grains of sand on her skin. But at least he knew what he wanted to do. He didn't want to be a movie cowboy or an architect or a novelist. He wanted to save those children to whom reading and writing and mathematics were all incomprehensible. He didn't care what was wrong with them: whether they stammered or whether they suffered from problems at home or whether they had the attention-span of a gnat. They all deserved to be rescued; and Jim studied for four years to give himself the ability to do it.

He reached the beach. He parked, and he lifted Mrs Vaizey's dust from the trunk. He went down the steps and walked across the sand. The ocean sounded uncomfortable tonight, and the surf was surging fretful and luminous all the way from Palisades Park to the Municipal Pier.

He went to the shoreline and the sea drew back as if it were afraid of him. Then, as he lifted up his plastic bag, it came flooding back in again, and warmly filled his shoes. He tipped the neck of the bag and the dust came flying out, into the wind, into the darkness, and blew across the water.

He had almost emptied it all when he remembered what Sharon had told him, after class. *"There's a way that you can show him up, so that everybody else can see him, too."*

The death dust: that was it. *'The physical body will decompose very quickly into death dust.'* Jim stopped pouring out Mrs Vaizey's remains and angled the bag toward the lights on the pier to see how much dust he had left. Enough to fill a coffee-mug, not much more. But he screwed the bag up tight, and carried it back to his car. He had a feeling that it might come in useful. He had dealt with Laura's dyslexia through research, and by talking to experts. He could deal with Uncle Umber in the same way. He was fighting against somebody who was practised in magic, and so he needed to equip himself with magic knowledge and magic skill and magic artefacts. Sharon had lent him her books; and now he had death dust, too. Maybe he could find himself a *loa* stick, if he tried hard enough.

He climbed back into his car and started the engine.

"Do you know what you are?" he asked himself. "You're a lunatic, that's what you are."

When he returned to his apartment, he found a message from Susan on the answerphone. "I'm sorry if I over-reacted, but I couldn't believe what you did. I like you, Jim, and if I gave you the impression that it was more than just a friendship, then all I can do is apologise. But I think maybe that we'd better keep our distance from now on, don't you?"

He listened to the message three times. He simply couldn't understand what had happened today. Yesterday,

133

Susan had seemed so eager. She had cuddled right up to him and told him how special he was and kissed him with her mouth open. Today, he was supposed to keep his distance. He had heard of fickle, but this was ridiculous.

Oh well, he thought, resignedly. At least he wouldn't have to rush around acquiring a whole lot of maps to show her.

There was another message, from Tee Jay's mother. "I just called to say how much I appreciate what you did, Mr Rook. You saved my boy. He's still with his Uncle Umber, but at least he's cleared of any blame for killing poor Elvin; and that's what means the most to me."

And the last message came from somebody who had a thick, gravelly, uncompromising voice. "Remember what you solemnly promised me, Mr Rook, and don't you go backing down on no solemn promises. My messenger will come to see you soon and tell you what to do. You make sure that you listen to what he has to say, and listen good."

Jim went through to the kitchen. He was suddenly feeling ravenously hungry. He opened the icebox and stared at his old piece of gorgonzola for a while. Then he opened the kitchen cupboard and stared at an out-of-date carton of Golden Grahams and at three cans of red salmon. Then he went to the phone and punched out the number of Pizza Express. "Thin and crispy, with extra pepperami, chillies and anchovies."

He showered and changed into a purple polo shirt and chino pants. He sat back on the couch and switched on the television. He had never felt so disoriented in his life. The way that Elvin had been killed; the way that Mrs Vaizey had died; the smoke and the spirits and the warnings of terrible tragedies – they had all completely undermined every belief that he had ever held about life and death and the supernatural. He had been certain that death was the end. Now he had been shown – in the most violent and extravagant way possible – that death was just a different state of being.

Restless, he went back to the kitchen to find himself a beer. On the floor, in the corner, was the bag containing Mrs Vaizey's death dust. He hesitated for a moment, then he took a blue china mug out of the cupboard, set it down in the middle of the floor and poured the dust directly into it. Then he covered the mug with clingfilm. Pretty damned funny way to end up, he thought. One minute you're sunbathing and drinking whiskey, the next you're a little heap of powder in somebody's coffee mug.

"'A heap of dust alone remains of thee,'" he quoted. "''Tis all thou art, and all the proud shall be!'" He smiled, and then he said to himself, *Elegy to the Memory of an Unfortunate Lady*. How true."

He drank beer and channel-surfed; and he was still flicking from one programme to another when the doorbell rang. Great – pizza at last. He went across to the side-table and picked up his billfold. The doorbell rang again and he called out, "Okay – okay! I'm coming, don't worry about it!" He licked his thumb and counted out twenty dollars as he approached the door. He was still counting as he opened up the door and there he was.

Elvin.

He was standing right outside the door, wearing a smart dark suit, as if he had dressed up to pay his college teacher a last respectful visit. But his face was distorted with twenty or thirty stab-wounds, his ears were gone, and his eyes were as blind as pebbles. His wounds had mostly healed, but his starched white shirt-collar was

135

stained with a few cranberry-coloured spots of blood and his eyes were still weeping.

Jim held on to the door and didn't know what to say. He was so frightened that he felt as if his skin had shrunk, and all of his insides had suddenly dropped out, leaving nothing in his stomach but a chilly vacuum of fear.

"Hello, Mr Rook," said Elvin. His voice sounded terrible, all foggy and bruised, as if his tongue were too big for his mouth. He stepped forward with an awkward, unbalanced shuffle, his feet dragging on the floor, and as he did so his wounds gaped open, so that Jim could actually see his bright white cheekbones.

"You're dead, Elvin," said Jim, retreating across the living-room. He stumbled against a chair but managed to right himself. "Umber Jones killed you. You're dead. You have the right to some peace, don't you?"

Elvin gave a tilted smile, and swivelled his head around as much as his wounds would allow. "I'm not going to hurt you, Mr Rook. I brought you a message, that's all."

"I don't want to hear it, Elvin. I want you to go."

Elvin stayed where he was. It was his blinded eyes that disturbed Jim the most, slit in half from top to bottom, so that his irises were split like cut-up mushrooms.

"I want you to go, Elvin," Jim repeated. "I don't want to have anything more to do with Umber Jones, and you can tell him that from me."

"You have to hear his message," Elvin insisted.

"I told him back at police headquarters, it's over."

"He says you're his friend, Mr Rook. He says you're the only friend he's got. But he said something else, too. He said that every time you say 'no' to him, one of your class is going to die, the same way that I died."

Jim said nothing, but licked his lips. His mouth

was so dry he felt as if he hadn't drunk anything in a year.

Elvin said, "There's a bar on Vernon called Sly's. There's a guy who hangs out in this bar called Chill. His real name's Charles Gillespie but he doesn't like nobody to call him that. All you got to do is to go see Chill and tell him that you work for Umber Jones and that Umber Jones knows that he's just taken delivery of two kilos of best Colombian nose candy. Then tell him that from now on *he's* going to be working for Umber Jones, too, and that he'd better make sure that he pays over ninety per cent of his profits. Tell him you'll let him know later how and where and when he can make his payment. And if he shows any sign that he doesn't want to co-operate, tell him that Umber Jones is going to be watching him, night and day, and give him this."

Elvin put one mutilated hand into his coat pocket and took out a small fragment of black cloth. He held it out but Jim wouldn't take it.

He laid it carefully on the table instead. "Tell Chill that times have changed. Tell him that he'd better change with them, if he values his life." With that, Elvin turned around and shuffled toward the door, groping and feeling his way between the chairs.

He opened the door but then he hesitated for a moment. "You'd better go tonight, Mr Rook," he suggested. "Umber Jones is a very impatient man." He walked through the door and closed it very, very quietly behind him, which Jim found much more frightening than if he had slammed it.

For a long time he couldn't move, but held on to the back of the couch, his head bent forward, taking deep, steadying breaths. He had read articles about the so-called 'walking dead', but he had always accepted the historical explanation rather than the magical myth. Zombies were the victims of unscrupulous sugar-plantation owners during Haiti's great labour shortage in 1918. The owners were said to have hired voodoo sorcerers to administer soporific drugs to any likely-looking worker – probably a cocktail of tetrodotoxin, from the puffer fish; datura, a powerful hallucinogenic; and an extract from the toad *Bufo marinus*, which gives extraordinary strength. These drugs lowered the pulse-rate and gave the appearance of death – so much so that the zombie-to-be could be buried, and could remain in the cemetery in a trance-like stupor for days.

The sorcerer would then exhume them, revive them and take them to the sugar plantations to work – but not before taking the precaution of cutting out their tongues, so that they would never be able to protest or to explain what had happened to them.

But Elvin – Elvin was different. Elvin had been repeatedly stabbed all over. His heart and his lungs and his liver had been pierced. His body had undergone a full post-mortem, which would have killed him even if he hadn't already been dead. Yet he had walked into Jim's apartment tonight and spoken.

At last, however, Jim began to pull himself together. The first thing he did was go to the door and put on the chain. Then he went to the kitchen and poured himself another drink. His hands were shaking so much that the neck of the whiskey-bottle clattered against the glass. He drank, swallowed, and half-choked himself.

Eventually he went back into the living-room. He sniffed. Elvin had left behind him a curious and distinctive smell, spicy and dry, like Uncle Umber's, but mingled with the underlying sweetness of decaying flesh. The small piece of cloth that Elvin had tried to give him was still lying on the table. He picked it up, and turned it over. It was coarse and very black, as if it had been cut from a priest's cassock. There were some signs and words written on it in dull red, scarcely visible in artificial light. He didn't know what effect this would have on the man who called himself Chill, but it didn't look very threatening to him.

Now he had to decide if he was going to talk to Chill or not. He had never been a coward, but the prospect of going to meet a drug dealer on his own turf and demanding ninety per cent of his income seemed to be tempting fate, to say the least. On the other hand, what if he didn't? He was quite sure that Umber Jones wouldn't hesitate to wipe his class out, one after another.

He checked his watch. A few minutes after midnight. He took his blue linen coat off the peg by the door and shrugged it on. He had never been so reluctant to do anything in his life, but he simply didn't have any choice. He took a quick look around the apartment and then he switched off the lights and opened the door. A tall black figure was standing outside, its head silhouetted by the glass globe light on the balcony. Moths fluttered and whacked around it, so that it looked like the lord of the flies.

Jim couldn't say anything else but "*Ah!*" He stumbled back into the apartment and stood staring at the figure with his mouth open.

The figure stepped forward. It was holding something in its arms, a book or a box. "Brought your pizza, man," it said, worriedly.

Jim switched on the light, and there was a lanky youth with a wispy little beard and an earring and a red-and-black Pizza Hut T-shirt, holding out his supper. "Twenty dollars, man," he asked, holding on tight to the

139

box. Then – as Jim opened his billfold and counted out the money, "You look like you just seen a ghost."

Jim handed him the money, all crumpled up, and a $5 tip. "Yes," he said. "Got it in one."

It took him over 20 minutes to find Sly's. It was a basement bar, reached from the street by a single dark doorway with the name *Sly* flickering in purple neon over the canopy. He managed to park around the corner and then he walked back to Sly's along a sidewalk still crowded with aimlessly-milling young people and watchful, hard-looking men. There were plenty of hookers around, too, in hotpants and short skirts and storebought hair of every conceivable colour.

Sly's doorway was guarded by a short, broad black man who looked like Mike Tyson after having an eight-ton block of concrete dropped on his head. "Sorry guy. Bar's closed," he said, as Jim approached, holding up the flat of his hand.

"I've got a message," Jim told him.

"Oh, yes? So where's your Western Union uniform?"

"Is Chill still here? Charles Gillespie? He's the one I've got the message for."

The doorman eyed him with piggy, glittering-eyed suspicion. "Don't nobody call him Charles Gillespie, excepting his mother. So you better not, white man, otherwise you know what they say about shooting the messenger, bad news or good."

"I have a message for Chill," Jim repeated, in the same tone that he used for his English comprehension class, very slow and very clear. "If Chill is here, I would very much like to speak to him."

"Okay, what's your name?" the doorman asked him.

"That doesn't matter. The message is all that matters. Don't tell me you don't know Marshall McLuhan?"

"Marshall McLuhan? He ain't never been in here," the doorman replied, suspiciously.

He picked a phone off the wall and spoke into it with his hand covering his mouth so that Jim couldn't hear what he was saying. After a few nods and grunts he hung up and said, "Okay, then, you can go on up. C'mere." He gave Jim a quick frisking and then he opened the door. "A word to the wise," he said, as Jim went down the first two steps. "Chill isn't feeling too happy tonight. He just had a root canal job. So, you know, don't like provoke him."

Jim didn't reply, but descended the narrow, black-carpeted staircase with growing trepidation. The walls on either side were covered in dark mirrors and he could see himself going down and down like a man on his way to hell. Another huge minder was waiting at the bottom, with sunglasses and an electric-blue suit. He let Jim pass through a swing door into the bar itself, which was ferociously air-conditioned and lit up in red and blue. A white man with an acne-scarred face was sitting at a black piano playing *I Will Always Love You* as if he were making it up as he was going along, and a large black girl in a small white dress was standing on a podium the size of a hatbox shrieking out the words.

In the darkest corner of the bar, in a semi-circular booth, sat a big black man with bleached hair, surrounded by five other black men with a variety of pompadours and crops and pigtails. They all wore black leather and heavy gold rings. The black man with the bleached hair was strikingly handsome, in a rough, unfinished way, as if he were a sculpture that had hurriedly been chiselled out of ebony, and then abandoned.

141

Jim went up to his table, drew out a chair and sat down. The six men looked at him like six cobras, ready to strike him dead. "Which one of you is Chill?" Jim asked, quite aware how close he was to committing the ultimate insult of disrespect.

"I'm Chill," said the man with the bleached hair, in a surprisingly high, carefully-enunciated voice. "You got a message for me, messenger boy?"

Jim's heart was beating so hard and so slow that he thought he was about to have a heart-attack on the spot. "I've got a message from Umber Jones," he said, unsteadily.

"Who the hell is Umber Jones? I don't know no Umber Jones."

"Well . . . this is just a message," said Jim. "Umber Jones says he knows that you recently took delivery of two kilos of Colombian cocaine."

Chill leaned forward in a menacing way, lacing his fingers together and looking Jim straight in the eye. "I told you, man. I don't know no Umber Jones. So how come this Umber Jones know so much about me?"

"He has – what can I call them? Very special abilities."

"Like what? To tap my phones? To pay off my runners? What? This Umber Jones wouldn't be the man, by any chance, would he? This wouldn't be no bust? Because if it is, messenger boy, you don't get out of here with two legs."

"Please, listen to me," said Jim. "Umber Jones says that times have changed. He says that he's taking over now and that he wants ninety per cent of everything you make out of this shipment. He says that he's willing to let you carry on, provided that you work for him, and provided that you don't give him any trouble."

Chill was staring at Jim in almost comical disbelief. One of his aides stood up, his earrings swinging, and reached inside his leather coat; but Chill snapped, "Siddown, Newton!" and the man reluctantly sat down again.

Jim continued, "Umber Jones will let you know later where you can pay him the money. He also said that if you lay one finger on me; or if you don't agree to do what he says; there's going to be trouble."

Chill slowly shook his head. "Never in the whole of my life, man, have I come across anybody with the nerve of you. Or this Umber Jones dude, if he really exists. I mean, let me get this right: he wants me to pay him ninety per cent of everything I make? He gets ninety per cent and I get ten percent, is that it?"

Jim nodded dumbly. The singer was approaching the climax of *I Will Always Love You* and her voice had risen to an hysterical screech.

"And if I *don't* give him the money, there's going to be . . . *trouble*?"

"Yes."

"Yes, what?"

"Yes, there is going to be trouble."

"You mean yes sir, Mr Chill sir, there is going to be trouble, sir. So what kind of trouble are we talking about here?"

Jim reached into his pocket and took out the small piece of black cloth. Now his heart was beating so slowly that it had almost stopped and he felt as if he could easily turn into a zombie himself. He laid the piece of cloth on the table and Chill pushed aside a heaped ashtray full of pistachio shells so that he could look at it. He picked it up. He turned it this way and that. He leaned back under a spotlight so that he could see what was written on it.

He looked at Jim with a wary expression on his face. "Where did you get this?" he asked.

"Umber Jones gave it to me, to give to you. I don't even know what it is."

"You don't know what it is? You bring me a voodoo curse and you don't know what it is?"

"Listen – I'm only the messenger here. I'm not a Catholic and I'm not black. I'm a college teacher. All I know about voodoo is what I've read in books and magazines."

Chill banged the table with his fist so that pistachio shells went dancing in all directions. "You brought me a voodoo curse!" he roared. He held the piece of cloth up in front of Jim's face and his eyes were bulging with rage. "You know what this is? This has been cut from the cloth of a murdered Roman Catholic priest and the warning has been written in his own blood! You know what this says? Here, look – *jama ebya ozias* – and here, the mark of Baron Samedi, the lord of the cemeteries! You dare to bring me this? You *dare* to bring me this?"

"I was – I was asked to, that's all. I didn't have any choice in the matter. I owe Umber Jones a kind of a favour, that's all. Don't ask me about voodoo. Don't ask me about narcotics. I'm just trying to stay alive and I'm just trying to protect some people who are very precious to me, okay?"

Chill looked down at him for a very long time. It seemed like hours. Then he reached into his coat and took out a pack of cigarettes. He tucked one into his mouth and instantly four lighters clicked into action. He ignored them all and lit his cigarette himself. "Who is he, this Umber Jones? He tired of living or something?"

"I wouldn't underestimate him if I were you."

Chill rolled the piece of cassock between finger and

thumb. "He knows his voodoo, I'll give him that. Sometimes somebody might take a splinter from the altar; or the communion host; and they'll dip it in chicken's blood, and that's enough of a warning. But this – this is like a death threat. Ain't nobody gives no death threat to Chill, believe me."

"I didn't know," said Jim. "He told me to bring it to you and I brought it."

Chill grinned, and smoke leaked out from between his teeth. "I don't know what somebody like you is doing mixed up in a business like this. But if I were you, I'd forget about this Umber Jones, whoever he is, and put as much distance between you and LA as you possibly can. Like I hear that Nome, Alaska, is pretty nice at this time of year."

"So what do you want me to tell him?"

"Tell him I'll see him in hell."

He said it as coolly as he could; as befitted a man with a name like Chill; but Jim detected an inflection in his voice that betrayed a deep underlying uncertainty. He had heard the same slightly-strangulated talk from countless college bullies. Chill had been seriously disturbed by Uncle Umber's patch of cloth. It was like Billy Bones in *Treasure Island*, being tipped with the black spot.

Jim waited for a moment, but Chill crushed out his cigarette and his minders began to shrug their shoulders and look threatening and the audience was obviously over. Jim got up and left the bar, just as the singer was launching into *You're Simply The Best*, wildly off-key. Quite honestly, thought Jim, if Chill was going to shoot anybody, he ought to shoot her.

Chapter Nine

To Jim's surprise, Tee Jay was back in class the next morning, wearing a Snoop Doggy Dogg sweatshirt and a strange, evasive look on his face. Jim came into the room with a bulging folder under his arm, dropped it on to his desk and stood for a while, taking in everybody's faces – Sue-Robin Caufield, flirting and chatting; David Littwin, frowning at his desk as if he couldn't understand why it was there; Muffy Brown, her head thrown back in laughter; Ray Vito, his eyes half-closed in a smooth Latin flirt with Amanda Zaparelli – he had taken a sudden interest in her now that her teeth were fixed.

Jim rubbed the back of his hand against his chin. He had been plagued by nightmares all night and he hadn't shaved very well this morning. His hair had refused to do what he wanted it to do and there had been no clean shirts in his drawer. He had discovered a blue checkered shirt that he usually used for working on the car. Two buttons were missing but at least it was pressed.

"Okay, class . . . this morning I'm pleased to welcome Tee Jay back to college and I'm sure that the rest of you are, too. What happened to Elvin was a terrible tragedy but in a way it makes it a little easier to bear knowing that the perpetrator wasn't one of us."

As he said "one of us" he turned and fixed his eyes on Tee Jay. He and Tee Jay were the only ones who knew that Tee Jay *had* been involved – and that even if he hadn't killed Elvin himself, he had stood by while Umber Jones had stabbed his best friend more than a hundred times. But Jim still wanted him to feel that he was part of the class – that he had a family to turn to. It was the only possible way of setting him free from his uncle's influence.

"Today we're going to read *Why He Stroked the Cats* by Merrill Moore. Page 128 in your *Modern American Verse*. I want you to read it silently to yourselves first of all, to see what you make of it. It's a difficult poem, strange. But I'd like to hear what each of you think it means."

'He stroked the cats on account of a specific cause,
Namely, when he entered the house he felt
That the floor might split and the four walls suddenly
melt
In strict accord with certain magic laws
That, it seemed, the carving over the front door meant,
Laws violated when men like himself stepped in,

But he had nothing to lose and nothing to win,
So in he always stepped—'

He was still reading the poem to himself when he saw what looked like black smoke pouring over the windowsill. It rose, and softly whirled, and eddied around, and gradually the shape of Umber Jones materialised, shadowy and distorted at first, but then quite clearly.

Jim tried not to look at him, but it was impossible, because Umber Jones came right up to his desk and stood in front of him. His face looked as if it had been powdered with ash and his eyes were glittering red. He looked like a zombie himself, but he spoke with his usual thick, threatening aplomb. "You did what I asked, and talked to the man called Chill?"

Jim nodded. He could see that Sharon had looked up from her poem and was frowning at him, as if she suspected that something strange was happening. He didn't want Umber Jones to think that any of his class were aware of his presence. But then he glanced at Tee Jay and it was quite obvious that Tee Jay could see his uncle as clearly as he could. He was giving Jim a small, mocking smile, as if daring him to speak.

"Okay, Mr Rook . . . and what did Chill have to say for himself?"

Jim said nothing. Umber Jones stepped closer to his desk and held up his right hand. "I didn't quite hear that, Mr Rook. Maybe you better speak a little louder."

Jim continued to stare at him and say nothing.

Umber Jones stared back at him for a while, and then he started to rotate his right hand, around and around, and take it off, exposing the blade that was concealed inside it. "You see this knife, Mr Rook? This knife has the power of Ghede, who is Baron Samedi's closest assistant. When Baron Samedi wants bodies, it is Ghede who provides them. Now, you wouldn't want to be one of those bodies, would you?" He held the knife right in front of Jim's face until the point almost touched his chin. "How about you telling me what Chill said to you last night?"

"He said he'd see you in hell."

"Well of course he did," said Umber Jones. "You didn't seriously think that he was going to give up ninety per cent of his income, did you, just because some college teacher told him to?"

148

"No, quite frankly, I didn't." Two or three more members of the class looked up.

"But you gave him the message, didn't you? And you warned him what would happen if he didn't do what he was told?"

"Yes, I did."

"So next time, when you go to see him, he'll be more amenable, won't he?"

"What do you mean? What are you going to do?"

"I'm going to *persuade* him, Mr Rook, in the time-honoured fashion."

"If anybody else gets hurt—" Jim began. But at that moment John Ng stood up, with an expression of panic on his face.

"Mr Rook!" he said, and held up his necklet. "Mr Rook, he's here now, isn't he? That's who you're talking to! Look at my stone! Look at it! It's turned completely black!"

Sharon stood up, too. "I can *feel* him, Mr Rook! You can't pretend he's not here!"

The other members of the class turned this way and that in confusion. "Who's here? . . . What are they talking about?"

"It's the man in black!" John shouted. "It's the man who killed Elvin! Nobody can see him, only Mr Rook, but he's here! He's here right now, in the classroom!"

Tee Jay twisted around in his seat. "Shut up, you Viet Namese loony! What the hell you say, man in black?"

Sharon said, "He *is* here! I know he's here!"

"You shut up too, bitch," Tee Jay snapped at her. "What are you crazy or something?"

"Tee Jay!" said Jim. And it was then that he felt a cold flick across his face, and the poetry book in front of him was abruptly spattered with a fine spray of blood.

He clapped his hand against his cheek, shocked. Umber Jones was glaring at him with his amber-coloured teeth clenched in a grotesque snarl. "I told you not to tell them but you told them, didn't you? You disobeyed me!"

The classroom was suddenly silent. All of the students stared at Jim wide-eyed. Blood ran down between his fingers and dripped off his elbow. "I didn't tell them anything," he said. "They were sensitive enough and intelligent enough to work it out for themselves."

Umber Jones seemed to rise and swell, so that he was nearly seven feet tall. His suit was black, with a black buttoned-up vest which Jim could clearly see, yet there was a shadowy transparency about it. He could faintly distinguish the faces of some of his students through it, Ricky and Beattie and Sherma Feldstein.

Umber Jones said, "Now they know about me, maybe they need a little lesson on what will happen if they talk about me to anybody else."

"Don't you touch them, not one of them!" Jim retorted.

"And who's going to stop me?"

"Listen, I'll do anything you want! You want me to go back and talk to Chill? Fine, I'll do it. But just don't touch my students!"

"You'll do anything I want, whether I touch them or not. You're my friend, Mr Rook, remember?"

Jim jumped up, knocking his chair over, and made a grab for Umber Jones' arm. His hand passed through it as if it were smoke. Umber Jones swished his hand down and cut Jim's left sleeve open. Then he swished it sideways, nicking the tip of Jim's nose. If he hadn't dodged his head back in time, Umber Jones would have sliced his entire nostril open.

All that his class could see was Jim dancing and

whirling on his own, his sleeve ripped open and blood flying in all directions. Muffy began to scream, and then Jim staggered against Jane Firman's desk and she began to scream too. The boys shouted in alarm. "Hold him! Somebody hold him! Go get Mr Wallechinsky! Don't let him fall!"

But Tee Jay suddenly stood up and shouted, "No! You hear me? Don't call nobody! Shut the hell up and stay where you are!"

There was a sudden hush, all except for Muffy, who kept up a monotonous self-pitying sniff. Umber Jones stepped away from Jim, holding his blade up high, his eyes almost crimson with cruelty. Jim pulled a bunch of Kleenex out of the box on his desk and pressed them against his cheek. He felt shocked and hurt but worst of all, he felt that he was weak. He was supposed to protect his students, but he couldn't.

Tee Jay said, "You listen to me good. You're all going to walk out of here today and you're not going to say one word about what you saw. Because the man in black that Mr Rook here was talking about, he's *real*, even if you can't see him for yourselves. I seen him. I seen him that day when Elvin died and I can see him now, as plain as day."

He stood in the centre of the class, looking at every one of them. "Maybe you didn't believe in him before, but take a look at those cuts on Mr Rook's cheek and tell me where they come from. If you don't want that to happen to you, keep your mouth shut and you don't say nothing to nobody. And if you need any further persuading, go to the funeral home and ask to take a look at Elvin."

"So who is this man in black?" Russell Gloach challenged him.

"He's like a ghost, that's all."

"A ghost?" said Ray. "There's no such thing as ghosts."

"Well, he's more like a spirit. He isn't dead . . . he's just walking around outside of his body."

"How come you know so much about him?" asked Sue-Robin.

"He's the spirit of somebody I know. That's why he's here."

"Can't you tell him to leave us alone?" said Jane, miserably. Her eyes were filled with tears and she was deeply distressed.

Tee Jay emphatically shook his head. "This spirit isn't the kind of spirit you can give any kind of orders to. You want to live a long, peaceful life? You give this spirit respect, and you give him plenty of space. You understand that?"

Jim came forward. He didn't look at Tee Jay, but he said, "Tee Jay's right, everybody. It's in your own interest if you don't tell anybody what happened here today. Even your family, or your closest friend."

"But what can we *do* about it, this spirit?" asked Beattie, looking nervously around the classroom. "Can't we do what they did in that movie when the girl's head went round and round?"

Jim looked at Umber Jones but Umber Jones kept his head lowered so that his face was obscured by the brim of his Elmer Gantry hat. "We can't do anything," said Jim. The class could sense the defeat in his voice and they quietened down.

Jim dabbed at his face. It had stopped bleeding, but it still needed cleaning up. He would have gone straight to the infirmary, but he wasn't going to leave his class alone with Umber Jones.

"Let's get back to the poem," he said. "Tee Jay – you want to return to your seat?"

Tee Jay gave him a shrug and sprawled back into his chair. Jim returned to his desk, picked up his chair, and sat down in front of his blood-stained poetry book. He glanced up at Umber Jones, but Umber Jones remained where he was, silently smoldering, his face still concealed.

The class whispered and shuffled their feet, half-bewildered and half-fearful. "Come on," said Jim. "Let's get back to the poem. He won't do you any harm if you do what he says, will he, Tee Jay?"

"If you say so, Mr Rook."

Jim said, "I want you all to think what the poet was trying to explain. I mean – is this real, the floor splitting and the walls melting, or is it an allegory? If so, what kind of an allegory? And what does he mean by 'certain magic laws'?"

The class remained silent. They knew that Umber Jones was still there, whether they could see him or not. But after a few moments, Umber Jones took off his hat, and ran his hand through his ash-powdered hair, and looked up at Jim with a sloping smile. "Chill frightened you, didn't he?" he said, in that sack-dragging voice of his.

Jim ignored him, but pointed to Greg, over in the corner, and said, "Greg – what did you think he meant by 'certain magic laws'?"

Greg squeezed his face into ten different expressions before he managed to say, "Superstitions . . . you know what I mean? Like spilling salt or walking under a ladder."

"That's very good, Greg. Taboos, that's what he was talking about. That comes from the Polynesian word 'tabu', meaning a sacred or significant object."

Umber Jones said, "You should have someone look at your cheek. Nasty cut, that."

"Don't interrupt," Jim told him, even though he was still shaking. "No matter what you do, these children still deserve their education."

They locked eyes for a moment. Then Umber Jones said, "Okay. I'll send you a messenger."

"Not Elvin, please. Let Elvin rest in peace."

"Elvin? Elvin doesn't want to rest in peace. Elvin's glad to be out and about."

Jim couldn't think what to say. But Umber Jones began to shudder and fade, and in a few moments his smoke had disassembled itself, and blown away, as if he had never been there at all.

"He's gone," said John Ng. "Look at my crystal. It's clear."

"Is he really gone?" asked Rita.

Jim said, "Yes. I think we can all breathe a little more easy."

"But what does he *want*?" Sherma insisted.

"Nothing that has to worry you," Jim told her. "I'm just sorry that you've all gotten involved."

"Come on, Tee Jay, tell us what he wants," demanded Russell. "I mean you seem to be such buddies with him."

Tee Jay said, "You heard Mr Rook. He doesn't want nothing that has to bother you. All he wants is space and respect." He put his fingertip to his lips, in the same way that Umber Jones had done when he looked through the classroom window. "And silence."

He turned to Jim and said, "You need to get that cut fixed, Mr Rook. How about I take you down to the nurse?"

There was something in his tone of voice that made

154

Jim immediately put down his bloodstained poetry book and say, "All right, Tee Jay. The rest of you . . . I won't be too long. Why don't you write me a poem of your own about your own superstitions . . . anything that frightens you. Breaking a mirror, treading on the cracks in the sidewalk, the number thirteen . . ."

The class looked up at him, still confused and upset. He left his desk and walked up and down the aisles between them, touching their shoulders, squeezing their hands. "Listen," he said, "something very strange and dangerous has happened here. But so long as we don't lose our nerve . . . so long as we all stick together, everything's going to work out fine."

Tee Jay stood up and took hold of his elbow. "Come on, Mr Rook. Let's get that face seen to."

They left the classroom and walked along the corridor. Mr Wallechinsky walked past, his cheek still covered in sticking-plaster, and Jim covered his own face with his hand. "How's it going, Mr R?" said Mr Wallechinsky, and Jim said, "Great."

They rounded the corner at the end of the corridor and Tee Jay stopped. "Mr Rook . . . I got something to say to you. I know you hate me. I know you think that I helped my Uncle Umber when Elvin got killed, but it wasn't that way at all."

Jim stood with his back against the wall. In the distance, he could hear the persistent squeaking of basketball boots on a polished wood floor. He wasn't feeling particularly friendly or amenable. His collar was sticky with blood and he was still trembling with shock. But all the same, Tee Jay was looking deadly serious, and much more like he used to be, instead of the furious swearing hoodlum who had beaten up on Elvin in the washroom.

"All right," he said. "What way was it?"

"It started six months ago, when my Uncle Umber turned up at the door without no warning at all. He said he was back from travelling all around Europe and Africa or wherever, and that he wanted to get to know us again. I didn't remember him. Like I was about two when he first left LA. Mom didn't seem to like him too much, but he was Dad's brother after all and what could she do? I thought he was great. He was funny and he was full of these wild stories about voodoo ceremonies and altars made out of human bones, and priestesses who could speak in languages that nobody had ever heard of.

"He taught me all about it. He *showed* me. He made me see that voodoo is the one true religion, you know what I mean? And it has to be, because it's the only religion that's real. It's the only religion with *evidence* for what you believe in."

"Well, I'll give you that," said Jim, taking his hand away from his face and showing Tee Jay the blood on his fingers.

Tee Jay said, "I'm sorry about that, Mr Rook. I wouldn't have had that happen for the world."

"And Elvin? What about Elvin? I suppose you wouldn't have had *that* happen for the world, either. But Elvin's dead; or what passes for dead."

"That's why I'm talking to you now, Mr Rook. When Uncle Umber killed Elvin, that was when I first found out just how far he was prepared to go. He said he was going to make Elvin show some respect. I never knew that he was going to *kill* him. I swear it."

"You were there when it happened. Why didn't you try to stop him?"

Tee Jay shook his head. "You can't do nothing to stop him, Mr Rook. He can call on all the strength of Vodun

156

and Baron Samedi and every spirit you never heard of. See – when he lived in Venice in the 'seventies, he was scratching for a living washing white peoples' cars and looking for handouts. He promised himself he wasn't never going to demean himself like that again. He was going to find the real black power. Not the political black power, but the *magical* black power. And he promised himself that he was going to come back to LA one day and take over everything, and be respected and rich, so that there wasn't one single white man who would ever be able to pop his fingers at him and call him boy. He wasn't going to let nobody show disrespect to him or his."

"And that's why he killed Elvin?"

Tee Jay swallowed and nodded. "Elvin was always laughing about voodoo. I tried to tell him that it was the only religion that a black man could proudly have. But all he did was diss me, on and on. I could take it for myself, but when he started dissing Baron Samedi, that was something else. He said, you going to start biting the heads off of poultry and strutting up and down with your face all white and your high black hat on? That's when I hit him. I'm sorry I hit him. But he shouldn't of said that. Not about something I truly believe in."

"Then what happened?" Jim asked him. "Your uncle came to college? How did he know you were feeling so upset?"

"I called him at home, because I was afraid that Dr Ehrlichman was going to can me. He asked me what had happened and I told him. He said he was going to fix it, and of course he did. Or his Smoke did, anyways."

Tee Jay took a deep breath and Jim could tell by the thistle in his throat that he was close to tears. "Uncle Umber told me to call Elvin into the boiler-house. I

157

told Elvin I was packing some speed. He walked in and Uncle Umber blew the goofer dust on him and he was paralysed just like he was dead. He couldn't move. He couldn't speak. But all the time his eyes were staring at me, like pleading, you know? Uncle Umber said that in Haiti they cut blasphemers one hundred and twelve times, one for each of the *loa*, to punish them for what they've done."

Tee Jay paused for a long, emotional moment. Then he said, "That's what he did to Elvin, right in front of me. I was scared, Mr Rook. I was so damned scared. I knew that if I tried to stop him, he would do the same to me. He'll kill anybody, Mr Rook, if they stand in the way of what he wants to do."

Jim said, "Why don't you leave him, if you're so damned scared? Why don't you go back home?"

Tee Jay looked down at the floor. "He won't let me."

"That's it? That's the only reason? He simply won't let you? Come on, Tee Jay, I know you better than that."

"That's part of the reason. But the other part is . . . I *believe* in voodoo, Mr Rook. I really believe in it. It gives you power, and I can feel that power for myself. In my hands. In my mind. I never felt so strong. I never felt so confident. For the first time in my life, I feel like I'm somebody important, with a future, you know? I feel like I've got a handle on my own destiny."

"I see. You've got a future, no matter who you hurt?"

"I didn't want Elvin to die, Mr Rook. I swear it. It won't ever happen again."

"So what if Chill refuses to give Uncle Umber ninety per cent of his profits? You can swear that you won't lay a finger on him?"

"Chill's a drug-dealer, man. He knows what the risks are."

"Oh, sure he does. But that doesn't give you *carte blanche* to kill him. That's a matter for the law."

Without looking up, Tee Jay said, "Mr Rook . . . this isn't easy. I'm stuck between a rock and a hard place. I respect you, right? You're just about the only white person I ever met who understands what's happening inside of my head."

But then he raised his eyes and said, "But voodoo . . . this is such a rush. This is *empowerment*. This is black people tapping the wells of their own heritage, right? I mean you're always telling us that we ought to be true to our heritage, aren't you?"

"I'm not prejudiced against voodoo," Jim told him. "I respect voodoo just as much as Roman Catholicism, or Shinto or anything else that anybody wants to believe in. But I don't respect violence and I don't respect extortion. Most of all I don't respect murder. You should go round to see Elvin's mom and dad and try to tell *them* how empowered you are, now that you've discovered voodoo."

Tee Jay said, "We'd better get you to the nurse."

"I think I can manage on my own, thank you," Jim told him. He started to walk toward the medical room, leaving Tee Jay behind.

Tee Jay watched him for a while, and then called out, "Mr Rook! Please don't chill me out, Mr Rook! I'm doing my best here, I swear it!"

Jim stopped, but didn't turn around.

"I promise, Mr Rook, I'm going to do everything I can to make sure that nobody else gets hurt."

"What if your Uncle Umber decides to kill somebody else? Who are you going to support then? Him, or me?"

"He's blood of my blood, Mr Rook. You got to understand that."

"Exactly," said Jim, and limped off toward the medical room.

The rest of the day was quiet and anti-climactic. While the boys went to the shop for welding and auto repairs, and the rest of the girls were given a talk on home management, Jim gave Jane Firman a one-to-one lesson in word recognition, and then worked with David Littwin on his stammer.

He liked David. In spite of his speech problems, he was always enthusiastic and co-operative, and he never took offence when he was teased by the rest of the class. Jim had never believed in pretending that his students didn't have handicaps. Sooner or later they were going to have to face the world outside, and the world outside wasn't forgiving when it came to bad stammers or thick accents or slowness of thought. Jim wanted to give his students confidence without pretending that their lives were going to be easy and that they were always going to be surrounded by understanding friends and politically-correct teachers. Some day, an impatient employer was going to ask David if there was any danger of getting an answer by Christmas, and David was going to have to deal with it.

David had improved immensely since he had started in Special Class II, but Jim had no intention of making him feel that people were going to wait for ever while he s-s-s. Struggled to s-s-s. Say what he meant.

At the end of the day, there was a knock on his classroom door. It was Susan. "Listen," she said, "when I said we should keep a little distance between us, I didn't mean three thousand miles, and I didn't mean forever."

"I'm sorry," Jim said, thrusting a sheaf of essays

into his briefcase and snapping it shut. "I've been extra-specially busy today."

"You've cut your face," she said, concerned. She came forward and touched his cheek and then his nose. "How did that happen? You look like Mr Wallechinsky."

"It's nothing. A window broke."

She frowned at him. "Is something *wrong*?" she asked him.

He kept thinking of the way that she had half-closed her eyes when she had told him that she loved him; and how furiously she had kissed him, as if she wanted to eat him alive.

"Everything's fine," he said. "I've had a crappy day, is all."

He tried to leave his desk but she stayed where she was, blocking his way. "I don't want you to think that I'm angry or anything," she told him. "I'd still like to see your maps, whenever you have the time."

"Susan," he said. "I don't have any maps. Ron Philips was stirring things up between us, that's all."

"No maps?" she blinked. "What do you mean, no maps? What about Martin Frobisher's chart of the North-West Passage?"

He shook his head.

"You *invented* it?" she asked him, incredulously. "Why on earth did you invent it?"

Even as she said it, of course, she understood why; and she blushed as fiercely as a teenager. "I'm sorry," she said, "I shouldn't have asked you that. That was stupid of me. Listen – I'm making a complete fool of myself here. I'd better go."

He took hold of her wrist. "Susan . . . I don't know what's happened between us. I don't know why you said you loved me so much and then you changed your mind.

161

I guess women are entitled to be fickle. But I'd quite like to know what it was that put you off me so suddenly. I mean was it my breath? Did you meet Richard Gere in the supermarket the next morning? What?"

"I'm at a loss here," Susan admitted. "You seem to think that we had something going when we didn't. All that happened was, you drove me home. We talked about maps, and that was it. You bumped into a hedge and got your pants wet."

"We didn't kiss?"

"We pecked."

"We pecked but we didn't kiss? No tongues or anything?"

"*Tongues*?" she said, startled. "Jim . . . we were talking about Mercator's projection, that's all. You don't go straight from Mercator's projection to *tongues*."

Jim pressed his hand to his head. "I'm missing something here. I thought we kissed. I thought you said you loved me and we kissed."

Susan took hold of his hand. "Jim . . . I *like* you. I *admire* you. All this work you do with Special Class II. But I'm sorry . . . I never said that I loved you. And believe me, please – and don't take this wrong – we never kissed."

It suddenly came to him. The memory powder. He had tested the memory powder by imagining that Susan was head-over-heels in love with him. He remembered that now. But in spite of the fact that he could remember it, he was still totally convinced that he and Susan *had* kissed. It was the strangest feeling that he had ever had. He could still feel her lips. He could still feel the softness of her hair and her breath against his cheek. "*I fell in love with you the moment I first saw you.*" She had said it so clearly that he could

162

imagine each word in shining fruity colour, like a roll of Life Savers.

"Jesus," he said. He was so dumbstruck.

"Listen . . ." she said. "Give it some time, then maybe we could go out for dinner together. Or maybe a picnic."

"Sure," he told her. He squeezed her hand. "I think I'd better be getting along home now. The feline formerly known as Tibbles will be wanting her supper."

"Jim," she said, as he left the classroom. He stopped, and turned.

"Nothing," she said, and let him go.

On the way back to Venice the atmosphere tightened and Jim could see snakes'-tongues of lightning flickering over the Santa Monica Mountains. By the time he was half-way home there was a deafening barrel-roll of thunder and the sidewalks were instantly spotted with rain. Soon water was cascading off the roof of his car and his windscreen wipers were flapping wildly from side to side. When he reached his apartment block he parked as close to the concrete staircase as he could and climbed out of the driver's seat with a copy of *National Geographic* on top of his head. Too bad about the fertility rituals of the Motu-speaking peoples of Papua New Guinea: they were just going to have to get wet.

He climbed the steps to his apartment. Myrlin was watching him out of his kitchen window but when Jim suddenly turned around and gave him the evil eye he promptly closed his venetian blinds.

There was a second burst of thunder as Jim opened up his front door, and the rain clattered down with even more intensity, gushing down the roof and leaping out of the gutters. Jim switched on the lights and dropped his sodden magazine into the wastepaper basket. He left the door a few inches ajar and a few seconds later his cat appeared, rubbing up against his legs and mewling for him to feel sorry for her. "All right, already," he told her.

He went through to the kitchen, opened up his freezer and took out a plateful of jambalaya that he had made for himself about two months ago. He didn't feel particularly hungry, after today, but he had a whole evening's marking in front of him and he knew that if he didn't eat properly he would end up at midnight building himself a disgusting Dagwood sandwich out of anything he could find in the icebox – pickles, gorgonzola, out-of-date prosciutto and peanut butter, and he would lie in bed in the early hours of the morning wishing he hadn't.

He slid the plate of jambalaya into the microwave and switched it to defrost. Then he popped open a can of beer, and pulled open a can of catfood. His cat came hurrying into the kitchen on speeded-up clockwork legs, and was gulping down reconstituted lumps of rabbit before he could spoon it all on to her plate. "Look at you," he told her. "You only love me for my food, and Susan doesn't love me at all."

He stood up and looked at himself in the mirror next to the phone, cautiously touching his cheek to see how much it had healed. Umber Jones's knife must have been sharper than a cut-throat razor, because the wound, although it was quarter of an inch deep, had closed together perfectly. The nick on his nose was more troublesome: it was a tiny semicircular slice close to the tip and it gaped slightly. He would have to ease off blowing his nose for a while.

Taking his can of beer, he walked through to the living-room. He picked up his remote control and switched on the television. News; baseball; *The Simpsons*; more baseball; disgusting insects in close-up, news. Lightning crackled outside his window and the television picture crackled too, and started to jump. He went over to the set and hit the top of it with the flat of his hand, but the picture continued to tremble. It was then that Jim heard his cat mewling again and he turned around to see a figure sitting on his couch. A shadowy figure, thin and bent and barely-visible; with no more substance than a silhouette cut out of a net curtain.

He stared at it, alarmed, but now that he had begun to accept the existence of wandering spirits, he wasn't as frightened as he had been when Umber Jones had first appeared. He watched it for a while, waiting to see what it would do, and then cautiously he approached it. It had none of the volcanic malevolence of Umber Jones. It sat with its head bowed and its hands in its lap, patient and quiet. He knelt down on the carpet in front of it, and then he reached out to touch it, to see if it would respond, but all that he could feel was a faint cold prickling, like dipping his fingers into a glass of tonic water.

The figure raised its head. Its face was wan and sad, its eyes concealed by dark shadows. But there was no mistaking who it was. Even after it has left its physical body for ever, a spirit can still be recognised. "Mrs Vaizey," said Jim. "Can you hear me, Mrs Vaizey?"

"I can hear you," she said. He wasn't sure if she had really spoken or not, but he could understand what she was saying.

"Mrs Vaizey . . . I'm so sorry for what happened. If I'd had any idea—"

"I knew what the risks were, Jim. And now that I'm dead, I think that you can call me Harriet, don't you?"

"Did Umber Jones catch you in his apartment?"

She nodded and said, "His smoke-spirit was out walking when it happened. His physical body was lying on the bed. His face was painted white with ash so that only his eyes looked out. His hat was propped up on the pillow beside him and he was holding his *loa* stick in his hand, just like Baron Samedi. I tried to take the *loa* stick away from him, but I was too late. His smoke-spirit returned and caught me and there was nothing I could do. He called on Ogoun Ferraille to help him, and Ogoun Ferraille forced me to eat myself."

"The pain—"

"The pain was more terrible than anything you can think of. But the mercy is that it didn't last long and now it's over. I'm never going to feel pain again."

"What's going to happen to you now?"

"I'll fade, Jim, like all spirits do, and then I'll be gone. There isn't a heaven. Beyond the light, there's just a kind of fading away, like a photograph left in the sun. One day there's nothing left but the faintest of outlines, and then there's nothing at all."

"I'm going to miss you. You know that."

"Well . . . so long as somebody still remembers me, I won't be gone for good. But you still have to find a way to deal with Umber Jones, or else he's going to plague you for the rest of your days."

"I've tried dealing with him," said Jim, turning his face so that she could see the cut on his cheek. "Look at the result. He's threatened to hurt my students if I don't do what he says."

He told her what had happened in the classroom today and she listened thoughtfully. In the end she said, "You'll have to take his *loa* stick. It's the only way. Do you think you might be able to persuade this boy Tee Jay to do it?"

166

"I don't think so. He's very upset about the way that his uncle killed his best friend, but he's very frightened of him. I don't think he'd want to risk his uncle's anger by messing around with something as sacred as a *loa* stick."

"Well, that doesn't surprise me. He must be a full convert to voodoo or he wouldn't be able to see his uncle's smoke-spirit. I guess *you'll* have to get it."

"You mean break into Umber Jones's apartment?"

"Either that, or do what I did, and visit it in spirit. Just make sure that he doesn't come back and catch you, the way he caught me."

"How can I do that? I don't have the first idea how to leave my body."

"It isn't difficult. You make a circle of ash and use your finger to make three signs – the moon, the sun and the wind. These will guide your spirit out of your body and guide it back again, like the markings on an airport runway. Then all you have to do is lie quietly on your couch and recite the three verses of leaving."

"I don't know the three verses of leaving. Was that all that Latin-sounding stuff you were saying?"

"You can say it in any language you like. In some languages it works much more quickly and whisks you out of your body almost at once. Creole, for example; and Yoruba, because they have very strong words for magic."

"My Yoruban is kind of rusty."

"Then say it in English. Set my spirit free . . . let it wander where it will. Let my body sleep without it. Set my spirit free . . . keep it safe from evil and darkness."

She repeated the words three times and Jim repeated them after her.

"You don't have to worry if you change them a little . . . it's your *will* that sets you free, not what you say."

"There's just one thing," said Jim. "What's it actually *like*?"

"You'll feel as if you've taken off a heavy coat which you've been wearing all your life. You'll feel so free that you won't want to come back. You'll fly. You'll flow. Once you've done it for the first time, you won't be able to wait to do it again."

Jim wasn't sure that he liked the sound of that. Up until Umber Jones had appeared on the scene, his life had been reasonably straightforward and contented. He didn't want to have his contentment disturbed by a strange craving which he could never satisfy. It would be like being an astronaut, forever yearning to go back to the moon.

"If I can fly . . . if I can flow . . . if I don't have any physical substance, how do I pick up the *loa* stick?"

"A spirit doesn't work by substance. A spirit works by will. A spirit's strength is its ability to concentrate, unhindered by flesh and blood."

Mrs Vaizey's outline began to dim. Jim said, "Listen . . . once I've got the *loa* stick, what do I do with it?"

Mrs Vaizey said something so faintly that he couldn't make out what it was. It could have been *take it* or *break it*. It could have been something quite different. She became so dim that she looked like nothing more than a faint shadow cast across the couch. Then she was gone altogether.

The feline formerly known as Tibbles gave a mystified miaow. Jim stood up and paced around the apartment for a while, wondering what the hell he ought to do.

There was a ring at the doorbell. He answered it, keeping the door on the security-chain. It was Geraint, in a violent green-and-scarlet shirt. "Do you have my mother in there?" he demanded.

"Your mother? Of course not. What gave you that idea?"

"Myrlin said he thought he saw you talking to her."

"And how did he manage to do that? Does he have X-ray vision or something?"

"He was just walking along the balcony and he just happened to glance over at your apartment."

"Oh, just *happened*? I might have known." Jim took the chain off the door and opened it wide. "You want to come in and search the place?"

"No thanks," said Geraint uncomfortably. "But I'm getting real worried about her, you know? She never took off like this before. I've looked all over, but zip."

"I wouldn't worry. You know what she's like. Wherever she is, she's bound to be happy."

Geraint was about to leave when he wrinkled up his nose and sniffed. "You know something . . . I'm sure I can smell her perfume."

Jim knew what he meant. She had left not only the smell of her perfume behind, she had left the vibrancy of what she once was. He laid a comforting hand on Geraint's shoulder. "I'm sorry, Geraint. Wishful thinking."

Chapter Ten

He managed to eat half his jambalaya and the rest he scraped into the cat's dish. Then he took a shower and changed into a black turtleneck shirt and black pants. He found a pair of black leather driving gloves, too, that his mother had bought him for Christmas and which he had never worn. He slicked back his wet hair and looked at himself in the mirror. He might not have any burgling experience, but he certainly *looked* like a burglar.

He opened the kitchen closet and took out the blue plastic container in which he kept his motley selection of tools. He chose a long screwdriver and a thin paint-scraper. There was also a bent piece of wire with which he had once opened a college locker when a student had lost his key, and he optimistically put that into his pocket, too.

He drove to Umber Jones's apartment feeling totally unreal, as if this couldn't be him at all. He parked across the street, tucked in closely behind a carpet-delivery van. There was a dim amber light shining through the blinds in Umber Jones's upstairs window and Jim could see the silhouette of a figure moving to and fro. From this side of the street, it looked like Tee Jay.

Jim checked his watch. It was 11:11 on the nose. He settled back in his seat, preparing for a long wait. It was going to be highly risky, breaking into Umber Jones's apartment when he and Tee Jay were asleep, but he would rather do it while Umber was in his physical form than when he was in the form of The Smoke, with all the destructive strength that the *loa* could give him.

He passed the time by reciting poetry to himself. "'*But death replied: "I choose him." So he went, And there was silence in the summer night.*'"

Unexpectedly, the street door to Umber Jones's apartment opened and Tee Jay emerged. He was wearing a blue-and-white nylon windbreaker with his hands thrust into the pockets. He looked right and left and then he headed off westward, walking fast.

Five or six minutes passed and then the light in Umber Jones's window was switched off. Maybe Umber Jones had retired to bed. Jim thought that he would give him about a half-hour, and then see if he could manage to break in. There would be a few minutes of maximum danger while he tried to locate the *loa* stick, but once he had it, there would be nothing that Umber Jones could do.

He waited twenty minutes. Umber Jones's window was still in darkness. He must be asleep by now. Jim gave him another three minutes and then climbed out of his car, leaving it unlocked in case he needed to make a quick getaway. "You're mad," he told himself, matter-of-factly, as he crossed the street. "This is never going to work. He's going to wake up and he's going to cut you to bits. Not only that, you're talking to yourself."

But what was the alternative? Continuing to act as Umber Jones's 'friend' – running errands for him and helping him to extort money out of pimps and drug dealers, under constant threat of him killing his students? Or staking out Umber Jones's apartment for days on end, waiting for him to leave it as The Smoke? But supposing

171

he returned, and caught Jim right in the act of stealing his *loa* stick, the way he had caught Mrs Vaizey? Jim didn't relish the idea of eating himself, and of ending his life as nothing but a heap of dust.

He reached Umber Jones's front door. He looked anxiously around but there was nobody in sight except for a very drunk man who looked exactly like Stan Laurel. He was leaning against a wall as if he were in love with it and occasionally bawling out random lines from *Moon River*: "*Wider than a mile . . . I'm croshin you in shtyle . . .*" The door was old and didn't fit very well. There was at least a quarter-inch gap between the frame and the door itself, and the wood looked pretty rotten. Jim took out his screwdriver and forced it into the gap, next to the lock. Then he pulled it back as hard as he could, and part of the frame splintered. Next he managed to work the screwdriver blade right into the gap until he could feel the tongue of the lock. He was just about to force it open when he suddenly became aware of a deep, thrumming sensation, as if a subway train were passing right beneath his feet. Except that here in Venice, of course, there *were* no subways.

Instinctively, he stepped away from the door. The thrumming grew louder, and as it did so it sounded more like drums beating. Furious, hectic drums. The door rattled and Jim turned around and ran. Half-way along the next block he found an empty doorway in front of an adult bookstore. He pressed himself against the security mesh, his heart beating as madly as the drums. Through the mesh, the faded picture of a plump white-fleshed girl smiled at him, her eyes encircled with thick black mascara.

After a moment or two he leaned out to see what was happening. The sidewalk was empty except for the drunk, who had managed to slide himself a few feet further away. *"Waiting . . . round the bend . . ."*

But then the air in front of Umber Jones's apartment appeared to tremble, like the hot air over a desert highway. The door opened, just a fraction, and smoke began to pour out of it. Dense, black smoke. Jim drew himself back. He knew exactly what this was. The smoke twisted and curdled and slowly rose upward; until it formed itself into the tall, dark, unmistakable figure of Umber Jones. He had emerged through an opening in the door that was no more than two inches wide.

Jim had two immediate choices. Either he could stay here and risk burgling Umber Jones's apartment, or he could follow Umber Jones wherever he was going, to see what he was planning next. It made more sense to break into his apartment. After all, once he had the *loa* stick, Umber Jones wouldn't be able to call on the spirits to give him strength; that was the way that Jim understood it, anyhow. He may still be capable of using a gun or a knife, but then so what? Jim had taught classes of fifteen-year-olds who had been capable of using guns and knives, and occasionally brought them to college, too.

Apart from that, Mrs Vaizey had died trying to bring him the *loa* stick, and he felt he had a moral duty to finish the job that had killed her. He owed her at least that much.

Umber Jones started to walk away from him, his black suit flapping like a crow's wings. He passed close to the drunk – who couldn't see him, of course, but who obviously felt him go by; like a shadow, like a dark summer draft; because he swivelled around on one leg, and stared at nothing at all.

Umber Jones crossed the street. As he did so, a taxi came speeding toward him, its flag lit up, its suspension bouncing on the patched-up roadway. It headed straight for him, its headlights shone right through his body, as if they were shining through fog. There was a moment when Jim thought that he was going to be killed, but the taxi drove right through him. The smoke that he was made of whirled and staggered, but then it blew itself back together again, and Umber Jones continued to cross to the opposite sidewalk as if he had been hit by nothing more than a sudden gust of wind.

He disappeared around the next corner. For a few long moments, Jim's courage failed him, and he stood where he was, pressed against the mesh of the adult bookstore. How could you fight a man who could leave his body and walk through the streets like smoke? But he gave himself his own answer: because you have to. Because nineteen young people are relying on you.

Because good has to overcome evil. It's the natural law.

He took two deep breaths. Then he left the bookstore and walked back to the front door of Umber Jones's apartment. He took out his screwdriver and carried on twisting at the lock. The drunk caught sight of him and began to shamble toward him. *"Waiting round the bend . . ."* he hollered. *"My huckleberry friend . . ."*

The light in Mr Pachowski's apartment was abruptly switched on, and the drapes drawn back. Mr Pachowski opened up the window and called out, "What's going on down there? Get out of here before I call the cops!"

Jim backed away from the door, lifting his hand in a conciliatory wave. "It's okay . . . I was looking for number 12002!"

"Wrong block . . . 12002 is three blocks west!"

"Great, thanks," said Jim. All the same, Mr Pachowski

stayed watching him as he walked away. He lifted his hand again. "Thanks," he repeated. "Good-night."

He crossed back over the street. The drunk came weaving after him, still singing. As Jim climbed back into his car he came up and leaned against the roof. Jim put down the window and said, "Go on, beat it. Find yourself someplace safe to sleep it off."

The drunk stared at him with eyes that refused to focus. "Tell me something," he said. "I've never been able to work it out for myself and nobody ever seems to know the answer. What the hell *is* a huckleberry friend?"

He went reeling off into the night with his arms spread wide, a scarecrow caught in a cyclone. Jim started up his engine and pulled away from the curb. He could see that Mr Pachowski was still keeping a beady eye on him. There was nothing left to do now but drive back home and work out some other way of getting his hands on Umber Jones's *loa* stick.

Or maybe there was something else that he could do. Follow Umber Jones, wherever he was going, and find out what he was up to. It could be highly dangerous, but on the other hand it might give him some valuable knowledge about Umber Jones's strengths, and maybe his weaknesses, too. There were one or two things that puzzled him about Umber Jones's behaviour. He had said that he wanted his existence to remain a secret, yet he had repeatedly appeared in a crowded classroom, where it had been almost impossible for Jim to conceal the fact that *something* strange was going on. He could have manifested himself just as easily in Jim's apartment, or in the street, and then there wouldn't have been any chance at all of Jim's students sensing his presence. There was something else, too: when Umber Jones had wanted to send Jim his instructions to talk to Chill, why had he sent Elvin, instead of visiting him in person – or at least in the form of The Smoke?

Jim drove to the corner where Umber Jones had disappeared. The street was deserted except for lines of parked cars and a man walking a brutish-looking dog. Jim turned left and drove slowly along to the next intersection, lightly drumming his fingers on the steering-wheel. He had been walking quickly, but he couldn't have gone more than four or five blocks. Jim stopped at the traffic signals – and then, when they changed to green, he turned right.

As he drove down the next block, he began to have a growing suspicion about where Umber Jones might be headed. He was now only three blocks away from Sly's bar, where Chill and his cronies hung out. Chill had told Umber Jones that he would rather see him in hell. Maybe Umber Jones had the same idea about Chill.

Jim still hadn't caught sight of Umber Jones, so he decided to risk it and drive directly to Sly's as fast as he could. He took a sharp left at the next intersection, his tyres squealing like strangled cats; and then a right. He arrived outside the bar just in time to see the dark shadowy figure of Umber Jones rounding the corner at the end of the block.

At the same time, he saw Chill and three of his minders standing on the sidewalk talking and laughing. Another minder was sitting on the hood of a green Cadillac Fleetwood, smoking a cheroot. Umber Jones approached them at unnatural speed, without once breaking his stride. His face was ghastly with ash and his eyes were scarlet, as if he had been rubbing cinders into them. He came along the sidewalk in his black suit and his black wide-brimmed hat and of course Chill and his minders couldn't see him at all. He didn't even throw a shadow.

176

Jim's grip tightened on his steering-wheel. He wasn't sure what he ought to do. Even if he shouted a warning to Chill and his men, they wouldn't believe him, because Umber Jones simply couldn't be seen. And it wouldn't help them, either. Umber Jones was not only invisible but untouchable. His only substance was his evil; but his power was the power of the *loas* who were helping him, Ghede and Ougon Ferraire.

Jim actually took an involuntary breath to shout, "*Look out!*" but his voice wouldn't work. All he could do was watch in horror as Umber Jones rotated his hand, revealing the knifeblade underneath.

Chill leaned back on his heels, his hands in his pockets, laughing. The minder who was standing next to him was wearing a black shirt and a white silk vest. Umber Jones came speeding right up to him and stabbed him straight in the stomach – once, twice, three times. He was even holding onto the man's right shoulder to steady himself. The man was too shocked even to shout out. He stood with his arms wide, staring down at his vest. It looked as if somebody had crushed strawberries all over it. Then – still silent – he dropped on to his knees. He coughed up a huge splatter of blood, swayed, and keeled over sideways.

The other minders spun around and around, their guns held high, trying to see who had attacked them. At first it looked as if they were blaming each other. After all, there was nobody else anywhere near them. One of them backed away, waving his automatic in all directions. Jim could hear them shouting, and for a moment it looked as if they might even start shooting. But then Chill yelled at them to stop acting like headless chickens. Appropriate, Jim thought grimly, for men being attacked by voodoo.

Chill pointed up at the opposite buildings and the

minders took off their sunglasses and peered frantically across the street, to see if their friend had been hit by a sniper. But one of them was down on one knee beside him, opening up his bloody vest, and he turned to the others and shook his head. These weren't bullet-holes: these were oval, gaping stab wounds.

All the time, Umber Jones was circling around them, his blade gleaming, his teeth gleaming, his eyes so wide and unblinking that he looked as if he were mad. He approached the minder who was kneeling over his fallen friend, bent over him, and hooked his arm around his throat. It looked as if he were holding him in a wrestling grip, but then he whipped his arm away and his knifeblade cut across the man's jugular vein and half-way through his Adam's apple. He tried to get up, but blood was pumping out of his neck so wildly that it sprayed all the way across the sidewalk and all over the windows of Chill's Cadillac.

That was enough for Chill. He shouted to his two remaining minders and they climbed into the car as if the devil was after them. And he was. Before Chill's driver could start up the engine, the black smoky shape of Uncle Umber glided over to the Cadillac and literally poured itself in through the half-open window at the back.

The Cadillac's engine whoofed into life. The tyres screamed, and smoke billowed out of the rear wheel arches. Then the car pulled away from the curb and out into the street.

It didn't get very far. It hadn't even reached the end of the block before it abruptly swerved and collided with a deafening smash into the back of a double-parked garbage truck. There was a moment's silence and then it exploded. A ball of orange fire rolled up into the night. The blazing spare tyre was hurtled thirty feet into the air and landed on top of a parked car on the opposite side of the road.

Jim thought that everybody in the car must have been killed. But suddenly the passenger door opened and Chill dropped out on to the road, the back of his hair smoking. He managed to get up onto his hands and knees and crawl away from the wreck like a beaten dog. The heat from the burning car was so intense that the soles of his yellow suede shoes momentarily burst into flame. At last he was dragged to safety by two garbage collectors, who laid him on the sidewalk and covered him with coats.

Jim stayed where he was, watching the car burn itself into a skeleton. Only he could see the ashy-faced figure in the Elmer Gantry hat who was watching the wreck, too; unmoving; but with a look of ghoulish satisfaction.

At three o'clock in the morning, Jim was awakened by a light, insistent tapping noise. He sat up in bed, suddenly alert, listening. There was a moment's pause but then he heard the tapping noise again, like somebody's fingernail against the living-room window.

He climbed out of bed. The feline formerly known as Tibbles had been curled up against his legs, and she opened one eye and gave him a look of intense irritation. He padded on bare feet across the living-room carpet. The cotton blinds were drawn down over the window, but there was a three-quarter moon tonight, and Jim could clearly see the shadow of somebody standing out on the balcony.

He stood in front of the blind for a very long time, wondering if he ought to put it up, or pretend that he was asleep and that nothing could wake him.

But then he could see the shadow raise its arm and tap at the window once again. It would probably tap all night if he didn't answer it, and he was exhausted enough already. After he had gone to bed, he had fallen asleep almost at once, but he had woken up after only ten minutes beating and flapping wildly at his bedsheet because he thought that he was on fire.

He had managed to get back to sleep shortly after two – but now he was faced with this. A shadow who stood outside his window, patiently tapping.

At last he took hold of the toggle and tugged the blind open. Standing in the moonlight was Elvin, so pale that his skin was almost luminous, his wounds looking even more than ever like the gaping mouths of dead fish. He tapped the glass yet again. He was smiling in an odd defensive way, the way that blind people smile when they think that they're approaching an unfamiliar obstacle.

Jim covered his face with his hands. He wasn't sure how much more of this he could take. But when he took his hands away Elvin was still there and he knew that he didn't have any choice but to open the door.

Elvin came shuffling into his apartment and stood staring at nothing at all.

"Hallo, Elvin," said Jim. The smell of decay was much stronger now and he thought that Elvin looked much worse. How long could Umber Jones's magic drag this poor mutilated body around, carrying his messages?

"Umber Jones wants you to go see Charles Gillespie again," said Elvin, his voice almost unintelligible. "He wants you to tell Umber Jones the same thing you told him the last time. If he still won't agree, he wants you to give him this."

He reached with a white, spongy hand into his suit and produced a chicken's wingbone tied with hair and feathers and coloured thread. It looked like a giant fishing-fly. Jim stared at it but he wouldn't touch it.

180

Elvin waited patiently for a moment and then laid it down on the table.

"Another voodoo curse, I suppose," said Jim.

"Another way to make Charles Gillespie see sense," Elvin replied.

He turned to go, but Jim sharply said, "Elvin!" and he stopped where he was, with his back turned. His hair was tufty with dried blood.

"Elvin – is there anything left inside you of what you used to be, before Umber Jones took control of you?"

There was an achingly long pause, and then Elvin said, "I don't understand the question."

"I just want to know if I'm talking to Elvin Clay, the real Elvin Clay, Mr and Mrs Clay's favourite boy, Elvira's brother; or whether I'm just talking to a lump of submissive meat."

"Umber Jones is my *houngan*. I do whatever Umber Jones asks me to do."

"I know you do, Elvin. But what I want to know is whether there's anything left of *you*. Any will-power. Any strength. Any mind of your own."

Elvin hesitated. Despite his revulsion, Jim put his hand on his shoulder. His flesh felt unnaturally soft beneath his suit. Jim could feel his putrescing muscles slide across his bones. Elvin bowed his head and the wounds around his neck opened up as if they were capable of speaking on their own.

Then he turned around, and his face – as hideously mutilated as it was – was filled with almost childish pleading. "Why doesn't he let me go, Mr Rook? Why doesn't he just let me die?"

"I don't know, Elvin. It seems like he needs you, the same way he needs me."

"Can't you just ask him to let me go? You don't

know what it's like, feeling yourself rot. It's like there's something gnawing inside of my guts, something that won't stop gnawing and gnawing, and I'm scared that it's maggots."

Jim swallowed, and then he managed to say, "Listen, Elvin . . . I'll do everything I can. I promise."

Elvin gave him a blind, pathetic nod. Then he turned around again and shuffled out of Jim's apartment. Jim watched him grope his way down the steps and out into the night. God alone knew where he was going, or where he stayed when Umber Jones wasn't sending him out on errands. Maybe the cemetery. Maybe some cellar. And what was going to happen to him when his body began to decompose so badly that he couldn't even walk?

He picked up the chicken-bone fetish. There was something indescribably nasty about it. It was dry and old but it had a strong, unpleasant smell that put him in mind of everything that had ever made him nauseous, from a lump of gristle to the stench of sewage. He didn't know what Chill would make of it, but it certainly frightened *him*.

He couldn't think of going back to sleep. He went into the kitchen and made himself a strong cup of coffee. He sat at the table, wearily staring at the fetish and wondering if he were ever going to be able to free himself from Umber Jones's service. He was still sitting there when he heard a sickening, regurgitating noise from the living-room. It sounded like somebody choking for breath on their deathbed.

Cautiously, he slid open the cutlery drawer and took out the largest knife he could find. Then he tiptoed out of the kitchen and stood outside the living-room door. The noise was repeated – a horrible gagging, cackling sound.

182

He said to himself: come on, you managed to face Elvin. You *touched* him, even. Whatever this is, this can't be worse.

He reached around the living-room door to find the light-switch. He counted to three, and then he simultaneously switched on the light and swung into the living-room with his knife held high, shouting, *"Right!"*

The feline formerly known as Tibbles looked up, startled. She had just vomited all of her supper on to the carpet. Jim stood and stared at her, his knife in his hand, and he was sorely tempted to use it. But then, well, it was his own fault for giving her jambalaya. He knew that chillis always made her sick.

He went back to the kitchen to find a bucket and a wet cloth. He had never felt so tired and dejected in his whole life.

When he came into class that morning he found his students all standing around or sitting on their desks, talking to each other. He dropped his folder with an emphatic slap, and then he said, "What's this? You've started a debating society? What's the motion for today? This house believes that all teenagers should tuck their shirts in?"

Russell Gloach came forward. He still had Twinkie filling around his mouth, and he wiped it away with the back of his hand. "No, sir. The motion is, what are we going to do about Tee Jay's Uncle Umber?"

Tee Jay was there, too, sitting at the back of the class. Jim approached him and said, "What do you think, Tee Jay? He's your uncle. What he's doing, it's all connected with your religion."

"He's gone too far," said Tee Jay. "I never knew that he was going to start wasting people."

"He's gone too far and you don't know how to stop him? You couldn't try appealing to his better nature?"

"Uncle Umber doesn't have a better nature."

Sharon said, "You can't expect Tee Jay to stand up to his uncle. He's going to get himself killed, same as Elvin."

David Littwin put in, "W-w-we've b-b. Been trying to find a w-w-way to g-get rid of him."

"Any ideas?" Jim asked them.

"We could go round to his apartment and beat the shit out of him," Mark suggested.

"What the hell good would that do?" said Ray Vito. "He hasn't done anything against the law, has he? Not that we can prove. We'll end up in the slammer ourselves, for assault and battery."

"We could wait till he leaves his body," said Titus Greenspan. "Then we could board up his front door so that he couldn't get back to it again."

Jim said, "That wouldn't work. In his smoke form, he can slide through any gap that smoke can get through."

Sharon said, "There's a voodoo ritual in one of my books. It's got all the words and everything. It's how to put a curse on somebody so that when their spirit goes out walking, it can't get back into its physical body."

"That could be useful," Jim told her. "But what we need more than anything else is Umber Jones's *loa* stick . . . the stick which he uses to call on the help of all of the lesser spirits. Without that stick, he has no power at all."

"Can't you lift it when your uncle's asleep?" Ricky asked Tee Jay.

Tee Jay shook his head. "If I could, I would. But I don't dare to touch it. It's like, sacred."

"Sacred or not, if it's the only way of stopping your uncle . . ."

184

"You don't understand," said Tee Jay. "It's *sacred*. It's carved out of a ghost oak which grew in a cemetery . . . a tree which was fed on dead bodies. The dead bodies belonged to Baron Samedi, and so the tree belongs to Baron Samedi – and that means that the *loa* stick belongs to Baron Samedi, too."

"Tee Jay," said Beattie. "Baron Samedi is one of those things that aren't real."

"A myth," said Seymour.

Tee Jay said, "Baron Samedi is as real as you and me, Beattie. And when I started to study voodoo, I gave my solemn oath that I would never disrespect his name or steal his property or defy his law. If I tried to take that *loa* stick away from my uncle, I would have the most powerful spirit in the whole damn Western world hunting me down. He'd have my ass. Let me tell you something, man: I'd be lucky to end up like Elvin."

There was hubbub of scepticism from the rest of the class. But Jim raised his hand for silence and said, "Listen – whatever the rest of us think about voodoo, Tee Jay's a believer and we can't ask him to compromise his beliefs. If he and his uncle were Muslims, we wouldn't expect him to disobey the will of Allah, even if it *was* a question of stopping a murderer. Plenty of people have found themselves in the same dilemma in the past, like Roman Catholic priests who hear confessions from serial killers. I think we can count ourselves fortunate that, whatever Tee Jay believes in, he's drawn the line here and said no more killing, and he's prepared to help us insofar as he doesn't commit a heresy."

Not many of his class knew what a 'heresy' was, but they got the gist. They also began to realise that Jim was making an effort to draw Tee Jay back into the family, and he was asking them not to isolate him.

185

Tee Jay had been attracted to voodoo because in spite of his popularity and his outward cool, he felt isolated and inferior. What was so good about being popular and cool if you were struggling to read *Green Eggs And Ham* in the remedial-teaching class of a trashy college like West Grove?

Sharon said, "Maybe Tee Jay can help us by telling us when his uncle's left his body . . . then we can go around and take the *loa* stick for ourselves."

"You won't be able to get in there," said Tee Jay. "When my uncle takes on The Smoke, he locks himself in good. He doesn't want nobody tampering with his body while he's away."

"Can't you let us in?"

"No way. He locks his room from the inside and he's also got this security bar. It would take a tank to get in there. Besides . . . that would be aiding and abetting you to steal the *loa* stick, and I'm pretty sure that Baron Samedi wouldn't take too kindly to that."

"I don't know why you ever wanted to start believing in a mean dude like Baron Samedi," said Muffy. "As if there aren't enough mean dudes in the world already."

Jim said, "If we can't physically break in and take the *loa* stick, then we'll have to break in another way. I don't know whether you're really ready for this, but since all of your lives are in danger, I think you're entitled to hear it." And as briefly and as matter-of-factly as he could, he told them what had happened to Mrs Vaizey, and all about Elvin, too.

When he had finished, the classroom was so silent that Dr Ehrlichman peered in through the window to make sure that they were still there. Jim walked up and down the aisles waiting to hear their reaction.

Jane Firman had tears in her eyes. "Is this really, really true?" she asked him.

Jim nodded.

Ricky said, "When that old woman swallowed herself . . . Jesus, you must have *barfed*."

"I can't believe a word of it," said Rita. "This is just a test, isn't it? Just play-acting, to make us think about impossible things."

"Oh, yes?" said Jim. "And why would I want to do that?"

"To educate us, right? To stretch our imagination."

"Well, I wish it was," Jim told her. "Sharon, what do you think?"

Sharon was very subdued. "I've read about this thing of people being forced to eat themselves, yes. It's supposed to be a punishment for sticking your nose in where it's not wanted. Like treading on magic ground, or walking through a cemetery, or watching a *banda* without being invited."

"A *banda* . . . that's kind of a dance ritual to honour Baron Samedi," Tee Jay explained. "Most of the time it's pretty sexy. You know, people dancing with no clothes on."

"This eating thing, though," said Sharon. "I never knew it could really happen."

"Lots of things you don't know about," Tee Jay told her. "You keep talking about our roots and stuff . . . you don't even know the half of it."

Sharon was about to protest but Jim interrupted her. "That's why we need your help, Tee Jay. You know more about this than any of us. And even when you can't actively help, at least you can try not to obstruct us. It's the least you can do, considering what happened to Elvin."

Tee Jay flapped up his hands from his desk as if to indicate, "OK, everything's going to be cool."

Jim said, "What I propose to do is this: Tonight, if and when his Uncle Umber goes out in his Smoke form, Tee Jay can call me at home and tell me that he's gone. That's all I'm going to ask you to do, Tee Jay – nothing else – but it has to be you, because you're the only other person who can see him. As soon as I get Tee Jay's call, I'm going to try to leave my body, using the technique that Mrs Vaizey taught me. If I go immediately, there's a good chance that I can get to Uncle Umber's apartment and get hold of the *loa* stick before he returns from wherever he's been."

"What if he catches you?"

"Then I won't need to worry about dinner tonight, will I?"

Chapter Eleven

He parked a block away from Sly's and walked the rest of the way. The bullet-shaped doorman was even more hostile than he had been before. "You got your nerve, Charlie. If I was you, I'd be in Nome, Alaska, by now."

"What is this place?" Jim asked him. "The Nome, Alaska, tourist board?"

"Chill won't see you. Chill's not seeing nobody."

"Tell Chill I have something for him. A little gift from Umber Jones." Jim's heart was beating more violently than usual, but all the same there was something indescribably exciting about talking to hard men like these and knowing that he had the upper hand. For the first time in his life he understood why some men turned to crime. It was pure adrenaline. He loved the terse, euphemistic conversations that barely kept a lid on ruthless acts of violence – beatings, knee-cappings, killings. He loved the constant threat of saying the wrong thing; of showing disrespect, or weakness; or pushing his luck just a little too far.

It was almost as exciting as teaching, he thought, wryly.

The doorman talked in the phone and then he said, "Okay . . . you know where to go."

Jim went down the darkened staircase and the bouncer

frisked him and nodded him inside. The same pianist was playing selections from the Broadway musicals. The singer was gone. Jim crossed the floor through the red lights and the cigarette smoke and there was Chill sitting in his corner booth with a white turbanlike bandage on his head and both hands wrapped up like finger-puppets. He was flanked by three stone-faced minders in reflective sunglasses, one of whom kept looking at his watch as if he had an urgent appointment with the hairdresser who kept his pompadour from collapsing.

Chill said, "Sit down," and Jim sat.

There was a very long pause. Chill said, "Cigarette," and one of his minders tucked a cigarette between his lips and lit it. Chill blew out smoke then leaned back in his seat and said, at last, "This Umber Jones . . . I need to know some more."

"I'm sorry. There's nothing I can tell you. I just bring the messages."

"What I'm saying is . . . would he be interested in a little gentlemanly negotiation?"

"No."

Chill made a squeezed-up face as if he were constipated. "You see, the trouble here – the trouble we're facing here is – there's no way ninety per cent."

Jim said, "That's up to you. I think it's only fair to warn you, though, that if you don't agree to Umber Jones's terms, the consequences could be pretty apocalyptic. For you, anyway."

"Say what? Will you talk English?"

"What I'm saying, Mr Chill sir, is that you and your people had better do what Umber Jones wants you to do, otherwise you'll be in for a major-league ass-kicking."

"*Hey!*" objected one of Chill's minders, but Chill waved his finger-puppet fingers at him to keep quiet.

He leaned forward across the table and said, "So who, may I ask, is going to be giving me this major-league ass-kicking?"

Jim didn't blink. "The same people who set fire to your hair, I should imagine."

"You know who they are?" said Chill, fiercely. "Don't you think you better tell me?"

There was a moment of spring-tightening tension. Chill stared at Jim with his eyes wide and Jim stared back at him, calm and unblinking.

After a while, Jim took out the chicken-bone fetish and held it up. At first Chill didn't want to look at it but then he had to. His eyes flickered once, twice, and then he took his eyes away from Jim's and focused on the fetish with the kind of expression you would normally see on a man who has been told by his doctor that the lump on his neck is not just an ordinary lump but malignant lymphoma; and that he has less than six weeks to live.

His minders backed away – clumsy, but with obvious cowardice. They knew what the fetish was, too; and they didn't want to be too closely associated with a man who was marked for sudden death. One of them crossed himself. Another one spat and made a sign in the air. The third one shielded his eyes with his hand, so that he wouldn't even have to *look* at the fetish.

"Maybe there's some room for manoeuvre," said Chill, without much hope in his voice.

"No," said Jim.

"Hey, come on. I should meet this Umber Jones . . . maybe we can talk this whole thing out between us, man to man."

"No."

Chill flared up. "I'm trying to be reasonable here, you understand? I'm trying to make some concessions! But you have to be fair! This is my turf! I been operating here for fifteen years, man. Everybody knows the Chill. How is this Umber Jones character going to take over from me? He don't know jack."

"He doesn't have to. You're going to do all the work; and he's going to take his percentage. It's either that or more of what happened yesterday evening."

Chill banged his fist on the table and immediately regretted it: his fingers were still sore. "You can't prove to me that Umber Jones did that! There wasn't nobody there!"

Jim held up the voodoo fetish and shook it like a tiny maracas. "Oh, yes," he said. "There was somebody there. Just because you couldn't see them, that didn't mean that they weren't there. You've heard of The Smoke?"

Chill's face drained of blood, and his cheeks were almost as white as his hair. "The Smoke? Is this what you're talking about? The Smoke? That ain't possible, man. That's just a superstition."

"Oh, I see. Your minders were stabbed by a superstition, were they? Unusual way to die." He held out the fetish.

Chill couldn't take his eyes off it. It was clear that he was deeply frightened. "Take that away. I don't even want to *look* at that, man."

"It's a gift. Umber Jones is going to be seriously upset if you don't take it."

"*Take it away, you hear me!*" Chill screamed at him. "Tell him he can have what he wants! Ninety per cent, one hundred and ten per cent, whatever!"

Jim leaned forward, one hand cupped over his ear. "Did I hear that right?"

"Tell him he can have what he wants! Anything!"

Jim said nothing for a second or two, but then he

nodded, and said, "Okay. I'll tell him." He stood up and walked out of Sly's. When he passed by, everybody gave him plenty of space, staff and customers both, and even the pianist stopped playing.

He detested Umber Jones for all of his cruelty and his greed and his mumbo-jumbo, but at that moment he felt a huge surge of power. He understood why Tee Jay had felt so attracted by voodoo. It was like sex. It was like beating a man to the ground. It was liberation. It was winning. It was like having the gods on your side.

He was sitting at his kitchen table eating Chef Boy-ar-Dee Ravioli with heaps of freshly-grated parmesan cheese when the telephone rang. He lifted it off the wall and said, "Yes, what is it?"

"Mr Rook? This is Tee Jay. Uncle Umber just left the house."

"You're sure?"

"He locked himself into his room about twenty minutes ago. I kept a watch on the street and I saw his smoke-spirit heading west."

"You're sure about that?"

"Sure I'm sure. I saw him with my own eyes. Like he was floating across the street."

Jim looked at the kitchen clock. It was 22:47. The feline formerly known as Tibbles was sitting at his feet, enthusiastically licking her lips. "Listen," he said, "you'll hate ravioli. Remember what happened yesterday."

"What happened yesterday?" Tee Jay asked him.

"Forget it. I was talking to a friend of mine."

"Come on," said Tee Jay, "I don't know how long he's going to be away."

"All right," Jim told him. "But don't go counting on

193

anything. I never did this before, and I might not be able to do it now."

"You'll do it, Mr Rook, I'm sure of it," said Tee Jay.

Jim had already marked out a circle of ash beside the couch, with his own improvised signs for the sun and the moon and the wind. He lay down and propped a cushion under his head. He felt ridiculous, to say the least. But it had worked for Mrs Vaizey. There was no reason why it shouldn't work for him. Countless people left their physical bodies at night and wandered around the universe as smoke, or spirits, or summer draughts. There was no reason why he couldn't, too.

The feline formerly known as Tibbles watched him with narrow-eyed interest as he started to recite the words that Mrs Vaizey had taught him, as well as a few elaborations of his own. "Set my spirit free . . . let my spirit go . . . let my body sleep without it . . . let me travel where I will. Keep my body safe from evil . . . keep my body safe from darkness . . . let my spirit go . . . *let my spirit go . . .*"

He felt strangely light-headed, as if he had spent all evening in a bar, drinking one shot of whiskey after another. He looked up at the ceiling, at its waves of combed 1950s plaster, and thought, *Let my spirit go . . .* The plaster began to undulate, wave upon wave, and all the time he kept repeating to himself *let my spirit go . . .* The plaster was the sea, and the couch in which he was lying was his boat; and in his boat he rowed on waving waters, out of his present consciousness, out of his cagelike bones and his heavy, restrictive flesh; shedding the weight of his physical body; and literally rising, into the air.

He turned, as if he were swimming, and saw himself

194

lying on the couch, his eyes closed, his arms crossed over his chest. He approached himself and stared at himself in fear and fascination. His face looked oddly lopsided, not quite himself. Then he realised that he had never seen himself like this before, except in photographs. Most of the time he looked at himself in mirrors, in which his image was the other way around.

His cat seemed to be aware that something strange was happening, because her fur stood up, and she took three or four tentative steps away from him. She didn't look at him directly, though, which meant that cats couldn't see spirits any more than humans could.

The kitchen clock read 23:00 precisely, and he knew that he had to go. The last thing he wanted was for Umber Jones to come back and find him in his apartment.

He swam across the living-room and slid through the quarterlight, which was less than three inches open. The sensation of having no physical substance was exhilarating. Mrs Vaizey had been right: it was like suddenly shedding a heavy topcoat and finding yourself naked. He glided along the balcony, past Myrlin's apartment, and through the window he could see Myrlin peering intently at a small mirror and clipping the hairs out of his nostrils.

He carried on, down the steps and out of the apartment block, on to the street. He found that he could glide much faster than he could walk. In fact he only had to *think* that he wanted to reach the next intersection and he was almost there, like a camera-trick. He flowed through the streets of Venice, crossing streets and sliding along sidewalks. Sometimes he passed within inches of people out walking, but nobody saw him.

He knew that he could cross the street right in front of speeding vehicles without any risk of injury. The vehicles would simply pass through him, the same way that they had passed through Umber Jones's smoke. All the same, he didn't feel confident enough to chance it, and he waited at DON'T WALK signs, invisibly, like everybody else. On the corner of Mildred he was standing behind a man in a beret who was walking his poodle. The poodle could obviously sense that he was there, because it kept whining and pawing the sidewalk and anxiously looking all around it. "What's wrong, Sukie?" the man wanted to know. "You're acting like you seen a ghost."

At last Jim arrived outside Umber Jones's apartment. He rose as lightly as a tissue-paper kite until he reached the second-storey windows. In one window he could see Tee Jay, sitting on the couch watching television with the sound turned off. Every now and then Tee Jay checked his watch, and glanced toward the window. Jim's first reaction was to duck, but while Tee Jay's initiation into voodoo had made it possible for him to see The Smoke, he couldn't see Jim's spirit at all.

Jim floated along to Umber Jones's window. The drapes were partly drawn, and the room was lit with only two floating night-lights fashioned out of black wax. As he came closer, however, Jim could see Umber Jones's body lying on his bed. His face was dusted gray with ash and he was dressed in a dusty black frock-coat, complete with grey spats and black funeral shoes. His top-hat lay on the pillow beside him. In his left hand he held a chicken-bone fetish, much more elaborate than the one which he had sent to Chill, with beads and feathers and knots of fur. In his right hand he held a long cane of pale polished wood, topped with a silver skull.

The *loa* stick. As much a symbol of Umber Jones's dark authority as a bishop's crook or a king's sceptre.

Jim had been reading about *loa* sticks in Sharon's books – how they were passed from one voodoo practitioner to another, but never owned by any of them. They belonged to Baron Samedi, the lord of the cemeteries, and technically speaking they had to be returned on demand.

The window to Umber Jones's window was slightly ajar, and Jim poured through it like warm water. The air-conditioner in the bedroom had been switched off, and it was almost unbearably stuffy and hot, and the smell of incense was so strong that Jim felt as if he were suffocating. Strange, he thought, that he had no visible substance, yet he was still aware of the need to breathe. Even spirits have senses, he supposed.

He approached the bed and stood looking down at Umber Jones. Unnervingly, Umber Jones's eyes were wide open, with pupils as red as garnets. But his spirit was absent, somewhere in the night, and his eyes were sightless and unblinking.

Jim cautiously reached across his comatose body and took hold of the *loa* stick. He could feel it, but his hand passed right through it. He tried again, but again his fingers couldn't grasp it. It was exactly like trying to pick up an unwilling eel.

Then he remembered what Mrs Vaizey had told him: a spirit works by *will*, not by physical strength. A spirit's strength is in the purity of its essence, its ability to concentrate on what it wants, unhindered by flesh and blood.

Again he laid his hand on the *loa* stick, and this time he concentrated on its rising out of Umber Jones's grasp and coming with him. He stared at it harder and harder, willing it to do what he wanted. Gradually he could feel it taking on substance, smooth and hard and shiny. It still didn't feel like a real stick, at least it didn't to him: he felt that his fingers could pass right through it at any moment. But he kept on concentrating – *rise – rise – you damned stubborn piece of wood* – and inch by inch he was able to draw it out of Umber Jones's fingers.

If anybody else had been watching, they would have seen the *loa* stick sliding out of Umber Jones's hand as if by magic. They would have seen it rise into the air and float unsteadily toward the window. Jim didn't realise it, but he was using the same psychic energy that so-called poltergeists use, to fling plates and furniture around the room.

It took all of his concentration to keep a grip on the *loa* stick – or, rather, to will the *loa* stick to stay in his insubstantial hand. But once he had 'carried' it to the window, he would be able to drop it into the street below, and then all he would have to do would be to hide it close by. He could come back later in his physical form to retrieve it. He still wasn't certain what he was supposed to do with it – break it, or bury it or throw it in the ocean – and none of Sharon's books made any mention of how to deal with a stolen *loa* stick. He guessed that the best way of getting rid of it would be to burn it and scatter its ashes, the same way that he had disposed of Mrs Vaizey, God rest her.

He reached the window and manoeuvred the tip of the *loa* stick into the gap. He looked down at the sidewalk below to make sure that there was nobody around. He didn't want some passing stranger to pick up the stick and walk off with it, not knowing what it was.

As he was just about to drop it, however, he saw a dark flicker on the other side of the street. At first he thought it was nothing but the shadow from the awning of Amato's Deli. Then – to his alarm – he saw a tall black figure come striding out of the darkness, making its way directly toward the apartment's front door. Umber Jones, with his ashy face and his glistening red eyes.

He lost his concentration and the *loa* stick dropped on to the rush-mat carpeting. Panicking, he knelt down and tried to pick it up, but he was too worried about Umber Jones's smoke-spirit flowing up the stairs. He grabbed and grabbed, but his fingers went through the *loa* stick every time. From the next room, he heard voices – Tee Jay's and Umber Jones's – and he guessed that Tee Jay was trying to stall his uncle's smoke-spirit for as long as he could. But it was still no use. He couldn't even *feel* the *loa* stick now, let alone pick it up. He would just have to save himself now, before Umber Jones discovered that he was here and used the power of Ghede to make him eat himself – or punish him in some other horrible and painful way.

He was about to flow through the gap in the window when he felt a strong, calloused hand snatch at his shoulder. He was wrenched around and slapped three times across the face. The slaps were silent, but they were so hard that Jim felt as if his neck had been dislocated. He was gripped by the wrists and pulled up straight, so that he was face to face with the smoke-spirit of Umber Jones.

Umber Jones, to his surprise, was grinning.

"So . . . you found out how to leave your body and walk the way that spirits walk?" said Umber Jones. Jim tried to struggle free but Umber Jones was gripping him far too tightly. "What brought you here, to my house?" Umber Jones asked him. "Thought that you'd pay me a visit, did you? Thought that you'd be sociable?"

Jim twisted himself sideways but still Umber Jones kept an unrelenting hold on his wrists. He looked around

199

the room – inspecting the cabinet crowded with voodoo bric-a-brac, at the tables with their charms and amulets and silver boxes. "You wouldn't have come here to *steal* something, would you, Mr Rook? I wouldn't believe that of you. I thought it was a teacher's duty to uphold our moral standards – set an example."

He gave a dry, thumping sniff. Then he said, "No . . . I don't think you came to steal anything, did you? I can't see anything missing." He was playing with Jim, taunting him. The moment he flowed into the room he must have seen that the *loa* stick was lying on the floor.

"Or . . . wait a minute, what's this?" he said, looking down by Jim's feet. "Isn't that my cane there, down on the floor? What do you think *that's* doing down there? I hope you weren't trying to make off with *that*, Jim, because that's a sacred cane. You can knock on any door with that cane and you've got the spirits with you, as many as you want. You've got Ghede and Ougon Ferraire. You've even got Vodun, if you dare."

Jim said, "You know damn well what I'm doing here. The killing has to stop."

Umber Jones tilted his head forward so that he and Jim were almost nose to nose. "The killing can never stop, Mr Rook. Not until everybody in this city pays their respects to Umber Jones. Not just their respects, neither. Their money, too, and anything else that might catch my eye."

"You're out of your mind."

"Maybe I am, Mr Rook. But you're something much, much worse. You're out of your body."

"You really think you can force every pimp and drug-dealer in Los Angeles to hand over ninety per cent of everything they make?"

"Think it? I *know* it. What did Chill say to you today? Don't tell me he's still holding out."

Jim said nothing. Umber Jones gave him a long, blood-coloured stare and then released his wrists. He leaned down and picked up his *loa* stick, sliding his hand down the length of it as if to reassure himself that it hadn't been bent or damaged. It was the *loa* stick that gave his smoke-spirit the ability to be able to intervene in the physical world – to pick up objects, to cut people, to stab them to death. He walked over to his body on the bed, opened up his own fingers, and returned the *loa* stick to its original position.

"I thought I could trust you," he said. "You don't know how much you've disappointed me. You've let your students down, too."

"Don't even think about touching my students."

Umber Jones came right up to him and towered over him. "You won't be able to stop me."

"Oh, I'll stop you. I'll find a way, believe me."

"And supposing I make you eat yourself, the way that I made your lady friend eat herself?"

Jim said, "You need me too badly. How are you going to talk to all of those drug dealers if you don't have me?"

"I can always find another friend."

"Maybe you can. But it isn't easy, finding friends, is it? Especially friends who are easy to blackmail, like me."

Umber Jones grinned at him. "You're right. But I think you need to be taught a lesson. I think you need to be given a little instruction in obedience and humility."

Jim didn't know what to say. He had never felt quite so frightened in his life. In his spirit form, outside his body, he felt naked and vulnerable, and as helpless in front of this smoke-black figure of spells and witchery as a newly-born child. He hadn't even known before Umber Jones had slapped him that spirits could even *feel* other

201

spirits, let alone hurt them. Apart from what Mrs Vaizey had told him, and what he had read in Sharon's books and *National Geographic*, his knowledge of spirits had been limited to Jacob Marley and *Casper the Ghost.*

"What are you going to do?" he asked Umber Jones, tightly.

"You'll find out."

"You're just going to let me go?"

"As you said yourself, it isn't easy, finding friends."

"So what about this little instruction in obedience and humility?"

"You'll find out."

With that, he turned his back on Jim and went back over to the bed. He stood beside his physical body and laid his hand on its chest. He crossed himself and muttered a few incomprehensible words. His physical body began to breathe more and more deeply, its nostrils flaring, its ashy black coat-lapels rising and falling. Soon its breath was coming in huge agonised groans, like a man trapped in a submarine.

The black image of Umber Jones's smoke-spirit began to tremble. With every inward breath that his physical body took, it seemed to be pulled toward it. Then it started to fold in on itself, and become smokier and even less substantial. Right in front of Jim's eyes, Umber Jones's physical body *breathed in* his smoke-spirit, little by little, until there was nothing left beside the bed except a few dark wisps that floated and curled until they were breathed in, too.

Jim heard Umber Jones murmur something, and his fingers stirred like spiders disturbed by rain.

Now was the time to leave. Jim turned away, and flowed through the gap in the window, into the night, floating down toward the street with the lights of Venice sparkling all around him. He reached the sidewalk and looked back toward Umber Jones's bedroom window. Umber Jones was standing there, silhouetted by the dim, flickering candelight, watching him.

Jim started to make his way home, gliding from one street to the next. All he wanted now was to be back in his physical body before Umber Jones decided to teach him his lesson. It didn't look as if he was going to be forced to consume himself, thank God. But not knowing what punishment Umber Jones had in store for him was almost as chilling.

He reached his apartment block and flowed in through the window. He crossed the living-room, where the feline formerly known as Tibbles was sleeping on the floor beside the couch.

The couch itself, however, was empty. Jim's physical body had gone.

Chapter Twelve

He glided through to the bedroom. His body wasn't there, either. With rising panic, he glided through to the bathroom. The tub was empty. The shower-head dripped with its usual plangent *plink, plank, plink, plank.*

He went back to the living-room. He laid his hand on the couch but he couldn't feel any warmth. He could see, however, that the ash had been scuffed, as if somebody had stepped on it. His cat must have felt his presence, because she lifted her head and opened one eye.

What the hell was he going to do now? Was this Umber Jones's punishment, to take his physical body away and leave his spirit without anywhere to go? From what Mrs Vaizey had told him, a body and a spirit could only survive for a very limited time without each other. What if Umber Jones had taken his body away and hidden it, so that he would have to beg to have it returned?

But then again, what if his disappearance wasn't anything to do with Umber Jones? What if Myrlin had seen him lying in a coma and had him taken away by ambulance? How could he find his body then?

He circled the living-room again and again. Nobody could have seen him, but as he circled he disturbed the air. Ghosts and spirits are not completely undetectable. They raise and lower temperatures, they slow down clocks.

Their breath can always be faintly felt, or sometimes even seen, especially on a fogged-up windowpane.

He was still frantically circling when he heard a familiar tap at the living-room window. He couldn't open the door, so he flowed out through the fanlight and reassembled himself on the balcony outside. Elvin was standing by the railings, smiling at nothing at all. He was even more decomposed than he had been before. The wounds in his face were gaping open and they had started to suppurate – a thick, glistening pus that had dried around each stab-wound like the crusts around a jar of mayonnaise. Blowflies crawled in his eye-sockets, giving Jim the impression that his eyes were sparkling, and that he could see.

"I suppose you've come with another message?" said Jim.

Elvin opened and closed his mouth. His tongue was so swelled up that it was almost impossible for him to speak.

"You don't happen to know the whereabouts of my body, do you?" Jim demanded. "If this is Umber Jones's idea of a punishment, then you can tell him that I'm sorry; that I'll never touch his *loa* stick again and that I'll do whatever he wants me to do, in perpetuity, no argument. But he has to give me my body back."

"Earth to earth, ashes to ashes, dust to dust," whispered Elvin.

"What the hell are you talking about?"

A blowfly flew out of Elvin's eye-socket with a sharp, echoing buzz. "I've taken your body to the place where it belongs . . . the place where everybody's body belongs."

"What do you mean? The cemetery?"

Elvin nodded. "All bodies belong in the ground; yours as well as mine."

"My body's been *buried*? Is that what you're trying to tell me?"

"Boxed and buried, Mr Rook. But don't you worry. I said some comforting words over your grave."

Jim felt even more naked and transparent than ever. It had been wonderfully liberating, to leave his body, but now he was beginning to feel as if he had been sitting in a cold bath for far too long. If a spirit could shiver, he was shivering. He began to long for his body. He missed its warmth and its security, for all of its heaviness.

Elvin said, "Nobody will ever find you, Mr Rook. You'll have to wait for Umber Jones to dig you up again."

"And how long is that going to be?"

"A day. Two days. A month-and-a-half. Three months. Maybe never."

"But my body's not going to survive without my spirit."

"Don't worry, Mr Rook. I'm going to show you where you're buried, so that you can slip back into your skin."

"But even if I do that – how can I survive if I'm six feet under?"

"Goofer dust," said Elvin, with a smile. "I blew some goofer dust on you, while you were lying on the couch. You don't need to eat. You don't need to drink. You scarcely need to breathe. You're a zombie, Mr Rook. You'll survive for months."

Jim couldn't think of anything to say.

Elvin shuffled closer and he smelled so sickly that Jim would have retched if he had had a stomach to retch with. "Follow me," said Elvin. "It isn't far." He turned and made his way back along the balcony.

Jim hesitated for a moment, but Elvin turned around

and beckoned him. "Come on," he said. "We don't have much time. You want your body back, don't you?"

Reluctantly, Jim followed him down the steps. Instead of going out into the street, however, Elvin turned right down the narrow path to the back of the apartment block where the dumpsters were kept. The path was dark and wet from a dripping garden tap, and Elvin's feet dragged along the concrete in the same shambling gait that had characterised the zombies in *Dawn of the Dead*. God, thought Jim, talk about life imitating art, if *Dawn of the Dead* could be classified as art.

Elvin crossed the yard and then made his way through a tangle of weeds and bushes until he reached a triangular patch of waste ground between the rear of the garages and the cinderblock wall of the property next door. It was dark and shadowy here, but Jim could see that the dry, clumpy soil had been recently disturbed.

"My body's *here*?" he asked, with a feeling of dread.

"Can't you feel it, Mr Rook? Can't you sense your own flesh?"

"So what do I do now?"

"Do what spirits always do when they come back from walking about. Slide into your body, and rest."

Jim said, "Did Umber Jones *know* that I was going to leave my body tonight?"

"Umber Jones knows a lot of things, Mr Rook."

"But only my students knew what I was going to do. Nobody else. And *they* wouldn't have tipped him off."

"Well," said Elvin, "you'll have plenty of time to think about it." He wasn't being sarcastic. In some way, his thick, obstructed voice sounded almost sad, as if he desperately wished that *he* was lying in a coffin under the ground, able to rest his decaying limbs.

Jim wasn't sure what to do. He stood on the broken lumps of dug-up dirt and tried to feel where his body might be. Several minutes went by, with Elvin patiently watching him, and the night all around them busy with the sound of traffic. Then Jim became conscious of a warmth beneath his feet; a sense of wellbeing. His body was below him, he could feel it. He could almost see it in his mind's eye. He allowed himself to sink. He closed his eyes and tried to think of himself as nothing more substantial than warm water, soaking into the soil. As he sank lower and lower, he felt his spirit trickling between each individual grain, deeper and deeper. In only a few moments, he was embraced by complete darkness.

He reached the lid of his coffin. It was only a plain pine box, and he soaked through that, too, like wood stain. He flowed back into his body, into his brain. He drew on his hands like pulling on a pair of gloves. He filled out his lungs and his stomach and he stretched out his legs until he reached his toes. For a few seconds, the sense of relief was huge.

Only for a few seconds. The next thing he knew he was trapped in a dark, stifling box, his arms pinned beside him, unable to move. A wave of claustrophobia rolled over him, but he couldn't even scream. He was still paralysed by the goofer dust, his eyes wide open, his mouth wide open, but his facial muscles completely locked. Once, when he was playing football, he had dislocated his jaw, but this was a thousand times worse. He was gripped by such muscular rigidity that he couldn't even express his hysteria by panting or kicking or beating his fists. He thought he was going to die.

After a few minutes, however, he tried to persuade himself to calm down. It wasn't easy. The coffin was so tight that his nose was touching the underside of the lid. His brain was telling his heart to beat faster but his heart refused. He felt as if the frustration of being paralysed was going to explode inside him like a bomb. But then he kept trying to tell himself, *you're buried, you're paralysed, but you're not dead yet.* Stop panicking and start thinking, otherwise you'll never get out of here – not until Umber Jones deigns to dig you up, anyhow.

You know for a fact that people in Haiti have been known to survive in their coffins for several days after their 'funerals'. You can survive, too, if you try to keep your head straight. Your lungs refuse to breathe, but that's all for the best. You need to keep your metabolism down to an absolute minimum. No mental struggling, no hysteria. You practically have to flat-line.

It took him almost twenty minutes before he was able to calm himself completely. He kept having little spasms of claustrophobia which made him shudder spastically from head to foot. In the end, however, he managed to suppress his terror and to quieten his mind like a glassy pool of water. He would survive, he was sure of it. Umber Jones needed him too much to let him die. He was being punished, that was all, for trying to steal the *loa* stick. If he could accept his punishment calmly, then he would survive.

He tried to think of what he could do next. He could either lie here and wait for Umber Jones to exhume him, or else he could try to escape. The trouble was, his body was paralysed and his spirit was incapable of any greater physical activity than picking up a stick. He lay in total darkness, underneath the earth, unable to cry out, unable even to weep. He now knew what it was like to be a zombie; and why so many of them were so subservient when they were finally brought out of the ground. Either they were totally traumatised, or else they were so grateful for being rescued that they were prepared to do anything that their rescuer wanted them to do. There was nothing more terrifying, nothing more lonely, than lying alive in your own grave, waiting and hoping for the sound of a shovel.

Jim could have believed that God had forsaken him.

By ten-fifteen, Special Class II were beginning to become restless. Not in their usual way: shouting and throwing paper pellets and drumming on their desks. This time they were quiet and worried, talking to each other in low murmurs and occasionally going across to the window to see if Jim's car had appeared in the parking-lot.

Russell Gloach was eating out of a family-sized pack of nacho-flavoured tortillas. "You don't think something went wrong?" he asked. "Tee Jay's uncle sounds like one real mean dude."

Muffy looked at her watch. "Where is Tee Jay anyhow? He's just about the only person who can tell us what went down, and he's not even here."

"Something went wrong," said Russell, with tortilla crumbs dropping from his mouth. "You mark my words. Something went wrong."

"Will you stop being such a pessimist?" snapped Seymour. "Mr Rook could have been held up by anything. Traffic, who knows?"

"Did you ever know him to be late? He's never late."

"Maybe he found the stick and now he's trying to get rid of it."

"M-m-maybe w-we should c-call him at home."

"David, that's the best idea yet," said Sharon. "Does anybody know his number?"

"It's in his desk," said Ray.

"How do you know it's in his desk?"

"Because I *always* look through teachers' desks, just to see what they've confiscated. Believe me, if you want chewing gum, penknives or porno mags, there is *no* more reliable source than a teacher's desk."

They found Jim's number in the small leatherbound diary he always kept in his left-hand drawer. Sue-Robin took her mobile phone out of her Moschino bag and punched it out, noisily chewing gum as she did so. She blew a large pink bubble while she waited. The phone rang and rang but Jim didn't pick up. Eventually Sue-Robin said, "He's not answering. Something must have happened to him."

"So what do we do now?"

"Well, let's check with the office, just to make sure that he didn't come in today. Then – I don't know – maybe a couple of us ought to go round to Tee Jay's place. Maybe Tee Jay knows where he is."

Muffy went to see Sylvia, Dr Ehrlichman's secretary, but Sylvia hadn't seen Jim either. "Don't you worry, it's probably that old car of his. I'll have Dr Ehrlichman set you some work to be getting along with."

"Oh, no, no. Tell him not to bother. We've all got plenty to do."

She returned to the classroom. The rest of the students were waiting expectantly, but all she could do was to shake her head.

"That's it, then," said Sue-Robin, decisively. "Ray and Beattie, why don't you go to Tee Jay's house. Ask his mom where his uncle's place is, and then go see if you can find him."

"Do I have go with Ray?" asked Beattie, with distaste.

211

Ray blew her a smoochy Italianate kiss and said, "Sure you do. I'm the one with the fastest wheels."

"Fast cars are a pathetic penis-substitute," Beattie sniffed.

"Fast cars get you laid faster," Ray retaliated.

"Exactly."

They were still discussing what the rest of them should do when they heard a scratching, squeaking sound. They all fell silent and stared at each other. Then, as if they had been choreographed, they all turned their heads toward the chalkboard. A stick of chalk was hovering in the air in front of it, tapping at it again and again, like a deathly-white dragonfly.

"Oh my *God*," breathed Rita Munoz. "It must be Tee Jay's uncle again."

"Oh shit I hope not," said Seymour. "What the hell are we going to do if it is?"

The stick of chalk hesitated and then suddenly dropped to the floor, making them all jump. Then, very hesitantly, it rose up again, back up to the board. It looked as if it were being held by somebody invisible, somebody whose fingers couldn't grip properly.

"Hey, look," said John Ng. "It's making some marks. It's writing something."

With excruciating slowness, the chalk made a single vertical line. Then it moved sideways a little, and drew what looked like an Indian tepee. Then two Indian tepees.

I A AA.

"What's that supposed to mean?" frowned Titus. But then the chalk moved sideways again and wrote what looked like an 8.

"I don't get this," said Ricky. "I mean if this is like spirit communication, he'd be better off giving us one knock for certainly and two knocks for whatever."

"How do you know it's a he?" Beattie demanded.

"Well . . . it could be a woman, I admit. The message is stupid enough."

Now, however, the chalk had moved again. This time it wrote a U, and then an R, and then another vertical stroke. Whoever the writer was, he seemed to be gaining in confidence and strength as it went on. I A AA 8URIED.

"I am buried," Titus interpreted. "That's what it says. I am buried."

It went on, growing defter all the time. The class watched it, spellbound. *I am buried in back of garages at my home. Bring shovels. Jim.*

After the word *Jim* the chalk stick dropped on to the floor again, and broke. The class remained silent for a moment, then they all broke out into whoops and screams and applause. He was *here* – Jim Rook's spirit was actually here.

Sherma shushed everybody for silence, and then she went up to the front of the class, looking this way and that. "Mr Rook . . . we know you're here. That was wonderful. That was one of the most moving experiences of my entire life."

"Hey, forget about the speeches," said Ricky. "Let's go dig him up."

They all crowded toward the door, just as Dr Ehrlichman appeared with a large folder of work under his arm. They stopped, and shuffled, and coughed. Dr Ehrlichman stared at them in bewilderment, and said, "It's another half-hour before recess. Where are you all going?"

"Field trip, sir," said Russell.

"*Field* trip? I don't know anything about any field trip.

Besides, you can't possibly go on a field trip without Mr Rook."

"Oh, we're meeting Mr Rook by the beach. We have to experience the beach and then write some poems about it. You know, the little dancing waves and all that stuff."

"Yeah and the babes in their bikinis," put in Mark, cupping his hands in front of his chest, and then went "*unh!*" when Russell punched him in the back.

Dr Ehrlichman said, "I'm sorry. I haven't given Mr Rook authorisation for any field trip. Until I can discuss this matter with him in person, you'll have to consider it cancelled." He sniffed. "I've brought you some basic maths papers so that you can keep yourselves amused for the next half-hour."

"Amused?" groaned Greg. Maths, to him, was about as understandable as Sanskrit. He would labour for hours over his maths papers, only to produce answer after answer that his maths teacher said were not only wrong, but *creatively* wrong.

"We can't leave Mr Rook waiting on the beach," said Ray. "He'll be wondering what the hell happened to us."

"All right . . . in that case you and John here go to the beach and advise him of the change of plan. Be as quick as you possibly can. The rest of you . . . please sit down, and I'll hand out your papers."

There were more groans and hoots and suppressed Bronx cheers, and the class shuffled unwillingly back to their desks. From the doorway, Ray made a circle between finger and thumb, and then gave Dr Ehrlichman the finger. Behind his back, of course. He was disrespectful but he wasn't suicidal.

It took them a while to find the scrubby patch of ground

behind the garages, but when they did they knew that they had come to the right place. The soil was heaped up in big dry lumps, and the shape of a grave was unmistakable.

They had unofficially borrowed two long-handled shovels from the janitor's toolstore, but they didn't start digging right away. They stood beside the mound of soil and looked at each other uncomfortably. Back in the classroom, it had seemed like a really cool adventure, digging Mr Rook up out of the ground. But now they were actually here, standing by his grave, they were filled with trepidation. Supposing they dug him up and he was dead? Supposing he wasn't dead, but horribly mutilated? Supposing it was all a mistake and it wasn't him at all? What would they say to the police then? "Like a spirit message appeared on our chalkboard at college and told us to dig up this body."

Ray said, "Maybe we shouldn't be doing this, man."

John doubtfully prodded the soil with the tip of his shovel. "What if he's down there, and he's still alive? We can't just leave him here."

Ray bit his thumbnail. "I don't see how he *can* be alive, do you?"

"He could be. This is voodoo . . . and those voodoo guys, they can keep people alive even when they're buried."

"I don't know, man. Maybe we should call the cops instead. Like an anonymous tip-off."

John thought for a while longer. Then he reached inside his shirt and took out his necklet. He held it up to the sun and it sparkled sharply, as bright as a diamond. "I think it's going to be okay," he said. "This place has a really positive aura. There's nothing evil here . . . and nothing dead, either."

Ray said, "I'm supposed to believe some stone?"

"You saw how dark it went, when Tee Jay's uncle came into the classroom. I trust it, even if you don't."

"Okay, then, let's get digging."

Underneath them, tightly enclosed in his dark pine box, Jim heard the first chipping noises of their shovels and thought *thank God*. He was feeling exhausted, as if he had run a full Olympic marathon. It had taken all of his strength for his spirit to leave his body this morning and soak back up through the soil. He had been capable only of gliding very slowly through the streets and he had almost given up before he was even half-way to West Grove college. He had stopped underneath the freeway, feeling as if the morning breeze could simply blow him away, in transparent rags and tatters, over the ocean and into oblivion.

He had managed to summon the will-power to write his message on the chalkboard by thinking of Umber Jones, and what he had done to Elvin and to Mrs Vaizey and to *him*, too. His rage had driven him. But after that he had been close to collapse, and he could hardly remember how his spirit had managed to drag itself back to his apartment block and sink back into the soil.

The chipping noises went on and on. Now that he was so close to being released he began to experience a rising surge of black claustrophobia. He wanted to beat on the lid of his coffin. He wanted to scream out that he was here. What if they stopped digging and went away? What if it wasn't one of his students at all? What if he was dug up by some complete stranger, who thought he was dead?

What if it were Elvin, or Umber Jones?

The shovels knocked against the coffin-lid. Then he heard scraping noises as the soil was cleared away, and the muffled sound of voices. After a few more minutes the tip of a shovel was forced underneath the lid. With a sharp creak, the lid was pried off. His face was showered in soil and his eyes were assaulted with dazzling sunlight.

Ray and John, God bless them. They were kneeling down beside him now, peering at him wide-eyed. He had never realised before that Ray was trying to grow a moustache.

"Is he dead?" said Ray. "He sure *looks* dead."

John took out his necklet again. He cautiously pressed it against Jim's forehead and held it there for a while. Then he held it up and inspected it. "Clear," he said. "He looks like dead but he's still alive. Let's get him out of here before anybody sees us."

Lifting Jim out of his coffin was a struggle that was almost comical. His muscles were so rigid that his elbows wouldn't bend, so they couldn't sling his arms around their shoulders and carry him between them. Instead they had to lever him bodily out of the coffin and carry him as if he were a cigar-store Indian. Gasping with effort, they carried him round to the front of the garages where Ray had parked his Caprice. They slid him on to the back seat – and while John went to recover the shovels, Ray looked through his pockets. Billfold, college timetable, keys. He found it deeply disconcerting, the way that Jim was staring at him with those bloodshot, unblinking eyes. But he patted him on the shoulder and said, "Don't you worry, Mr Rook. We dug you up. Now we're going to fix you up."

John came back and threw the shovels into the trunk. "Where now?" he wanted to know.

"I think we'd better take him back to his own apartment; that'll be best. Then we can call the rest of the class and decide what we're going to do next."

John looked into the car, where Jim was lying stiffly across the back seat. "Do you think he can hear us?"

"I don't know. For Christ's sake, I don't even know if he's going to survive. But we have to do the best we can, right? He tried to take care of us. Now it's our turn to take care of him."

Between them, they managed to carry Jim up the steps to the balcony and drag him along to his apartment door, his shoes scraping along the concrete. They opened the door and manhandled him inside. The feline formerly known as Tibbles came mewling around their ankles as they carried him over to the couch. They laid him down flat on his back and John leaned over him and pressed his ear to his chest. "I was right. He's alive. You can just hear his heart beating."

"So what do we do now?"

"Let him rest, I guess. Whatever they've given him, it has to wear off sooner or later."

With the tips of his fingers, Ray did his best to close Jim's eyelids. He managed to shut the right eye, but the left one remained open, watching them both accusingly from under a drooping lid. At least it *looked* accusing, but in fact he was willing them to understand that he was still conscious, that he was still very much alive.

More than anything else, he was willing them to call their classmates – especially Sharon, with her knowledge of African culture and African spells. He was locked in this unrelenting physical paralysis, but he knew that there had to be a way of breaking it. After all, what did the voodoo sorcerers do, when they had to bring their zombies back to life? It was a chemical spell and there had to be a chemical antidote, even if it was made out of ground-up skulls and spiderwebs and the bitten-off heads of sacrificial chickens.

218

Ray said, "I'm going to call the rest of the guys, okay? We have to have a group discussion, do you know what I mean? Mr Rook isn't just *our* teacher, yours and mine. He's everybody's teacher." He paused, and then he said, "Besides, I don't know what the hell to do, do you?"

He picked up the phone and dialled West Grove Community College. "Hallo?" he said, dropping his voice an octave. "May I speak to Sue-Robin Caufield, please? It's her father. Yes, I'm afraid it's urgent. Her grandmother's suffered a very serious heart attack. Yes. She may not live the night."

While he did so, John sat down on the edge of the couch and looked at Jim with a mixture of mystification and sympathy. "Mr Rook, sir? Can you hear what I'm saying? Can you talk at all? Can you tell me how you feel?"

Jim stared at him one-eyed. He could see him and he could hear him, but he couldn't say a word because his tongue felt as if it were carved out of balsa wood and his cheek-muscles were clenched tight. He wanted his lips to move; he wanted so much to say something, but his nervous system had literally forgotten how to speak.

"We're calling the whole class together," John told him. "We're going to find Tee Jay's uncle and we're going to teach him a lesson if it's the last thing we do."

Jim lay there, rigid, one eye open and one eye closed. All he could do was wait for Umber Jones's goofer dust to wear off, or for somebody to bring him something to counteract it. If Elvin had been telling him the truth, it was quite possible that the effects would last for days, or even weeks.

Ray hung up, and came back over. He took hold of Jim's shoulder and gripped it tight. "If you can hear me, Mr Rook, everything's going to be okay. The whole class is coming over. We're going to see that Umber Jones doesn't get away with nothing no more. Nobody buries *our* teacher; *nobody*."

He picked up the feline formerly known as Tibbles and stroked his head. Jim watched him and didn't move. All of a sudden, however, Ray said, "Shit. That's it. I understand it now."

"What?" asked John.

"I understand it. *Why he stroked the cats.* In the poem, you know. Because the whole world was falling apart, all around him, and stroking the cats was like reality. You stroke a cat and it doesn't give you nothing back, so why do you enjoy it? Because people give something for nothing, sometimes; and they enjoy it."

John Ng looked very solemn. "If you say so, Ray."

The sunlight was shining through the cotton blinds, and it gave Jim's face a terrible radiance, as if he were closer to the angels than he was to earth. Inside his mind, however, he was beginning to feel a coming-together, a new sense of relaxation. He managed to open both of his eyes, and he could feel the sides of his mouth flexing a little, like a ventriloquist's dummy. He still couldn't speak and his arms and legs were still totally paralysed, but he knew now that he wasn't going to die.

He tried to say, "Thank you," and it came out as "mah-hoo". But that didn't matter. He was rapidly coming out of his paralysis. He was out of his coffin. He was back at home, with people who cared whether he lived or died, and that was one of the best curatives of all. "Mah-hoo," he repeated.

John looked up at Ray with a serious face. "What's he saying, for Christ's sake?" Ray asked him.

"He's saying 'mah-hoo'."

"Oh. Right. 'Mah-hoo'," said Ray, and knelt down beside the couch. He wiggled his fingers and said, "Hallo, Mr Rook! Can you hear me? Mah-hoo, Mr Rook! Mah-hoo!"

Chapter Thirteen

The rest of the class arrived within twenty minutes. "We didn't ask no permission," said Muffy, with bright-eyed bravado. "We just walked right out of the door. Didn't nobody ask where we was going. Didn't nobody try to stop us, neither."

"It was cool," said Russell. "We came down here in a convoy, right. Six cars and a pick-up, nose-to-tail. Cool."

They gathered round the couch where Jim was lying, and he looked up and saw all of their faces. The slow, the dyslexic, the fat, the disturbed. The children who would never be bright. The children who would never be glamorous. They were rebellious, most of the time. They bullied more successful students, and they caused disruption everywhere they went. Special Class II had always been a synonym for educational mayhem. But Jim had learned that if he showed his students that he cared about everything they tried to do, no matter how crass or clumsy it might seem to a non-remedial teacher, then his students cared, too. They couldn't spell, they couldn't add up, they couldn't draw a dog without making it look like a trash compactor. But Jim encouraged every one of their efforts – "Come on, let's not call this 'Fido'. Let's call it . . . trash compactor." In return, they were here, when he was paralysed, trying to get him back on his feet.

"Mr Rook?" said Sue-Robin, leaning over him so far that all he could see was her wide blue eyes and her warm, Babe-scented cleavage. "Are you still alive, Mr Rook?"

"Meathin," said Jim, between clenched teeth. He was trying to say "breathing", but it didn't matter. He must have been breathing to have spoken at all.

Sharon X was in the kitchen, furiously leafing through the books that she had lent him. "Here—" she said at last, lifting her hand.

"What?" said Ricky.

"It's here . . . the stuff they use to bring you back to life. It's called vive mixture."

"They got a recipe for it?" asked Russell.

"Well, it's kind of vague," said Sharon. "Something called blood root and something called betony, mixed with chicken's blood and celery."

"Sounds delicious," said Titus. "Where are you going to find that?"

"There's one of those occult herb stores two blocks down," said Muffy. "My aunt Hilda used to go there for musk oil and myrtle wood. She used to make this little fire every morning to bless her day."

"Right," said Russell, "I'll take Sharon down there right now. The rest of you . . . see what you can do to wake him up. He's starting to talk, right? Maybe you can get him to move."

Jim still lay rigid on the couch. His face was as white as a papier-mâché mask, and his eyes were circled in red. His whole system was gripped by tetrodotoxin – 160,000 times stronger than cocaine. He still had a chance of revival. In the 1880s, a Japanese gambler had been poisoned with tetrodotoxin after eating *fugu* fish and recovered in a mortuary over a week after he was declared dead. But Jim had been poisoned with *datura*, too, and *bufo marinus*. He was a classic zombie – pale, rigid and unmoving – waiting to give his gratitude to anybody who brought him back to life.

Sue-Robin stroked his forehead. "Don't you worry, Mr Rook. You're going to be fine. You're going to be back in that classroom boring our asses off with all of that poetry before you know it."

Jim's eyes flickered. He looked up at Sue-Robin's smile and thought that if any one remark could be guaranteed to bring him back to life, that was it. Sue-Robin had sat at the back of the class, dewy-eyed, while he read out *Wild Peaches* by Elinor Wylie. It had bored her ass off, had it? He wouldn't read any more poetry. She could sit in class reading *Igrat, Hell's Assassin* comics, for all he cared.

He didn't know how much time went by before Sharon returned. He saw her in the kitchen under the strong fluorescent light, her hair decorated with beads, pulping up roots and powders with the pestle-and-mortar that he usually used for crushing mustard seeds. He slept with his eyes open. He heard voices moving to and fro. The feline formerly known as Tibbles jumped on the couch next to him and purred loudly in his ear; more of a death-rattle than a purr.

Then his head was lifted by Sharon's hand and something bitter-sweet and liquid was being poured between his lips. He could feel it running down his neck and into his collar, but he didn't care. He lay back and closed his eyes. He didn't even realise how significant it was, the fact that he could close his eyes.

He slept – and as he slept, his toes relaxed, and his legs shifted sideways; and suddenly he lifted one arm and flung it across his chest. The class sat around and watched him, not saying much; passing round the beer they had found in his icebox. Sharon stood a little way away from the rest of them, very quiet, because she knew what a risk she had taken, giving Jim the the vive potion. Betony and bloodroot could have killed him, instead of bringing him back to life. Bloodroot was so dangerous that mystics always labeled it under a false name. If betony leaves were placed in a ring they were supposed to keep out all evil spirits, but betony taken as a drink could cause death by vomiting.

Hours went by. The class watched television, smoked, and read all of Jim's copies of *Playboy*.

"No wonder he's one of the those men who looks down on women," said Beatrice.

"Oh, come on," said David Littwin, "j-just b-because you d-don't have b-b-big enough t-t-t . . ."

Myrlin peered into the window to see what was going on and eighteen pairs of eyes stared back at him. He retreated into his apartment and pulled down the blinds.

David Littwin said, "Tits," and everybody turned and stared at him.

At three o'clock in the afternoon, Jim slowly sat up. "My God," he said, pressing the heels of his hands against his forehead.

"What is it?" said Sue-Robin, hurrying over to the couch and busily parking her bottom next to his.

"I'm fine," Jim told her. "I feel like I've been drinking all night, that's all." He reached around and kneaded the back of his neck. Then he stretched and tried to stand up, but he couldn't quite make it. He looked around at Special Class II and he couldn't help smiling in pride. "You made it, then. You saved me."

They all nodded wildly. "Ray and John dug you up, but we all saw the message."

Jim looked around. He still felt stiff, and oddly detached, but Sharon's elixir had definitely broken the grip of his paralysis. "I messed up," he admitted. "I managed to get out of my body and float down to Umber Jones's house, but it took me far too long to pick up the *loa* stick. I mean, when you're a spirit you don't have any hands, not in the physical sense. You have to *will* that thing into your fingers, otherwise it won't come. Same as that stick of chalk. Did you ever see that film *Ghost*, with Patrick Swayze, when he was trying to pick things up? That was exactly the same. I could only write with that stick of chalk by willpower. Nothing to do with muscular strength.

"But the trouble was, while I was trying to steal Umber Jones's *loa* stick, Umber Jones was taking my physical body right off this couch and burying me. With Elvin's assistance, of course. When I tried to come back to my body, it wasn't there."

"Hey, man, that must of freaked you out," said Ricky.

"You're right, it did. But Elvin showed me where my body was buried, and I was able to slide right back into it. Don't ask me how I did it. I just kind of soaked right into the ground. Mrs Vaizey told me that if I managed to leave my body just once, I'd always want to do it again. But after today . . . let me tell you something, no way."

"So you didn't get the *loa* stick?" said Sharon.

Jim shook his head. "We're going to have to work out another way." He looked at his watch, and said, "I'm going to have to grab some zees. If you guys want to stay here, you're welcome. Order some pizza or something. Then we'll talk about what we're going to do next."

A little after six, when they were all drinking mugs of coffee and talking about spooky encounters, Jim walked into the living-room and gave them a quick, short hand-clap to catch their attention. He had showered and changed. His hair was still wet and he was wearing his pink checkered shirt and his owlish Armani glasses. "Okay . . . I think that I'm pretty much recovered. I'm a little stiff – but then, who wouldn't be, after their own funeral? I had some dreams, but that was all. Nothing too frightening, unless you count a sexy dream about Dr Ehrlichman. Next time you see him, don't mention black stockings and garter belts, okay?"

The class laughed, but they were aware of Jim's tension, as well as his tiredness.

Much more quietly, he said, "We're dealing with some serious voodoo here. No point in trying to be sceptical. Umber Jones has *amazing* supernatural powers. He can use his *loa* stick to call on any one of two hundred different spirits. He can walk through the streets like smoke and he can kill people without them seeing who did it.

"I've been thinking about the way that he caught me last night. To begin with, I couldn't understand how he knew that I was going to be out of my body. But when I was buried in that coffin, I had plenty of time to chew it over, you know, with all of the benefit of total silence and total darkness. It's really incredible how clearly your mind can work, when you don't have any external stimuli to distract you. No airplanes passing overhead. No hookers bouncing the bedsprings in the room upstairs."

Again, the class laughed – not because he was funny, but simply because they were relieved to have somebody back in control. A class lost all of its cohesion without a teacher, no matter how laidback that teacher might be.

"Okay, informal registration," said Jim. "Is everybody here?"

"Everybody excepting for Tee Jay," said Seymour.

"Well, that's what I expected," Jim told him.

"You expected it? Why?"

Jim said, "Think about it. You all knew that I was thinking of leaving my body yesterday evening and trying to break into Umber Jones's apartment – but I was only going to do it if his smoke-spirit was out walking somewhere else. Only Tee Jay knew that his uncle had done it, and, when. So only Tee Jay knew exactly when *I* was going to leave my body to come looking for the *loa* stick. He sent Elvin here to bury my body, and that was that."

"It was a trap," said Sharon.

"That's right," Jim nodded. "It was a trap. I wanted to believe that Tee Jay wasn't totally dominated by Umber Jones. I wanted to believe that all of his interest in voodoo was a teenage fad; that one day soon, he'd get over it. But he knew what he was doing when he called me last night . . . and as much as I hate to say it, I think he knew what he was doing when Elvin was killed. It was nothing to do with a fight in the washroom. He was making a human sacrifice to Vodun."

"Jesus," said Mark.

"It says in Sharon's book that making a human sacrifice is the quickest way to have yourself accepted as a voodoo convert."

"All the same. Jesus."

228

"So what are we going to do now?" asked Titus, blinking behind his glasses.

"If you're willing, we'll tackle this problem together. I realised today that I can't handle it all on my own. I need my class to help me."

They glanced at each other. Jane said, "Not me. Not if it means looking for ghosts."

"Hey, come on, you can count me in," said Russell.

"Me too," said Mark.

David Littwin raised his hand and said, "You c-c-c. Can. C-c-c."

"Thanks, David," said Jim. He didn't want to be unkind, but he didn't have all night.

All but two of them wanted to join in. Jane was shy and badly dyslexic; Greg Lake had to be home early because his grandparents were visiting. Jim knew that Greg's parents were very severe: that accounted for his facial grimaces. He didn't want to give Greg any more stress in his life than he could handle.

In the end, he lifted one hand for silence, and said, "We're going to have to deal with Umber Jones on two fronts. The next time he leaves his body, a bunch of us will have to follow his smoke-spirit and keep it busy while two or three others break into his apartment and take his *loa* stick. They should also recite the chant that stops a smoke-spirit from re-entering his physical body. He won't have a *loa* stick, to call on the *loa* to help him. He won't be able to return to his body. After a while he'll simply fade away, like everybody else fades away, when they die.

"I think it would be a good idea if the group that's following the smoke-spirit is divided into two smaller groups. I can go with one group, because I can actually see him. The other group can take Mrs Vaizey's

229

ghost-dust. If you suspect that he's anywhere near you, you can throw some dust and it should show him up.

"We have three mobile telephones between us, don't we? That's okay . . . we can all keep in touch."

"What about Tee Jay?" asked Sharon. "The way he's been talking about voodoo, he could be pretty powerful, too."

"Well, for one thing, we don't know where he is, do we? And for another thing, I may be wrong about the sacrifice, and he may not have tipped off Umber Jones that I was leaving my body. He's still our classmate, until we can prove him otherwise. Let's cross that bridge when we come to it."

They staked out Umber Jones's apartment from eight o'clock onwards. In Ray's car sat Ray and Sharon and David Littwin. In Jim's car, a few spaces behind them, sat John Ng and Beattie McCordic and Muffy Brown. Across the street, facing in the opposite direction, was Russell's Mustang Mk II, with Sue-Robin Caufield and Seymour Williams. Russell had the coffee-mug filled with ghost-dust, on strict instructions that he wasn't to eat it.

In Ray's car they all ate Big Macs with their mouths open and noisily drank strawberry milkshakes. Sharon had brought her book of voodoo ritual so that she could say the words that would prevent Umber Jones's smoke-spirit from returning to his body. They were written in a very old African language and she could barely pronounce them. She kept repeating them over and over again, until Ray said, "For Christ's sake, Sharon. You sound like you're bubbling in your bathwater."

Babai babatai m'balatai . . . hathaba m'fatha babatai . . .

230

Jim felt exhausted but he was determined to see this through. He sat slouched down in his seat, wearing Ray-Bans and a green West Grove baseball cap in case Umber Jones recognised him from across the street. He probably wouldn't – especially since he must still believe that Jim was six feet under, in a tight pine box, suffering a well-deserved punishment for trying to steal his *loa* stick. All the same, Jim didn't underestimate Umber Jones's cunning; nor Tee Jay's either, if Tee Jay really *had* betrayed him.

Over an hour went by and Jim was beginning to think that he ought to call it a night. He got all of his students to call their parents to tell them that they were working late on an English project, and to hold supper for them. Beattie McCordic wouldn't eat pizza or hamburgers, and much to her embarrassment her stomach began to gurgle, although John kept saying, "It's quite all right. Even your stomach has the right to express itself."

"Spare me," said Beattie.

At that moment, without any warning, the front door of Umber Jones's apartments was flung open and out strode a tall, dark man wearing a wide-brimmed Elmer Gantry hat. It certainly *looked* like Umber Jones, but was it? "You see him?" he asked Beattie. "Just across the street there . . . passing the telephone booth . . . passing the trash bin."

Beattie frowned across the street. "I don't see anybody. There's nobody there."

"Good – that's definitely him, then," said Jim. "If you could have seen him, he might have been a decoy. Let's go." Beattie gunned the engine and swerved away from the curb. Jim said, "Not too fast. He's just passing that grocery store. That's it. We don't want to get too close, just in case he gets the idea that we're following him.

He won't be too alert, though. He doesn't realise that anybody can see him."

Umber Jones reached the end of the block and crossed over without even looking at the passing traffic. A truck passed less than three inches away from him, and his smoke whirled up, but he didn't even flinch.

"Keep going, keep going, left a bit," said Jim. "He's still headed in the same direction, but I think he may take a right at Colonial."

Beattie was driving so that Jim could concentrate on their pursuit. He was an edgy passenger, but he knew that he might have to jump out at any moment and follow Umber Jones's smoke-spirit into a house or a store or a restaurant. He wanted to have a 'getaway' car ready, too, in case anything went seriously wrong. He didn't have a gun – not that a gun would have had any effect against a smoke-spirit – and he had already seen from his dealings with Umber Jones that running away was the better part of valour.

"Right," said Jim. "He's definitely turning right." He dialled Sue-Robin's number. "We're following him north-westward on Colonial. Why don't you meet up with us at Colonial and Warren?"

"Where do you think he's going?" asked John.

"I don't know . . . but wherever it is, he'll be causing mischief."

The Smoke turned left and then right again, along a street of shuttered stores and cheap hotels. Outside the Glencoe Hotel two men were talking to a girl with fluffed-up hair and a short sequin mini-dress. One of the men was dressed in a white suit and built like an oak front door. The other was thinner, with greased-back hair and sunglasses. The thin one was remonstrating with the girl about something, because he kept jabbing his finger at her and every now and then he would make a slapping gesture in the air as if he was angry enough to hit her.

"Oh God," said Jim. "Here we go again."

The Smoke-figure came sweeping down the street and as it came nearer and nearer to the hotel entrance it appeared to swell in size, until it was even larger than Mr Oak Front Door. Jim didn't see its hand twisting, but the streetlight caught the flash of its knife.

This time, he couldn't let it happen without saying a word – whether the men deserved what The Smoke intended to do to them or not. He put down the car window and shouted out, "Hey! Look out behind you!"

Immediately, the thin man in sunglasses dodged behind the girl. Chivalrous, thought Jim. Mr Oak Front Door swung around with his fist half-raised just as The Smoke glided into him and stabbed him in the side of the belly.

"What's happening?" shrieked Beattie. "Look at that man!"

Blood spattered all over Mr Oak Front Door's suit as Umber Jones stabbed him again and again. Nobody except Jim could see The Smoke. All they could see was a heavily-built man performing a jerky dance on the sidewalk, while his coat was covered in one bright red splash after another. He made one more stumbling step and then he fell face-first on to the concrete.

Umber Jones turned toward Jim's car with a hideously frightening expression on his face. His eyes burned and his cheeks were powdered with ash. For a moment Jim thought that he was going to come rushing over to attack them. His bloody knife was lifted and he even took two or three steps across the sidewalk. Then, suddenly, he stopped. Jim could almost hear him thinking aloud. If Jim had escaped from his coffin and was following him with some of his students – what were the other students doing?

He bared his teeth and screamed, "Curse you, Mr Rook! I'll kill you for this!" and he turned and went rushing back the way he had come.

"Follow him!" Jim shouted, forgetting that Beattie couldn't see him.

"Which way? Which way?"

"Back that way! Quick! He's headed back to his own apartment!"

Police sirens began to wail in the distance as Beattie performed a jerky, bouncing seven-point turn in the middle of the street. Jim picked up his mobile phone again and punched out Sue-Robin's number. There was a long burst of crackling static, but then he heard her saying, "Yes? Yes? I can't hear you, Mr Rook!"

"Can you hear me now? Good! Then head right back to Umber Jones's apartment, and step on it!"

Next he tried Ray's number, but he couldn't make any contact at all.

"Can you still see him?" Beattie asked desperately.

"It doesn't matter – he's seen us now. Just get back to his apartment as fast as you can. I'm trying to raise Ray but I can't get through."

Ray, Sharon and David were round at the back of the Dollars&Sense store, gingerly picking their way between orange-boxes and vegetable crates and stacks of sacks of potatoes. The store was still open. Through a wired-glass window they could see the back of a young man's head as he was talking on the telephone. Sharon accidentally kicked a fruit-box, and the young man turned and peered outside. There were no lights in the back yard, however, and he soon turned away again, still talking. The three of them dodged across to the black-painted fire-escape without being seen.

They climbed the fire-escape as quietly as they could. They knew that they wouldn't disturb Umber Jones's body, but Jim had warned them about Mr Pachowski, and it was quite possible that Tee Jay was there, too. When they reached the second-storey landing, Ray pointed toward Umber Jones's bedroom and whispered, "That's it. All we have to do now is break in and grab the stick."

He reached the window, and tried to lift it up.

"Is it l-l-locked?" asked David.

"Not only locked, it's been screwed down, too."

"What do we do now?"

"We use subtle Italian skills handed down from father to son for generations." With that, he took off his pointy-toed shoe, swung his arm back and smashed the whole window with it.

David said, "For C-c-c. Christ's sake, Ray!" pressing his hands to his ears. Glass pealed and tinkled into the yard below, but Ray unhurriedly put his shoe back on and gave them a shrug. "This isn't the kind of neighbourhood where anybody's going to come running at the first sound of broken glass. In fact they'll probably go running in the opposite direction."

He cleared away a few remaining splinters. On the other side of the window hung a heavy black curtain, and he had to pull that aside, too, in order to climb over the sill. He gave it three sharp tugs. And there he was, lying on his bed, with his black nightlights floating beside him – the body of Umber Jones.

"There's the stick – I can see it," hissed Sharon. "Come on, Ray, all you have to do is grab it, then I can say the words and we can get the hell out of here!"

Ray eased himself in through the window and walked across the bedroom. He looked down at Umber Jones in fascination. "Look at him, his eyes are open but he can't see me. Creepy, isn't it?"

"Just grab the stick!" Sharon urged him.

Ray put out his hand and grasped the silver skull on top of the *loa* stick. As he did so, however, the bedroom door burst open so violently that it juddered against the wall, and Tee Jay came hurtling in. He seized hold of Ray's shirt and flung him aside.

"You dare to touch the sacred property of Baron Samedi!" he roared. He didn't sound like Tee Jay at all. He sounded as if his voice had been composed from a hundred slowed-down screams – harsh and agonised, but totally commanding. He didn't look much like Tee Jay, either. His face was plastered white all over, except for black circles painted around his eyes and a black slit of a line painted across his lips. He was bare-chested, and his skin was decorated with scores of tiny barbed hooks, each of them tufted with red-dyed fur or clumps of chicken-feathers. He stood amidst the clouds of incense-smoke and he looked like a visitor from hell.

Ray climbed to his feet. "Listen, man," he said, "I don't want any trouble here. But we have to have that stick, man. Your uncle can't go on killing people. You know that."

Tee Jay stared at him with eyes like glistening black beetles. Then, without warning, he swung his fist and knocked Ray back against the door-jamb. Ray toppled sideways and hit his head on the edge of the table.

As Tee Jay went over to hit him again, Sharon managed to scramble in through the window. She reached out for the *loa* stick, but Tee Jay must have been able to sense her. He pivoted around and slapped her open-handed across the side of the head. She fell to the floor with her ears ringing. "Touching the *loa* stick is blasphemy!" he roared at her.

"Tee Jay!" she begged. "It's Sharon!"

He ignored her. He picked Ray up from the floor but Ray was out cold, with a swelling bruise on the side of his head. Tee Jay let him drop.

"You stay where you are," he told Sharon. "My uncle will be back here soon, and then you'll find out what we do to blasphemers."

Sharon tried to crawl back toward the window but he stepped forward and slapped her again. "Stay where you are, bitch! I've been waiting for this!"

Outside the window, David kept himself pressed against the wall, hardly daring to breathe. He couldn't even call for help, because Ray was carrying the mobile phone. He listened and waited and prayed that Tee Jay wouldn't look outside.

"It wasn't your fault," said Jim. "I shouldn't have told you to drive so fast."

They were only two blocks from Umber Jones's apartment, but the police had flagged them down for speeding, and now they were waiting with almost intolerable tenseness while a pot-bellied officer pedantically wrote out a ticket. "You just remember, little lady, ten miles on your speed puts another hundred feet on your stopping distance. There are kids around here, at this time of night; and people with too much alcohol inside them. You don't want to go killing nobody, do you, just because you're one minute late for some appointment?"

Jim was grimacing and squeezing his hands into fists. For God's sake, cut the road safety lecture and let's get out of here.

But before he tore off the ticket, the officer stepped back and walked very slowly all the way around the car, peering at the tyre-treads, checking the lights, tapping at the bodywork. Anybody would have thought that he was thinking of buying it. "All righty," he said, at last, and handed Beattie her ticket. "Just remember the golden rule."

"The golden rule?" asked Beattie, anxiously.

Come on, thought Jim. *Come on, come on, come on.*

"Better to be late in this world than early in the next."

Oh, please.

They drove slowly away, leaving the police officer standing in the street watching them go. They turned the corner, and then Beattie slammed her foot down. The rear tyres howled like slaughtered pigs, leaving twenty–foot slashes of burned rubber on the concrete.

Russell and Sue-Robin and Seymour had already arrived outside the street door that led up to Umber Jones's apartment.

"No sign of Ray and Sharon yet," said Seymour. "I just hope they've managed to grab that stick."

Russell tried the door but it was firmly locked. "Best thing we can do is stand here and wait. He may be smoke, but even smoke needs an eentsy-weentsy gap to get through."

"I'm scared," said Sue-Robin.

Russell peeled the clingfilm off the top of the coffee-mug. "There – you don't have to be scared. If he comes anywhere near, we'll be able to see him."

"And then what?"

"I don't know. Run, I guess."

Sue-Robin peered into the mug and wrinkled up her

nose. "Do you think that really works? I mean, that's just some old woman's ashes, isn't it?"

"Mr Rook seems to think that it's going to work."

He took a pinch between finger and thumb and sniffed it. "Doesn't smell like anything much."

"Oh, *gross*, Russell. You're breathing somebody in."

Russell threw the ghost dust away. As he did so, however, he was sure that he momentarily saw something in the air in front of him – something that looked like disembodied fingers. He flattened himself back against the door, and he was heavy enough to make it shudder.

"What's the matter? What's wrong?" asked Sue-Robin, in fright.

"He's here," said Russell, in a tiny, squeezed-up voice. *"He's here! He's standing right in front of us!"*

Sue-Robin snatched the coffee-mug and flung the ghost dust into the air. For a few terrifying seconds they saw the outline of Umber Jones, ten feet tall, with his knife raised up in the air. His teeth were clenched and his face was rigid with fury.

He vanished; but Russell rolled himself away from the door just as the shoulder of his shirt was sliced open. "Get back!" Russell yelled at Sue-Robin and Seymour. "Get the hell out of here! Run!"

The door rattled ominously; and then there was a long sucking sound, as if a current of air were streaming underneath it. Russell couldn't see it, but Umber Jones had just poured under the bottom of the door, and now he was making his way back upstairs.

Russell said, "What's Ray's number? Tell him that Umber Jones has come back!"

Sue-Robin scrabbled with her mobile phone, but even

when she managed to get Ray's number right, she heard nothing at all.

"Oh, Jesus, this is all getting out of control," said Russell.

They heard a car speeding toward them, and then a squeal of brakes. They turned around and saw that Jim had arrived, with Beattie and John.

Jim looked at Russell's shoulder. It was bleeding slightly, but the wound wasn't too deep. "What happened?" he said. "Where is he now?"

Russell nodded up toward Umber Jones's apartment. "I think we blew this one, Mr Rook. All we've managed to do is to make him pissed off. And I mean *seriously* pissed off."

An upstairs window opened and Mr Pachowski peered out. "What's going on down there? Get away from that door or I'll call for the cops!"

Jim ignored him. He gave the front door a hefty kick with his left foot, then another. The frame cracked a little but still the door wouldn't move.

"Hey! What are you doing down there?" Mr Pachowski demanded. "That's vandalism! That's criminal damage!"

"Oh shut up you old idiot!" Sue-Robin retorted.

Jim kicked the door again but still it wouldn't budge. Russell said, "Here – get out of the way. You got to leave this kind of thing to experts." He stepped back six or seven paces, and then came running at the door shoulder-first, all 300 pounds of him, and knocked it clear off its hinges and into the hallway.

"Come on," said Jim. "Let's hope to God we're not too late."

They reached the door of Umber Jones's apartment. It was an inch or two open. Maybe Tee Jay had left it like

240

that so that his uncle's smoke-spirit could return more easily. From inside, they could see only the dimmest flicker of candlelight, and they could hear voices, too.

Jim eased the door wider. He turned around to Russell and Sue-Robin and Seymour and put his finger to his lips. "Ssh, follow me."

They crept across the darkened living-room to the bedroom. For all of his bulk, Russell was remarkably graceful. The bedroom door was wide open, and Jim could see Umber Jones's feet in their dusty black patent shoes, lying on the bed. The candles circled and dipped in their saucers, making the light swivel across the walls. He stepped closer. Through the crack at the side of the door he could see Tee Jay, standing with his back to him, tufted with feathers and fur. He could see part of Sharon's skirt, too. Ray lay sprawled in full view, his face pale, unconscious.

Jim edged just a little bit nearer, so that he could see around the doorframe. There he was, Umber Jones's smoke-spirit, standing beside the bed on which his own body lay comatose. Thank God he hadn't yet decided to breathe his smoke-spirit back in.

"We will cut them one after the other," said Umber Jones. "One hundred and twelve cuts each. A great, great sacrifice to Vodun and to Baron Samedi."

"To die for Vodun is the greatest honor of all," Tee Jay told Sharon. "It is the most painful death of all . . . so painful that you will welcome Baron Samedi when he comes for you."

"Screw you," said Sharon, although Jim could tell how frightened she was.

He glanced back at Russell and Sue-Robin and Seymour. "Russell," he whispered, close to Russell's ear. "You go barging right in and tackle Tee Jay. I'll make a grab for

241

the *loa* stick. If I miss it, you go for it, Sue-Robin, and when you've got it, run like hell. Into the car, and away, OK – as far and as fast as you can."

"You are conscious," Umber Jones told Sharon. "We will kill you first."

Jim could see him slowly twisting his right hand and exposing his knife. Right, thought Jim. It's now or never. He touched Russell's shoulder, and said, *"Go!"* and they went.

Russell cannoned into the room and knocked Tee Jay flat to the floor with one of the greatest body-tackles that Jim had ever seen. Sharon screamed. Umber Jones whirled around, his eyes staring in surprise and fury. He slashed at Jim's face, but Jim managed to duck his head sideways.

He reached across for the *loa* stick, but Umber Jones slashed at him again and again, and cut the edge of his hand. "This time I'll kill you, my friend," he spat. "This time I'll bury you for ever."

Jim dodged toward the *loa* stick again, and again Umber Jones's smoke-spirit sliced his knife in the air from side to side. But as he did so, Sue-Robin scrambled right under the bed to the other side, reached up with one hand, and dragged the stick out of Umber Jones's grasp.

Umber Jones's smoke-spirit bellowed with rage, and sprang around after her. But Sue-Robin called, "Catch, Mr Rook!" and tossed it over to him.

Jim caught it, and threw it to Seymour. "Go, Seymour!" he shouted. Seymour immediately disappeared out of the door and ran through the living-room on to the landing, colliding as he did so with Mr Pachowski.

Umber Jones started to go after him, but Jim suddenly

thought: *if I could will myself to leave my body — if I could will my spirit to pick up solid objects — then I can will myself to stop Umber Jones.* As Umber Jones rushed toward the door, Jim went after him and punched him hard in the jaw, and then the stomach. Totally taken by surprise, Umber Jones fell back against the wall, staring at Jim in astonishment.

Jim went to hit him again, but this time his fist went through nothing more than wind. All the same — he had delayed Umber Jones for long enough. Outside in the street he could hear Seymour's tyres shrieking as he drove away.

Umber Jones stared at Jim for a long, long time, his eyes hollow with malevolence. Then he started to shuffle back toward the bed, where his physical body lay. "One day, my friend, I will find another *loa* stick, and then I will come back for you. I promise you that."

He stood beside his body and laid his hand on its chest. Then without warning, David Littwin came climbing in through the window. He ignored everybody else, and walked right up to Umber Jones's body. Sticky-outy ears, with the light shining through them. Serious expression.

"Careful, David," said Jim. Although Umber Jones's smoke-spirit no longer possessed a *loa* stick, and couldn't call on the *loas* to help him to hurt human beings, it was better to be cautious.

But David pointed his finger at Umber Jones's body and said, loudly and clearly, *"Babai babatai m'balatai . . . hathaba m'fatha habatai."*

Umber Jones's smoke-spirit stared at him in disbelief. Then he twisted around and stared at Jim. His expression was one of utter horror. "He has hexed me! Your child has hexed me! I can never go back into my body!" He

243

rushed from one side of the room to the other, a tornado of smoke – but only of smoke, with no power or influence at all. At last he came to rest in the far corner, shuddering with fear and desperation.

Jim walked up to him and said, "Let's hope that all the people you killed are going to be more forgiving than you ever were." With that, he twisted the knob of the air-conditioning unit under the window.

"No," whispered Umber Jones, as the motor whirred into life. "I want to keep my shape . . . I want to keep my soul." But he was helpless. The air-conditioner began to fray the edges of his coat, and then it sucked in his sleeves. Umber Jones gradually collapsed into a spiral whirl of smoke, and was drawn through the air-conditioning vents like nothing more substantial than a bad memory.

Jim went over to Russell, who was still sitting on top of Tee Jay. "Thank you, Russell, for a memorable performance. Thank *you*, Sharon, for being so knowledgeable about your own heritage. And thank *you*, Sue-Robin, for a pretty cute move."

He put his arm around David's shoulder and said, "As for you, David, you're excused speech therapy for the rest of the semester."

He met Susan as he walked across the parking lot after college. She came right up to him and kissed him on the lips. "Hi," she said. "Where are you going to take me tonight?"

"I don't know. I was thinking about a barbecue *chez* Rook. Salmon steaks and a little salad?"

"That sounds good."

They walked arm in arm toward his car. "Have you heard anything about Tee Jay yet?"

"He has to take a whole bunch of psychiatric tests. His Uncle Umber really messed him up. But, you know, give him a little time . . ."

"He really thought he was a voodoo sorcerer?"

"Oh, yes. And in a way, he was. He was young, you see, and strong. He had an aura filled with energy and life. Other spirits love that energy . . . that's why ghosts so often appear to young children, rather than old people."

"I really don't know what you're talking about."

"Well . . . it doesn't matter now," he said, opening the car door for her. Although he understood now why Umber Jones had appeared so often in his classroom. His dark and dried-up soul had reveled in all that youthfulness. He had literally devoured it, and it had made him stronger. The past feeding off the future.

That evening, as they sat by the pool, Susan snuggled up close to him. She kissed his lips and nibbled his earlobe.

"You know something," she said, "the moment I set eyes on you . . . it was love at first sight."

He smiled and kissed her back and said nothing.

"You know something else?" she said. "I had such a sneezing fit today. I think I must be allergic. It was just after lunch . . . just after you and I were talking together. I sneezed and I sneezed and I couldn't stop. I felt as if I'd been sniffing up pepper."

Jim kept on smiling at her. Not pepper, sweetheart. Memory powder. And now you remember falling in love with me; the same way that I remember falling in love with you.

The charcoal in the barbecue briefly glowed, but it was starting to die. Jim disentangled himself from Susan's arm and said, "There's something I have to do. Hold on a minute."

He left the side of the pool and walked across to the parking-lot. He opened up the trunk of his car and took out the *loa* stick.

Myrlin was walking past, and he stared at the stick and commented, "Ankle problems, Jim?"

Jim gave him the sweetest of smiles. "Nose hair problem, Myrlin?"

Myrlin looked confused and hurried off.

Jim returned to the barbecue carrying the *loa* stick. He held it up for a moment and looked at the silver skull on the top. He couldn't even guess what power this stick contained, but then he didn't really want to know. He lifted his knee, and broke it in half, and then he dropped the pieces into the barbecue charcoal.

They smoldered for a while, while Jim and Susan lay watching them. Then they suddenly flared up, and began to burn with a crackling, firecracker fierceness. Thick grey smoke poured out of the flames, and rose up into the evening sky. For a moment, Jim could have sworn that it took on the shape of Umber Jones.

He didn't see the faint outline of an old woman standing in the shadows; a faint outline with the faintest of smiles. She was smiling because her prophecy had come true, and Jim's fate had been sealed by fire.

"I love you, Mr Rook," said Susan, and kissed him again.

Jim didn't say anything, but watched the smoke drifting through the yuccas; until a cross-breeze caught it, and whirled it out of his life for ever.